When Love and Rage

Rip the Veil

Pauline Potterill

Pobo

INTRODUCTION

When Zoe inherits a hotel, it turns out not to be her only possession.

To claim her inheritance Zoe, and best friend Natalie, head north to the sleepy little sea-side town of Wanton Ness. On their first night, a blast from the past propels them both into a world of horror, challenging their beliefs and their sanity.

Can Natalie and new friends Toby and Kyle, unravel the mystery of the hotel, in time to save Zoe, and themselves.

When Love and Rage Rip the Veil

(a Ripped Veil novel)

Sometimes a rip appears, in the veil separating the living from the dead.

Sometimes the dead can't rest in peace.

Sometimes, the dead won't.

Prologue

She fell. Lurching, falling, grasping at air, finding only dust: choking, blinding dust. With sickening solidity, she landed and lay, unmoving: her mind numb with disbelief, her body numb with shock. Dispassionately, she examined the experience: comprehension beyond her grasp: fear scratching, clawing. There was a shuddering and she dropped again, half rotating, falling, bouncing. Through it all she was aware of the silence, an oppressive silence with an energy all of its own. Unable to control her limbs she felt the pain as they flailed through the tumbling debris. It seemed an eternity, then merciful oblivion.

There was a hand on her face: its touch clumsy, abrasive. Fingers in her mouth, poking, gouging, and clearing. She gasped for air, inhaling brick dust. She coughed uncontrollably, in spasms, unable to get enough air. Pain racked her chest, her arms, her legs. Briefly she felt relief as something heavy was lifted off her. Then the return of sickening pain and heart-thumping panic. She blinked against the grit in her eyes, desperate to see and make sense of it all. The silence persisted: surreal and enveloping and then, blessed oblivion again.

There were faces looking down at her. They looked concerned. Their mouths formed words but made no sound. Behind them was the sky, dark and uncaring with stars beginning to appear through the settling dust, emphasising the fleeting irrelevance of her being.

A familiar voice and an arm round her shoulders, tenderly guiding her. She was on her feet, grass between her toes. The person was hugging her, supporting her, and leading her through a corridor of people, their faces all showing concern. She stared back at them. They were in dressing gowns. She was in her pyjamas. It was the middle of the night. Why were they all outside? Her guide was speaking to her, muttering soothing words. It was Natalie, yes Natalie. As a doorway loomed ahead, the bright internal lights contrasted starkly with the dark external night. Zoe stared in horror at the glow, screamed and dropped to her knees.

Chapter One

Two weeks earlier

A clunk and a light patter, and the crisp white envelope landed on the hall mat. It lay there, smug, sandwiched between a double-glazing flier and a money-off pizza voucher, patiently waiting to deliver the new life it held. It got trodden on a couple of times before it was finally picked up and handed to Zoe. The young woman put down her phone, took hold of the envelope, and inspected it. Ms Z Spencer, it announced. She stared at the formal form of her name, then raised her perfectly shaped but somewhat bold brows. Embossed on the top left-hand corner was 'Titherington and Sons, Solicitors'. She turned it over, long nails sparkling. The back was blank: no clues as to its contents. She frowned and worked her little finger under the flap. A thin red line began to ooze on her knuckle. She sucked in her breath, and then sucked her finger. After a brief pause, she extracted an A4 sheet and unfolded it. Her eyes warily scanned the page. Then she greedily read it again and felt guiltily thrilled. A relative she barely knew existed, had died. She, it seemed, was the only known descendant. The letter requested her presence at Titherington's solicitor's, at 11am Monday morning, a week and a half hence. Not wanting to go alone she had persuaded her friend Natalie to accompany her. They would go up on the Saturday and spend the week there. From what they could see on-line, Wanton Ness was a lovely little coastal town in Northumberland. It was set into and on cliffs, where a river entered the sea. A small fishing town, it had a couple of hotels and a number of guest houses, several pubs, some shops and a town store.

Friends from school, Zoe and Natalie had done everything together. When Zoe lost her parents and grandmother at the age of 14, Natalie's family had adopted her. They had taken her in and treated her as one of their own. Natalie became the sister Zoe, a single child, never had. Equally, Zoe became the sister, Natalie didn't have. The two girls went everywhere together. They shared more or less the same likes and dislikes. They were inseparable. So, going to Northumberland together, during their university Easter break, was natural.

As the time for the trip grew nearer, they grew more and more excited and planned what they would do. They also speculated as to what it might be that Zoe was about to inherit. Top of the fantasy was a castle, unlikely, but they were just dreaming. As Zoe had been asked to appear in person, they felt that it was likely to be something substantial. If it was just money, then a cheque would have been quicker and easier and cost next to nothing. Instead, the solicitor had booked them into a hotel, costs to be met from the deceased's estate. When Zoe had asked if Natalie could come too, stating that they would be happy to share a room, the answer had been 'yes, they could have a room each if they liked'. However, not wanting to risk incurring any cost herself, she had declined. Two train tickets arrived through the post with a note saying that a car would meet them at the station when they arrived. It was all very exciting and mysterious and a little scary. The arrangements made life easier but also removed Zoe's control. She knew very little about the dead relative and didn't think that they had ever met.

The train journey was long, and lugging cases between platforms at Birmingham and Leeds was exhausting. Clutching a coffee apiece, they collapsed into their seats and settled down for the final leg of the journey. Zoe snuggled into the window seat and rested her head on her scarf which she'd scrunched into a pad against the damp window. As Natalie idly stirred her coffee, a weary ticket inspector appeared at the other end of the carriage. Three rows nearer he settled into a practiced leaning position on a seat arm, one foot wedged against a table leg opposite, rocking slightly. He checked his watch a couple of times as a passenger frantically scrolled and stabbed at his mobile. There was a brief exchange. Then, leaning across, the ticket inspector took hold of the phone, gave it a few deft swipes, and handed it back. As he crept down the carriage Natalie gave Zoe a nudge. When the girls handed over their paper tickets he took them reverently, cherished them briefly and then handed them back; order had been restored in his day.

By the time they reached their stop it was going dark, and Zoe was glad that she had Natalie with her. It was a small station and very few other passengers got off the train. The girls dragged their cases along the platform and then carried then up and over the bridge to the other side of the station, following the exit signs. Emerging from the station they found that they were alone, the other passengers having quickly dispersed. A single vehicle was parked in the waiting area outside. The door opened and a man got out and addressed Zoe by name.

Settled in the car, they set off and soon found themselves out in the countryside, heading along a dark tree-lined road. At first, they headed uphill, the road rising gently but twisting as it climbed. Then they started to descend. They got the impression of a river off to the right and below them. Zoe, wide awake now, chatted away to the driver. She asked him about his family. She asked him if he enjoyed driving a taxi. She asked him if he had driven any famous people. He had, but wouldn't say who, despite Zoe's persistence. He seemed happy to talk and Natalie, very quickly, learnt everything that she would ever want to know about the man.

Soon, they could make out lights ahead and buildings began to appear out of the gloom. A sign stating 'Welcome to Wanton Ness, please drive carefully through our town' flashed by. On both sides of the road sat single-storey terraced houses which intrigued the girls, having not seen this type of housing before. Elevated from the road by banks of earth the tiny homes had a narrow, flagged pavement running along their fronts. The walls appeared to be white-washed, and Zoe could just make out the odd tub of flowers in the taxi's headlights. As they continued, the buildings got larger, two and three stories high. Soon there were shops and other business premises. The car slowed and pulled up at the kerb.

They were outside a three-storey stone building with a wide front door set into an arched porch. The driver got out and opened the doors. As the girls stepped out into the street, they were met by a stiff breeze carrying the distinct smell of fish and salt; the sea wasn't far away. As the driver retrieved their cases from the boot and set them on the pavement they glanced around. Asymmetrical, the building had one bow window projecting over the street whilst the other ground floor windows were flush with the stonework. A large Union Jack flapped noisily halfway up the wall, whipping back and forth in the wind. Their eyes drawn upwards by the noise, they saw a large sign stating, 'The Dolphin Hotel and Lido'.

Overhead, the screech of gulls assaulted their ears from the building's ledges. As they were about to take their luggage a man in uniform appeared. He placed their cases on a rack and wheeled them into the foyer. They thanked their driver and followed their cases.

The entrance hall was low-ceilinged and panelled, making it quite dark. A couple of wall lights and a lamp on the reception desk were its only illumination. The effect was cosy and welcoming but rather old-fashioned. Looking round at the décor and furniture the place appeared to be stuck in a time-warp. Leaning on the reception desk Zoe fully expected to see an old telephone with separate mouth and earpiece and a dial with finger holes. However, what she saw was a modern phone and a computer screen. The receptionist greeted them and handed over their room key which, despite the IT on show, did fit the décor: it was large and metal and was attached to a heavy wooden fob shaped like a big smiling dolphin.

They followed the porter up to their room which was on the top floor at the back of the hotel. Zoe automatically went to the window to look at the view, but she was going to have to wait until morning; it was now too dark to see. The porter ran through his usual speech explaining about the hotel facilities and the opening times of the dining room, not too subtly informing them that it was just about to close. Zoe asked what the wi-fi code was.

"Oh, I'm sorry. We don't have wi-fi," said the porter.

"What?" said Zoe, aghast!

"I'm sorry," repeated the man as both Zoe and Natalie stared at him.

"What sort of hotel is this?" asked Zoe in disgust.

"The town is promised broadband, but it hasn't arrived yet. None of us are happy about it," said the man pointedly.

"But you've got IT on the reception desk," blurted Zoe.

"Yes, we have internet access via the phone line, but it isn't very good. The computer is mainly for internal use."

"We can just use our phones," interjected Natalie.

"If you can get a signal," said the porter with a sigh, heading for the door and attempting to ignore the expletives coming from Zoe. "Unless there is anything else I can help you with, I will leave you to settle in. Please be aware that the restaurant stops serving dinner at 9pm but will provide something if you can be down there in the next 15 minutes."

"Whatev's," Zoe huffed and threw her bag on the nearest bed. The porter pursed his lips and let himself out realising there was no tip coming his way.

They quickly changed out of their jeans and into dresses, combed their hair and touched up their make-up. Natalie was eager for Zoe to hurry up; she didn't like to keep the hotel staff waiting. Zoe, however, was determined to ensure that she looked perfect; it was a hotel, and they were on holiday; who knew who they might meet. She ran her fingers through her blonde hair, attempting to increase the volume. She gave her lipstick a final application, pursing her lips to check the effect. Once ready she followed an impatient Natalie down to the dining room.

As they were led to a table by the window, they looked around to discover that they appeared to be the only guests. Further inspection indicated that there had been other diners, as there were tables that needed clearing, but now they were the only ones. Disappointed, they studied the menu which was somewhat reduced due to the lateness of the hour.

The service was excellent, and the food was good, despite a limited choice. They quickly wolfed their way through it, eager to get to the bar in the hope of finding other guests and in particular, ones of interest to two young women.

Entering the bar, they were pleased to see other guests there. However, they were considerably older than the two of them. Having obtained drinks, they went and sat in a pair of armchairs at a little table in the corner of the room, where they had a good view of everything and everyone. The bar staff were very attentive, keen to ensure that the girls were looked after. Maybe it was because the staff were roughly the same age as the pair of them that they seemed to be getting more attention than the other guests. One of the barmen, Jez, seemed particularly eager to ensure their glasses didn't run dry, suggesting cocktails they may wish to try. He had a sparkle in his eye and an engaging smile, and he laughed easily at their jokes. From a distance they would never have looked at him twice but the more interaction they had with him, and the more they drank, the more likeable he became. It wasn't long before the other guests drifted off to their rooms and Zoe and Natalie were the only guests left. At some point Jez had gone, and one solitary female remained behind the bar, obviously there, until the lounge was empty. So, no reason to stay, they headed upstairs.

A little tipsy, Zoe stumbled into the wall as they headed along the corridor to their room. However, she succeeded in unlocking their door. Noisily she closed it behind them, put the key in the lock and turned it. Taking a moment to steady herself, she stared at the fire escape plan on the back of the door. Curiously, it seemed that their part of the building was much more uniform than the rest of it, the rooms less 'higgledy piggledy' than those at the front of the hotel. It looked like they were in an extension. Realising that she had had too much to drink she decided that a coffee would be a good idea. Natalie, having had the same idea, was busy trying to get the kettle to fit under the tap in the ensuite. The solution they discovered was to fill it using the cups.

The stiff breeze from earlier had increased in intensity and the windows rattled intermittently. It didn't however drown out the noise of the gulls, on the ledges outside, which were voicing their annoyance at having their feathers severely ruffled. The girls watched TV for a while and drank their coffee. Having eaten all the biscuits and nuts and downed a second cup they were just considering going to bed when a knock at the door caused them to stare at each other. The knock came again, and Natalie went and opened it. Standing in the corridor was a prim looking member of staff, smartly dressed in dark blue. The woman politely, but firmly said, "Would you mind turning down the volume of the TV, please. We have had complaints from other guests."

"It is the only way we can hear it over the noise of the gulls and wind," snapped Zoe. "Perhaps some double glazing might help. After all, we aren't living in the dark ages."

"The hotel does have double glazing, but unfortunately..."

"It is okay," interjected Natalie. "We will turn it down. We were just about to go to bed anyway. We are sorry."

With that the woman left and they went to bed, quickly falling asleep.

Natalie woke with a start, heart pounding. Somewhere in the dark something banged violently, whipped back and forth by a howling wind. She was cold and disorientated. Clutching her bedding about her she looked around the room, her eyes alighting gratefully on the alarm clock. It was 1.10am and she now remembered that she was in a hotel, with Zoe. She glanced over at Zoe's bed but couldn't make out much. However, she sensed that it was empty. The window slammed again, making her jump. It was open and flapping in the wind and rain. She switched on the bedside lamp. Yes, Zoe's bed was empty. She got out of bed and leant out into the rain and took hold of the window handle, getting a wet arm in the process. As she pulled the window to, the wind caught it and forced it back, flat against the outside of the building and out of her hand, nearly dragging her out. Shaken and wet, she waited for a lull in the wind, leant out again and this time managed to pull the window to and lock it. Then she knocked on the door of the ensuite.

"Zoe, are you in there?" Getting no reply, she opened the door. The room was empty. Puzzled, she grabbed her dressing gown and went to the door; it was locked, and the key was hanging on the hook next to it. With growing alarm, she ran at the window and, using her hands to shield her eyes from the light in the room, peered out. On the ground, about 6 metres in front of the building a blurry white shape could be seen, sprawled and unmoving. She threw open the window and yelled, "Zoe!" Her voice went nowhere, lost in the noise of the storm. "Zoe! Zoe!" Zoe didn't move. Pulling the window shut she raced for the door. Clattering the large key in the lock she fought with the mechanism until it opened. She flung the door wide, crashing it against the wall. How she found her way through the hotel she later had no idea, but she arrived in the garden with several other people in tow, no doubt awoken by the noise she made.

Zoe was wet through and getting slowly to her feet. Natalie tried to restrain her, "Don't move. Stay still!" Muddy and slippery from the rain-soaked ground it was impossible for Natalie to hold her. Zoe made it to her feet. Shouting against the storm, Natalie put her arms around her friend and tried to shepherd her back into the hotel. As they approached the open doors, Zoe stopped and stared, a look of sheer horror on her face. Then she let out an ear-piercing scream: a scream so tortured, so despairing and so heart-stopping that Natalie was, in that moment not just afraid to help her friend, but deeply afraid of her. Unsupported, Zoe dropped to her knees.

"Zoe, what's wrong? Are you hurt? Tell me where it hurts." Overcoming her fear Natalie crouched down in front of Zoe and gently took her head in her hands. "Zoe, talk to me." As she looked into Zoe's eyes, illuminated by the light from the hotel, Natalie went cold, shaken to the core. Zoe's face was completely blank, and her eyes had lost all comprehension. Natalie stared, uncertain of what she was seeing and feeling. As other guests took over and guided Zoe inside, Natalie followed, watching as her unsteady friend briefly braced herself against the hall wall, leaving behind a muddy smudge, before being deposited in the nearest available chair. Blankets were brought and an ambulance called. As others took charge, Natalie was despatched up to their room for clothes to take to the hospital.

Natalie sat and waited and the clock on the corridor wall ticked slowly on. What were they doing? Initially she had been bombarded with questions, 'how far had Zoe fallen?', 'what had she landed on?', 'had she lost consciousness?', 'did she have any medical conditions?', 'had she taken any drugs?' Then there was the Police Officer, asking question after question, as if Natalie had shoved Zoe out of the window. Now she was on her own, and no-one stopped to ask or tell her anything. Zoe had been wheeled away for an MRI scan and Natalie didn't know what to do. Should she call her parents? It was 3.30am and there was nothing they could do, and it would take them half a day to arrive. Besides, she had nothing to report other than that Zoe was in the hospital. The staff hadn't found anything physically wrong with her bar a few minor cuts and bruises, but she wasn't responding, just staring into space and she didn't appear to be able to hear anything.

The ceiling was a grimy cream, and peeling. A single dark red metal shade hung from the centre of the room. Its glaringly white lining reflected dazzling white light. She stared at it. The light was painful, but it was something to focus on, to hang on to. Every part of her body hurt. She wanted to scream but her chest had enough to do just drawing in each successive breath. Desperately she wanted to close her eyes. Desperately she wanted to sink into oblivion, to give in, but she couldn't. She couldn't and wouldn't give in. Someone came close and peered at her, mouthing words that she could neither hear nor understand. She felt something sharp in the crook of her arm, barely distinguishable from the rest of the pain. Then something tightened on her other arm, cutting off the circulation to her hand before releasing its grip again. Various other tests were carried out, all painful, and she tried to protest, but this only produced sympathetic smiles and more prodding. She opened her mouth, but only a strange gurgle came out when she tried to speak. She had to make someone understand.

Finally, one of the doctors came to see Natalie and explained that none of the investigations had shown any physical injury. Zoe's chest, skull and spine were fine, her blood tests were all normal and her alcohol level, although over the legal driving limit, did not account for her semi-unresponsive state. They were going to monitor her overnight and assess her again in the morning. Natalie may as well leave. So, she took a taxi back to the hotel to wait for midday when she had been told to ring the hospital for an update.

Chapter Two

Despite not getting to bed until nearly 5am Natalie barely slept. As light crept round the side of the curtains, she at last fell into a deep sleep. When her alarm went off at 10am she awoke with a start and stared at the other bed. Yes, it was empty. Zoe was in hospital, and it hadn't been a dream. She crawled out of bed and went and drew open the curtains. The sun streamed into the room, blinding her. As her eyes adjusted, she barely took in the view as she looked down to the ground outside the window to see where Zoe had landed and to try to make sense of it all. Below the window, was a huge privet bush. It appeared to be split down the middle: its thick trunk was snapped and its branches in disarray. It had broken Zoe's fall and probably saved her life. Looking further away the ground was a muddy mess, the grass badly trampled.

As she got dressed Natalie became increasingly annoyed. Zoe should not have been able to fall out of the window. If the hotel was complying with Health and Safety, then it shouldn't have been possible. Incensed, she headed down to reception. A young man, she hadn't seen before, sat behind the desk. He stood up and smiled and asked what he could do for her.

"I would like to know why it was possible for my friend to fall out of our bedroom window and end up in hospital. There should have been safety catches on there. I nearly fell out too trying to close it."

"There are safety catches on all the windows. It is possible to undo them in an emergency, but they don't come undone easily – they are supposed to be child proof." As he looked Natalie in the eye she raised an eyebrow, not sure if the comment was loaded. "We were waiting for you to get up so that we can investigate."

"Well, you'd better. I am not letting this drop. Is it possible to have some breakfast?"

"I am sorry, but they stopped serving breakfast 15 minutes ago. The restaurant will be open for lunch at midday." Seeing that Natalie wasn't impressed he offered, "There is a café just down the street that does all day breakfasts."

Outside it was cold and miserable but no longer wet. The wind had stopped howling, but the gulls were still noisily voicing their opinions. It was a lovely little café. She stepped inside and shut out the noise of the gulls. There was an eclectic collection of mismatched chairs round little tables covered in pretty linen cloths. The walls were covered in a selection of local artworks, each with a hefty price tag. Most were seascapes and beach scenes, but some depicted local buildings: pretty in their own way. Natalie seated herself at a table near the window so that she could watch people passing in the street outside.

Soon a delicate China teapot and matching cup and saucer arrived. Picking up a teaspoon she removed the teapot lid and stirred. Steam rose and she watched as leaves swirled and the liquid turned a satisfying rich brown. Before it was cool enough to drink, a plate of hot bacon, eggs, sausage, beans, mushrooms, tomato and fried bread were placed in front of her. She hadn't realised how hungry she was: the lack of sleep and worry, taking its toll. The mustard and ketchup she had asked for were presented in two tiny white dishes and she spooned dollops from both onto her plate. Then she sprinkled a little salt and pepper onto her eggs. Knife and fork in hand she chopped off a piece of fried bread and dunked it into the yolk of an egg, and then carefully into the ketchup to pick up just the right amount. It was fabulous. As she savoured the first mouthful she inhaled, savouring the smell of the bacon, inspecting the rest of her plate, contented. It was strange how some foods didn't need company. Some foods provided companionship all on their own. Briefly she forgot that her friend was in the hospital and then felt guilty that she was enjoying herself. She must bring Zoe here.

It didn't take her long to eat it all, so she ordered some toast whilst she sipped her tea and waited for midday. After what seemed a very long wait, and a second pot of tea, she phoned the hospital. When she eventually got through to someone who knew what she was talking about she was told to please ring back in half an hour, as the 'ward round' had taken longer than expected. Deflated, she paid and decided to go for a walk around the town to pass the time.

Outside the café she turned away from the hotel and headed into the breeze. The street sloped slightly and, she noted, grew steeper further down. It would be uphill on the way back but at least she would no longer be walking into the wind. The shops were typical tourist ones, and she stepped inside a couple and looked around. She had no intention of buying anything, but it was a good way to pass the time. At the end of the shops the street curved, and Natalie found that she now had a view of the sea. Drawn forward, she walked as far as she could, coming to a halt at a green painted railing that marked the edge of the cliff. What a view! Sweeping her eyes along the horizon she caught sight of some fishing boats and a container ship. Up the coast to her left were cliffs and to her right what looked like a port; she could see cranes and other metal structures and warehouse buildings. Nearer, in both directions, was coastline. Below, she could see evidence of sandy beaches in little coves. They would have to investigate.

It was time. Sitting herself in the corner of a small wood and glass shelter, out of the wind, she tried to phone the hospital. No signal. Frustrated she headed back to the café and stood outside. Yes, she had a signal. She rang and this time there was news. Zoe was okay. They could find nothing wrong with her. After a sleep, she had woken, alert and fully orientated, had eaten her breakfast and was now ready to leave if someone could come and pick her up.

Within 45 minutes Natalie was back at the hospital with a coat for Zoe and a warmer set of clothes than the ones she had provided the previous night. As Zoe got dressed a nurse gave Natalie a set of instructions and explained that if Zoe demonstrated any of the listed symptoms, she was to bring her back.

"The night staff said she kept calling for Meg. Well, it sounded like Meg. At one point they thought she was saying leg. However, this morning, apart from understandably being a little subdued, she seems perfectly okay. She was very lucky. Does the name Meg mean anything to you?" asked the nurse.

Natalie shook her head. Everyone Zoe knew, she knew.

Chapter Three

When their taxi pulled up at the hotel, Natalie got out. Zoe, however, stayed put. "I'm not going in there. It is way too embarrassing."

"What? At least get out. I am not paying more for this taxi than necessary," and she dragged Zoe into the street. With the taxi gone, Natalie stared at her friend. "You aren't serious, are you?"

"Can't we just find a pub, eat out this evening and then go up to our room when there is no-one about. Then, after the solicitor tomorrow, we can go home."

Natalie was about to argue further but there was something about Zoe's demeanour that gave her pause. This reluctance to face people, Natalie completely understood, she faced it every day, but any reluctance, any lack of confidence in social situations, was completely out of character for Zoe. She was the outgoing, gregarious one who frequently embarrassed Natalie, dragging her into situations that she wouldn't even have considered. She remembered a theatre trip to London when Zoe fancied a look backstage and had found an open door. In she went with an increasingly worried Natalie in tow. When they were finally challenged Zoe just beamed her way out of the situation, heaping praise on everyone and everything and gaining a personal tour for the two of them and drinks with the cast.

Now, Zoe rested herself against the hotel wall, arms folded, firmly stating her intention to stay put. Seeing that she was adamant, Natalie took the spare clothes up to their room, and then re-joined Zoe in the High Street. They found a café, a different one to the one Natalie had had breakfast in, and ordered tea and cake.

"So," said Natalie, "What happened? How did you manage to fall out of the window? Actually, I know how you managed to fall out. I nearly fell out myself when I went to close it, but why did you open it in the first place? I know it was noisy what with the storm and those horrendous gulls shrieking but opening the window makes like, absolutely no sense."

Zoe didn't reply. She was staring into space. When Natalie nudged her arm, she looked as if she was surprised to see her.

"Zoe! Talk to me. Are you feeling okay? The hospital said to take you back if you weren't right."

Slowly Zoe gathered herself and looked at Natalie. "I, I'm, no I'm fine." Seeing that Natalie wasn't convinced she added, "Really, I'm okay."

Natalie wasn't sure, but she was certain that she wasn't going to get much more out of Zoe, so she suggested that they went for a walk and explore the town. Maybe a bit of fresh air would do them both good.

After the first 100 metres Natalie buttoned up her jacket and wrapped her scarf round her neck a couple of times before tucking the ends inside her lapels. Then, as they walked along the pavement, she pulled gloves out of her pockets and put them on. Zoe, it seemed, was oblivious to the cold. Natalie chatted away, telling Zoe what she had seen on her morning outing, suggesting that they head to the cliff top as the view was lush. She knew that she was talking a lot. She felt the need to fill the gap left by Zoe who normally filled any silence with non-stop chatter and giggles. When they reached the cliff top, they headed left, along the backs of the High Street buildings, most of which were holiday flats and cafés, with terraces enjoying spectacular views of the sea. They walked as far as they could and then stopped at what Natalie assumed was the wall of their hotel. A sign on a large gate stating, 'The Dolphin Hotel and Lido - residents only', providing confirmation. It seemed that the hotel had its own cliff top garden, which made sense with what she had seen from their room window. She gave the gate a rattle, but it looked like a swipe card was needed. Maybe they should ask for one. They turned and headed back the way they had come.

A gap in the railings, which ran the length of the promenade, revealed a set of steps zigzagging their way down to the shore. Green painted railings marked the edges of the path, and similarly painted green benches, which were placed at intervals, provided rest along the way for the weary. Natalie and Zoe went part way down and took a seat on the first bench. It was less windy here, below the cliff top, and they were able to sit and enjoy the view. Looking down they could see that the path currently went nowhere as the tide was in. They watched as straggly bits of seaweed were slapped onto the concrete and then dragged back into the surf. It looked cold, violent, and uninviting. Cawing and hovering, a gull tried to touch down on one of the rocks but was repeatedly reprimanded by the waves. Giving up it soared in an arc, caught an updraft, and rocketed skywards.

"I don't know about you, but I'm just getting cold sitting here," said Natalie. "Let's go back. We can look in a few shops to pass the time."

They trudged their way back up the cliff and back into the wind, which appeared to have increased. It was bitterly cold now and the light was starting to fade. It looked like they were in for another storm. As tiny drops of rain started to fall, they arrived at their first shop and almost fell through the door. It was a gift shop which turned out to be a bit of an 'Aladdin's Cave'. It was crammed floor to ceiling with all sorts of seaside gifts and the shop space extended into the depths of the building and up two floors. It stocked everything from postcards to cheap ceramics, books, artwork and expensive ornaments and handbags. Natalie soon found a bag she liked. She didn't, however, like the price. They wandered round for a bit, Zoe trailing after Natalie as she picked up random items and inspected them, rejecting and mentally selecting goods for possible purchase later. After a few more shops Natalie's head was buzzing. She wanted to sit down. Back on the street she headed in the direction of the hotel, hoping that Zoe would follow her in when they got there. They got nearer and nearer, and Zoe said nothing. Natalie kept her fingers crossed. As she reached the hotel door, she realised that she was alone. Zoe had stopped a few feet away.

"Really! You aren't going in?" said Natalie.

Zoe looked stricken.

"Let's at least go in and change."

Zoe didn't move.

"Fine, but I am coming back here to change before we go to eat," and she set off up the High Street and turned into the first pub that she came to, a swinging board over the door declaring 'The One-Eyed Seagull'. She bought a couple of J2O's and headed over to a table in the corner. Zoe followed and sat down. After a couple of refreshing glugs Natalie turned to Zoe, "Look, you need to talk to me. This isn't like you. You are normally, like, so bubbly..."

Still Zoe said nothing.

"Is something hurting?" She reached out and took her friend's hand. It was cold and almost lifeless: a barely perceptible shake present. "Please talk to me. What happened last night? I was so scared when I saw you lying on the ground. Zoe, I thought you were dead. I couldn't bear that."

"I'm fine. If you want to go change, I'll get us another drink and then we can go find somewhere to eat."

Leaving Zoe at the bar, Natalie headed back to the hotel.

Someone had been in their room. There was evidence of work being carried out on the windows: the catches were new. However, they looked identical to the old catches which had been left behind on the windowsill. She picked one up and turned it over in her hand. The plastic appeared to be stretched and snapped. Had the staff deliberately left the old ones behind? Why? To show that there had been catches or to show the damage Zoe had done. Either way the break shouldn't have been possible. Or, were they just designed to stop children breaking them! She wasn't happy. Quickly she changed and then packed both her and Zoe's belongings. On her way out of the hotel she demanded a new room. The only room available was the bridal suite which they could have for two nights but they would then have to move to another room. Concealing her delight, she accepted. Then she realised that there would only be one bed. Still, at least she might notice if Zoe got up in the night.

Re-entering 'The One-eyed Seagull', which was considerably busier than when she had left, she couldn't see Zoe. The table they had been sitting at was now occupied by a couple of elderly gentlemen playing Dominoes, and cradling pints of frothy white topped stout in their spare hands. Then, above the general noise she heard a familiar laugh. She couldn't see her friend but heading over to the bar she found Zoe surrounded by three young men. Two were smartly dressed, obviously out for the evening, but the third looked like he had come straight from work: odd for a Sunday. He had steel toed boots, covered in either paint or plaster, with similarly splattered trousers, and a donkey jacket over a paint splotched T-shirt. She smiled: glad to see that Zoe appeared to be back to her normal self. Being the centre of attention was how Zoe lived her life. If they weren't such great friends, Natalie could have hated her for it. Instead, she accepted the situation, generally content to observe from the sidelines, but occasionally interjecting her own brand of charm to focus the attention on herself, just to check she could.

"Natalie, great, you're back. Stan," and she gestured to the barman, "a drink for my friend."

"I'll get this," said the nearest of Zoe's three companions. "What would you like?"

"She'll have a rum and coke," said Zoe, and then, to Natalie, "You were so long I drank yours as well as mine."

Assessing the state of her friend, Natalie said pointedly, "I'll have a mango J2O please."

"Really? You've got to have something stronger than that."

"Yeah, get her a rum and coke."

Looking directly at the barman Natalie repeated, "J2O please."

After introductions, they chatted and consumed another two rounds of drinks. Then a phone rang and was pulled out of one of the lads' pockets. After a quick scrutiny its owner said, "Charlotte and Amy are wondering where we are. Better go." As the two smartly dressed lads made to go, they slapped their mate on the back and said suggestively, "Have fun, Kyle."

Kyle, the quietest of the three lads, now looked a little uncomfortable and started to mumble that he too had better be going.

"No, no, stay," said Zoe as she put her arm around him.

"Isn't it time we got something to eat?" said Natalie.

"Yes. Kyle, where would you suggest? I'm starving. Not too expensive mind."

"Er, there is a good fish and chip place. It has a great view of the estuary, and it is licensed."

"Excellent!"

So, the three of them headed outside and, arm in arm with Zoe, Kyle led them down the High Street, Natalie trailing behind.

The restaurant was beautifully lit with shiny gold lettering lighting up the High Street and looking very inviting. The three of them went in and were given a table by the back window. Being dark now, it was difficult to see beyond the prettily lit terrace and it was a shame that they couldn't see the sea. However, plates of cod, chips, mushy peas, and a pint each, soon took their minds off it.

Kyle turned out to be great company. Quietly unassuming he had a gentle sense of humour. It took the girls a little while to realise that he was joking as his dead-pan delivery was initially a little off-putting. Once they understood, they thoroughly enjoyed his company. He was single, a plasterer by trade but had just started his own decorating business. With lots of holiday accommodation in the area he was kept busy as competition for business, amongst owners, was fierce. He had grown up in the town and was very enthusiastic about the area and its history. Fishing was the main source of income but there were issues, both environmental and political which were having an impact, and trade was turning more and more to tourism.

When they finally left the restaurant, he walked them back to the hotel: although later Natalie couldn't have said if he was going that way anyway. He told them that he would be in 'The

One-eyed Seagull' again the following night, if they fancied meeting up again.

This time Zoe didn't put up any fight as they entered the hotel. There was no-one at the reception desk and Natalie steered her towards the lift, deciding that the stairs would be too much of a challenge of co-ordination. She wasn't sure how much Zoe had drunk, but it was obviously too much. The lift doors opened noisily, and they stepped inside. Was it the weary fluorescent light in the lift, or did Zoe look slightly green? The doors closed with a juddering clang, and the lift rose. Zoe's knees sagged slightly, but she steadied herself and beamed. Natalie realised that Zoe was trying to demonstrate that she was fine. However, she just looked slightly demented: not something you want in a friend, especially if you are sharing a room, and a bed. As the doors opened Natalie stepped out, crossed the corridor, and put the key in their door. Behind her she heard the lift doors start to close, accompanied by a strangled retching noise. Spinning round, she was just in time to see the doors close on Zoe's head as she spewed green fish and chips into the gap. The doors parted briefly, and Zoe's head disappeared. On their second attempt, and now lubricated, the doors managed to close. Natalie leapt at the lift call button, stabbing frantically. The mechanism groaned and she heard the lift descend a couple of floors before creaking to a halt. Then, slowly, it returned. The doors opened to reveal Zoe on her knees staring at a mushy green mess. She watched in fascination as it spread, oozing between the cracks to drip down the lift shaft. Natalie held the doors open and helped Zoe out. Depositing her in the ensuite she went back to the lift with a toilet roll and a couple of towels to try to clean up the mess. As well as on the floor, Zoe had managed to get the lumpy slick all down the insides of the doors. Holding one hand in the air on a level with the sensor, to avoid the lift closing and moving floor, Natalie was able to crouch and mop with the other, but it was exhausting. Every time she stopped, the doors closed, dragging more mess out from the recess of the lift and depositing more green slime down the lift shaft. For as long as she lived, she didn't think she would ever be able to face mushy peas again. When she finally gave up, and went back to their room, she found a fully clothed Zoe sprawled on the bed amongst a delicate scattering of pink rose petals, another pile of vomit on the carpet outside the bathroom door. Incongruously, floating on the slick was a bedraggled origami towel swan. This ridiculous item of hospitality had been on the bed with a small selection of cellophane wrapped chocolates and a dolphin-motif label saying, 'With the compliments of The Dolphin Hotel and Lido'. Natalie briefly wondered where the chocolates were.

Irritated, she did her best to clean up the mess. Then she dismantled the swan and rinsed out the towels in the bath, picking bits of pea off the previously white material, before using the base of a tiny bottle of hotel shower gel to squash the chip remains down the plug hole. Finally, with a quick spray of air freshener, she managed to make the bathroom presentable. Exhausted, she removed Zoe's shoes, covered her with a blanket and then crawled into bed. As she settled silently between the sheets, she became aware that Zoe was snoring. With difficulty she rolled her friend onto her side and the snoring stopped. However, she was now facing Natalie's side of the bed and breathing, open-mouthed, in Natalie's face. Natalie turned her back, but the fragrant fog was all enveloping. Briefly she tried turning Zoe the other way. Despite the width of the bed, there wasn't room without pulling her nearer to its centre, which she failed to do. In desperation she un-tucked the sheets, grabbed her own two pillows and placed them at the foot of the bed. Having her head next to Zoe's feet wasn't pleasant but preferable and she soon fell asleep.

Chapter Four

In the morning Zoe was wide awake and, incredibly, not feeling too shabby. She was however, mystified as to what she was doing in a bridal suite with Natalie but relieved that they were no longer in their original room.

Once dressed they headed down for breakfast, Natalie steering Zoe away from the lift, which now had an 'Out of Order' notice dangling from its call button, and towards the stairs.

When they stood by the 'Wait here to be seated' sign the duty manager almost ran to them and guided them to a table by the window. His manner was professional but with a slight edge to it of which Natalie was acutely aware. Zoe however, seemed oblivious. He took their order for coffee and pointed out the buffet. They filled up their plates with a full English breakfast and returned to their table. Zoe sipped her coffee and toyed with her beans: now uncertain whether eating was a good idea.

Looking out of the window, Natalie wasn't sure why they had been seated there as the view wasn't very picturesque. It wasn't the only window seat available, and it had the worst view. Outside the window was a very tatty privet bush, badly mangled with a split trunk. Then she realised that it was the one below their original window. This was the bush that had broken Zoe's fall. It looked to be beyond repair. Feeling uncomfortable she turned her attention back to her food and the table. In amongst the condiments was a metal stand with postcards. She pulled out the first one and stared in dismay at a large green dolphin. This beautifully shaped bush must have taken years to grow and shape, painstakingly clipped year after year. Zoe had destroyed The Dolphin Hotel's iconic topiary dolphin. Quietly she placed it back and faced it away from Zoe.

The taxi arrived on time and drove them inland to the solicitor's office. Zoe gave her name at the reception desk, and they were told to 'please take a seat'. They sat, surrounded by pot plants and county magazines, and exchanged smiles with a lady sitting opposite. Following a quick phone call, made by the receptionist, a gentleman appeared and introduced himself as George Titherington.

"Which one of you is Zoe?"

"I am," said Zoe, "and this is my friend Natalie."

"Good. So," he said, now turning to the elderly lady, "You must be Miss Hardcastle." She nodded and he continued, "Ladies, please follow me."

All three women stood and stared at one another. Miss Hardcastle looked positively shocked and very displeased. She turned and marched quickly after the solicitor, her back straight and her shoulders stiff, clutching her handbag to her bosom. Behind Miss Hardcastle Natalie mouthed, "Who is that?" Zoe wrinkled her nose and shrugged her shoulders.

Once they were all seated in Mr Titherington's office he began, "Thank you all for coming. As you are aware, the late Mr Walter James Brammar named you in his will."

Natalie, sitting slightly to one side, was able to observe Miss Hardcastle. The woman really wasn't happy that Zoe was there. It was increasingly obvious that she had thought she was the sole heir.

The solicitor began to explain the terms of the will. To Zoe, his great granddaughter, he had left his property and investments: the details of which he would go into in private with Zoe. First, he needed to explain the provision made by Mr Brammar for Miss Hardcastle. For Zoe's benefit he explained that Miss Hardcastle was Mr Brammar's hotel manager and in the latter part of his years, companion. In gratitude for her selfless commitment to the running of 'The Dolphin Hotel and Lido' and for her superb care of him, she was to retain the use of her hotel apartment. Now Zoe interjected, whilst Natalie stared in wonder, "The Dolphin Hotel and Lido, he owned the Dolphin Hotel?"

"Yes," said Mr Titherington, "You didn't know!"

"No," said both Zoe and Natalie.

"So," said Zoe slowly, "I've inherited a hotel? *That hotel!*"

"Yes, but there is a provision attached; to ensure that the hotel continues to run efficiently, and that Miss Hardcastle has somewhere to live, she is to retain the use of her hotel apartment whilst continuing to manage the hotel."

At this point he asked Miss Hardcastle to wait outside as he needed to talk to Zoe in private. He would call her back in when they were done. Miss Hardcastle stood and swept out of the room, crashing the door into the wall. It remained open. The solicitor got up and carefully closed it.

"I can see that this has come as a bit of a surprise to you. Taking on a business is a big task which is why your great grandfather wanted Miss Hardcastle to continue managing the place for you. Also, in order to inherit you must run the hotel, successfully, for 5 years. If you choose to sell before that time, you inherit nothing, and the money will go to the local lifeboat station. Your great grandfather always gave 5% of the hotel profits to the lifeboat station, and that must continue. Have a look at the hotel, think about what you are taking on and let me know by the end of the week. If you decide to go ahead, we can sign the paperwork then."

After several questions and further discussion, they stepped out of the office, and

Miss Hardcastle stood, lips pursed, and headed in to see Mr Titherington.

In the taxi the two girls were stunned. *A hotel*! Zoe had inherited a hotel, *and lido*. It was so exciting. They couldn't wait to explore it and investigate the grounds.

Before they knew it, they were back at the hotel. Laughing and giggling they burst through the front door.

"Ah, Miss Spencer, Miss Walker, I am so glad you are here. The Duty Manager would like to talk to you," said a frosty faced receptionist. As they approached the reception desk the woman rose, stuck her head into the room behind the reception desk and spoke to someone, who then appeared.

"Hello, I am Mrs Johnson, the Duty Manager," pausing, she looked Zoe and Natalie up and down. The two young women felt like they were back in the headmistress's office, something that had happened to Natalie only once. Zoe, a frequent visitor, had been responsible for that occasion. Zoe stared insolently back, and the woman continued, "Following a number of complaints, and 'INCIDENTS' I must ask you to pack and leave the hotel.

"What? You can't do that," said an indignant Zoe.

"Yes, we can. We have had a number of complaints of noise from guests, complaints of rudeness from staff, destruction of property, i.e. dirty handprints on the wall by the back door, muddy carpet, an expensive chair which needs professional cleaning and possibly reupholstering, forced window catches, a lift which needs deep cleaning, parts of which will need dismantling in order to do that, a wedding suite which is currently unusable due to a badly stained carpet and chocolate impregnated silk bedspread AND, most distressing of all, the destruction of a 100 year old topiary dolphin. That dolphin survived World War Two bombing, but not you! So, yes, we *can insist* that you leave."

"No, you can't," said a resigned voice from the doorway. Miss Hardcastle had just returned. She walked behind the reception desk as the two members of staff stared at her. "You can't ask them to leave. This here," and she waved her hand dismissively in Zoe's direction, "is Mr Brammar's great granddaughter. She is now the owner of the hotel, and your new boss."

Several expressions crossed the Duty Manager's face: annoyance that her authority had been publicly challenged, disbelief that Zoe was the new owner, and then dismay that she had tried to evict her. Finally, it looked like she now feared for her job. Miss Hardcastle seemed to take brief satisfaction in the woman's discomfort. The wrinkles at the side of her mouth, highlighted by the bleed of her lipstick, narrowed and turned up slightly. Then, turning her attention to Zoe she said waspishly, "You will probably wish to address the staff. I will gather them together for you. Shall we say 2pm in the Conference Room?" With that she disappeared into the back office and shut the door leaving the receptionist and Duty Manager to wait uncomfortably whilst Zoe and Natalie headed away upstairs.

Back in the Bridal Suite a sickly-sweet smell assaulted their nostrils. An attempt had been made to clean the carpet, leaving a large wet patch by the bathroom door. Hopefully it would be less obvious once dry.

Trying not to wretch, and pressing her fingers to her temples, Zoe sat on the edge of the bed. "I can't address the staff. What am I going to say?" She picked up the key fob she'd thrown on the bed and played absent-mindedly with its wooden dolphin. "What time is it? No-ooh! It is nearly half one. I've got 35 minutes."

"Well, you could just cancel. Tell the receptionist you aren't ready to speak to the staff yet. You will let them know when you are. Or, you could 'take the bull by the horns', after all, you are good at that. Just be yourself, tell them that it has come as a surprise and you want to have a look round, see what you've inherited, take a look at the books..."

"Yes, brilliant – look at the books. That sounds professional and it sounds like I have a plan," said Zoe.

"And go do something with your face. You look like crap."

Having both smartened themselves up they headed down. Big wooden signs with gold lettering, announcing 'to the Conference Room' led them to a room over the reception area. The double doors were closed, but failed to contain the noise of people on the other side. As Zoe pushed open one of the doors the room fell silent and about 20 pairs of eyes all turned and stared at her. Feeling distinctly uncomfortable she and Natalie walked round the edge of the room to a table in front of the staff. There was no chair. Was that deliberate? A quick glance round the room showed that there weren't any spare ones to hand. So, they perched on the edge of the table. Zoe looked at her audience and smiled her best smile. From the comfort of the crowd Miss Hardcastle could be seen, smugly waiting to see what would happen. She plainly had no intention of introducing Zoe or attempting to make her feel welcome.

"Thank you all for coming, and to Miss... sorry, what was your name?" All eyes now followed Zoe's gaze and turned towards Miss Hardcastle. Natalie tried not to smirk as the woman straightened her shoulders and sat up

45

straight in her chair. Pushing her wire rimmed glasses back up her nose she cleared her throat.

"Miss Hardcastle."

"Yes, thank you Miss Hardcastle for organising this meeting," said Zoe brightly, letting her audience know this gathering wasn't her idea. "For those of you who don't already know, Walter Brammar was my great grandfather. I am Zoe Spencer. This is my friend Natalie Walker. I have just discovered that he left The Dolphin Hotel and Lido to me." She paused, and appraised her audience. A variety of expressions met her gaze. Most of the staff just looked interested or indifferent, but some were distinctly hostile. "As you can imagine, inheriting a hotel has come as a bit of a surprise. So, before making any decisions, on the running of this place, I intend to have a good look around, and inspect the books, etc. Once I have done that, I will be in a better position to talk to you all." Then she beamed and said brightly, "Perhaps we can gather here again at 2pm on Friday – Miss Hardcastle, perhaps you could see to that. In the meantime, please, just carry on as normal. Thank you. Could I have a volunteer to show me round?"

"Perhaps, the Duty Manager," suggested Natalie, pointing to the woman, she had spotted, sitting two rows back.

"Yes," said Zoe, appreciating what Natalie was doing. "Please, we didn't get your name before. I am Zoe, and this is Natalie. And you are?"

The Duty Manager joined them, looking uncomfortable but putting on a brave face through a crooked smile. She looked on the verge of an apology but other than saying her name, Karen Johnson, and smoothing down her suit, she stayed silent.

Zoe decided to try and make a friend of her and to put her at her ease. So, she smiled, as she waited for the room to empty. Once the three of them were alone she held out her hand, "Hi, I am sorry that we have been like... such terrible guests and speaking now, as owner, I have to say that you did the right thing, telling us to leave. I wouldn't want us here wrecking the place."

"We aren't normally like this," said Natalie, "and we were mortified when you went through that list, but it all came about as a result of Zoe falling out of the window, which wasn't her fault. She has been having a terrible time coping with the experience. We still have no idea how that happened. The rest, well, neither of us ever drinks that much normally."

Karen appeared to relax and agreed that it all must have been quite traumatic and said she hoped Zoe was okay now. She told them that the hotel had no idea how the catches came to break. They were designed for an adult to be able to unfasten them in an emergency, but not to break. Happy that her job now seemed secure she gladly showed them round.

Miss Hardcastle sat in her apartment and wept. It was so unfair. Why had he done this? The hotel should be hers. 12 years of managing the place: 10 years caring for him after his wife died; the last 2 feeding, washing, and dressing him. Why had he given the hotel to this... this child: a child who didn't even know how to behave in a hotel, let alone run one? He should have given it to *her*, Doreen. Instead, her only thanks after all those years, was to carry on. To carry on doing what she had been doing, and to live in the flat which came with the job. "Walter, how could you?"

She stood and looked out of the window. She considered going for a walk. Really, she wanted to leave. Leave, and not come back. Leave that spoilt child to manage, but Doreen had nowhere to go, no family to stay with and no friends to speak of. The hotel had been her life and her social circle for as long as she could remember. She couldn't leave. To make things worse, they all knew that she had expected to inherit. She hadn't said anything, but they knew; they expected it too. Some of them had sympathised with her, but she despised their pity. Others were amused, and she loathed them for it. As she stared through the wet glass her eyes filled again and she let the tears fall.

It was a large hotel with 62 guest rooms, a bridal suite, 2 conference rooms at the front, a bar and lounge, and 2 dining rooms, one for hotel guests and one to accompany the function room on the ground floor at the back. From an upstairs room Karen pointed out the landscaped garden and explained that there was access to the beach via steps and a lift. As it was raining again, they agreed to leave viewing the pool and its changing facilities, for another time. They trailed round after Karen, looking in room after room, the function rooms being the most interesting. There were several 'back' rooms, offices, stores, and finally the kitchen. Zoe and Natalie nodded and smiled at the kitchen staff as Karen introduced them all. Then she turned to leave.

"Where does that door go?" asked Zoe.

Karen looked at a large oak door in the corner of the room and said, "I believe it goes down to the cellar," looking at the kitchen staff for confirmation, which none of them provided.

"Can't we see?" asked Zoe. She walked over and took hold of the handle. It was locked.

Karen looked at the kitchen staff and the kitchen staff all stopped what they were doing and looked at one another. Then they all looked at Karen, whilst taking, what might have been, furtive glances at the cellar door.

"It is just a dusty mess. No-one goes down there, anymore," said the head chef. "I'd have to find the key."

"Then please find it," said Zoe as she followed Karen out into the reception area.

"Please wait here whilst I find Miss Hardcastle," said Karen. "She has the keys to Mr Brammar's private apartment. She probably has a spare key for the cellar, too," and she set off upstairs.

"There was a key on a hook next to the door," whispered Natalie.

"What? Come on," said Zoe, and led the way back to the kitchen. As they walked in, conversation ceased and vacant faces eyed them suspiciously. Natalie wanted to leave but Zoe marched straight to the cellar door, grabbed the key, and fitted it in the lock. It wouldn't turn. She pulled it out and inspected it.

Natalie looked. It wasn't the same key. She was certain of it. She whispered to Zoe, "I'm sure the key I saw was an old brownish metal one."

Zoe whipped round and glared at the staff, "Where is the key?"

No-one spoke, but a couple glanced at the head chef and everyone else followed their gaze. All eyes now on her, the chef squared her substantial shoulders, held her head up and said, "I don't know. It has been missing for some time."

Zoe strode towards the woman and thrust the key at her face. Almost squinting, the woman looked at the key. Then she stepped slightly to one side and looked Zoe in the eye. "You really don't want to go down there. We don't use that space anymore."

"Well, I would still like to see it."

"As I said, the key is missing."

"Well, as I say, you'd better start looking."

At the top of the hotel Miss Hardcastle handed over the keys of Mr Brammar's apartment, "No I don't have one for the cellar but there should be a spare one in my office safe. I'll have a look next time I'm down." Having no intention of bothering anytime soon she closed her apartment door. Then, she started to wonder what the kitchen staff were hiding. None of them had been at the hotel that long. Certainly none had been there at Zoe's mother's final visit.

It took a while but when Karen returned, she took the girls to a door marked Private, on what appeared to be the upper floor. Opening it, she led them up a staircase to the very top of the hotel. The apartment took up most of the roof space and included a large terrace overlooking the grounds and, of course, the sea. The remainder of the top floor space contained Miss Hardcastle's flat which also had an area of terrace, adjacent to Mr Brammar's.

"I don't know what your plans are, but I suppose you could move in here, now that you own the place," suggested Karen. "I believe that there are a couple of bedrooms. I have never been in here before. It is a lovely apartment, isn't it?" she said, glancing round.

"Yes, it really is," said Natalie. "Let's get our stuff. Then," and here she looked at Karen, "hopefully you can get the Bridal Suite back into use again. Will it need a new carpet, do you think?"

"Possibly," said Karen, and then laughed, "That list, you really achieved quite a lot, in quite a short space of time: less than 48 hours. I can't remember having guests that caused so much trouble, ever before, and I've worked here for going on 10 years."

Natalie started laughing and then Zoe joined in, "I am so sorry, it was all my fault. Natalie isn't to blame for any of it."

"But how on earth did you manage to fall out of the window?"

"I don't know, I really don't know. I, I just..."

Natalie noticed the brief internalisation. There was something that Zoe wasn't willing to admit to, or, was afraid to own.

Oblivious, Karen ploughed on, "You just what...?"

Zoe blinked, a barely perceptible shudder, "I just remember waking up outside."

"You must remember something. Do you sleepwalk? I have a cousin who does that: gets herself into all sorts of situations. I remember once..."

"No," snapped Zoe. "I don't sleepwalk. Never! I just don't remember. Okay!" But Zoe did remember. Natalie could see that. She could also see that Zoe was scared. It would be perfectly understandable to be unnerved by falling out of a third-floor window. To get up in the night to close a window and be unbalanced by the force of the wind, as Natalie had, would unnerve anyone. Nearly falling out had shaken Natalie, but she knew that actually falling out, wasn't it. There was something else. This wasn't about accidentally slipping or being careless. This was something different. This was something deep seated and primal. Natalie had seen it in Zoe's eyes as she helped her back into the hotel after the fall.

"Come on, let's go and get our things. I suppose I get *that* room," said Natalie pointing at the smaller of the two bedrooms, being as I am just a guest of her ladyship."

Zoe didn't laugh, so Natalie shepherded her to the door whilst raising her eyebrows at Karen.

It didn't take Doreen long to locate the spare key. When Karen came back down, she bid her follow. Back, ramrod straight, she marched into the kitchen. Brandishing the key, she launched into the head chef, "If you really can't find the cellar key we will have another cut, but what I would like to know, is why didn't you report it missing?"

The chef just stared. At first, she looked wary, glancing between Miss Hardcastle and

Karen. Then the dynamics changed, and she almost smiled, "I don't answer to you anymore." Her eyes travelled briefly to Karen, implying her inclusion.

Doreen raised an eyebrow, said nothing but held the woman's gaze. Then she turned and pushed the key into the door's lock. A bit of jiggling and it turned. She pushed the door back and reached inside for the light switch and switched it on. Then, ensuring Karen followed, she went down.

Chapter Five

Having gathered their belongings and moved them into the flat they spent some time arranging them and checking out the kitchen. Someone had cleaned out the fridge, but the cupboards were still stocked. It looked like the flat had been tidied and the bedding stripped from the bed in what they assumed had been Zoe's great grandfather's bedroom. On a trunk at the foot of the bed was a pile of clean bedding. As Zoe was still a little distracted, Natalie set about making up the bed for her. She was surprised at how feminine the bedding was: not something you would expect an old man to have. Then it dawned on her. This wasn't his bedding. This was Miss Hardcastle's bedding, placed ready to make up the bed, for her. Miss Hardcastle had been expecting to move in. Briefly it crossed her mind to make up the bed and force Miss Hardcastle to ask for it back but that would have just been mean. So, she folded it back up and went in search of alternative bedding. A large dresser in the hall outside the bedroom supplied what she needed. When the bed was made, she suggested that they go out and get some milk and a few other supplies, like lunch. But then, Zoe owned a hotel; they could just order room service. When she suggested this, Zoe brightened and headed for the phone.

Karen stepped carefully down the stone steps behind Miss Hardcastle, their heels clicking on the cold granite, hands clutching the wooden handrail. Karen sniffed slightly and wrinkled her nostrils, but dutifully followed. Ahead, Doreen had reached the bottom and was fumbling for another light switch. One light came on, and as she flipped another switch a second one illuminated the far end of the underground space, casting shadows. Wrapping her arms about herself Karen stepped carefully down the last step and looked around. It didn't look like anyone had been down there for years. Along one wall was a series of cupboards with large heavy doors, some of them newer than others. The opposite wall contained shelves. Dusty bottles lay stacked on their sides and a few sagging cardboard boxes lay brooding in the gloom. Karen had no difficulty believing that the cellar was no longer used. It was dark, dank, and dusty. Even the spiders had abandoned the place. Garlands of old cobwebs festooned the lights. In the heated glow they heaved slightly, wraith-like. She shivered as a slight breeze briefly lifted the hair at the back of her neck. She turned, looking for the source, but found none. Miss Hardcastle marched about the room looking left and right, up and down. Karen watched puzzled as the other woman poked the odd item, moved another. Then she began wiping a finger along each surface, apparently checking for dust, which was ridiculous, because it was everywhere. There was a crunch as Miss Hardcastle trod on a broken bottle. To Karen's amazement she crouched and picked up a piece of glass, rotated it in the light and then sniffed it. Karen had a brief vision of the woman popping the glass in a forensics' bag.

Karen felt the breeze again. She whipped round in a full circle, unable to locate its cause. Then, something moved in her peripheral vision, just a slight shift. She turned her head but there was nothing to see. Eyes darting, she studied the shadows. She scanned their form and shape, unable to make out anything tangible. As she held her breath, depths of darkness coalesced, thinned, and reshaped. Fear pricked in the corners of her eyes. She blinked but could make out nothing more. There was nothing there, yet there was. She felt it, an almost palpable emotion. There was rage, prowling and building. She could almost hear it, an angry throbbing of the veil; the veil that separates the living from the dead. It was beginning to rip. Every sense alert, she backed towards the steps and looked to see if Miss Hardcastle had sensed it too. Doreen seemed oblivious, intent on her search, but for what? She was now poking the remains of a bag of flour which was ripped and scattered on the floor, its contents grey and congealed. Delicately she took hold of a paper corner and peeled it back, causing more of the contents to ooze about the floor as damp clods of flour broke and cascaded. From the far corner of the room, beyond Miss Hardcastle, something scraped. This time she heard and looked. Both women turned their gaze to the end of the cellar. Both women held their breath, their feet rooted to the spot. Something was moving in the space at the edge of the light. Something was impinging on the visible spectrum, bending, and applying torque. It pulsed and rocked, like a bull pawing the ground. Without warning, a metal mug flew across the cellar and clattered against the wall. Before the echoes died, a second mug flashed past Miss Hardcastle's head. There was a tinkling of glass and a brief sparking flash, and the light was extinguished, plunging that end of the cellar into darkness. Karen almost swallowed her tongue as she gagged on a scream. She could see it now; it had visible form. Without the ceiling light it had its own energy, its own glow. It was getting stronger, and it began to move. Karen backed into the wall, but Miss Hardcastle stood still, eyes wide, darting. The thing began to circle her, testing, probing. Karen fumbled her way along the crumbling plaster then scrambled, tripped, and clambered her way noisily up the flight.

When she emerged into the kitchen, a sea of faces studied her. She was unable to speak, barely able to breathe. The head chef stared at Karen's ashen face, a look of knowing sympathy on her own. Then she turned to the open cellar doorway and waited, watching for Miss Hardcastle to emerge; the corners of her mouth turned up slightly.

It wasn't long before a tray arrived with some chicken wraps, a couple of cans of coke and two large slices of chocolate cake. Zoe and Natalie went and sat by the window. Had the weather been better they would have ventured out onto the terrace. The sun was shining but the wind was such that a couple of gulls could be seen flying into the wind without making any forward progress. They changed wing angle slightly and cartwheeled away, diving out of sight.

"Pity it isn't warmer; it would have been lovely to try out the pool," said Natalie. "Still, it will be good to explore, find out what this place is like: help you decide what you want to do. You gotta keep this place. Owning a hotel is just too brilliant!"

Zoe said nothing; just continued eating her wrap.

"Zoe, talk to me. Tell me what's wrong. This isn't like you. I know it must have been a huge shock falling out of the window like that, but this isn't like you. Please talk to me. I know there is something else..."

"I'm fine. Okay."

When Miss Hardcastle finally emerged from the cellar, she ran her eyes over each of the kitchen staff in turn, who were all gaping at her. She stared defiantly at them, back straight. Powerful. Smug. Then she turned, locked the cellar door, and pocketed the key. Giving Karen a look of scorn she marched out of the room and headed for the stairs. Karen looked at the kitchen staff as they returned to their work, clearly disappointed.

As the afternoon wore on, Zoe and Natalie went to do a bit of shopping. They wanted to get some milk and a few other items so they could make their own drinks. As they passed the reception desk Karen smiled at them, and they smiled back. Maybe they had one friend.

As they made for the door Natalie had a thought. "Karen, the back entrance into the garden, could we have a key card?" Then she looked closely at Karen, "Hey, are you okay?"

"Yes, no problem. Key card. Certainly! Just give me a minute."

"Are you sure you're okay? You look like you've seen a ghost! You seem…"

"Yes, fine." She busied herself behind the desk. "So, what are you planning to do with the rest of the day?"

Zoe said nothing so Natalie answered, not convinced that Karen was okay; she looked very pale and seemed distracted, "Not sure: get a few supplies, take a look around, possibly head to the One-Eyed Seagull this evening, and yourself?"

"Oh, er, probably just watch a bit of TV if the kids will let me."

"Oh, you have children! How many?"

"Three, a boy and two girls."

"Oh, that's nice. How old are they?"

"The boy is 7 and the girls are 11 and 8." She handed over two key cards. "Have a good day."

"Let us know when the cellar key is found," said Zoe and headed for the door.

Natalie briefly studied Karen and noted that she now had the same expression that the cook had worn, when asked about the key!

Out in the street it was sunny and not too breezy for a change. They headed up the High Street, past the One-Eyed Seagull, to a small supermarket. They wandered up and down the aisles collecting the items they wanted as they went.

"Hello, how are you?"

Natalie and Zoe turned and stared. They were being addressed by a middle-aged gentleman clutching a packet of Imodium and a bottle of bleach. "Are you alright love? When they took you off to the hospital, I was so worried. You were white as a sheet."

"Oh, I remember," said Natalie, "You are the man who wrapped a duvet round her whilst we were waiting for the ambulance."

Natalie and the man looked at Zoe, who was staring speculatively at the man's shopping. Realising she was expected to respond she said, "I'm fine," and after too long a pause, "Thanks for asking."

"Well, must get back. Glad you are okay." As the girls watched he trotted off to the till, scooping up a newspaper as he went.

"Hmm", said Natalie, "that raises a number of questions for a hotel owner," but Zoe didn't laugh, and Natalie sighed. This wasn't Zoe.

That evening Natalie suggested that they head to the One-Eyed Seagull as Kyle had said that he would be there, and Natalie hoped that, as before, Zoe would be a bit more like her old self again. They bought drinks and found a table next to the pub's fireplace: then decided to move as it was a bit too warm. It wasn't long before Kyle arrived. It seemed that he was keen to meet up again. Zoe brightened and Natalie soon began to feel that her presence was a little superfluous.

There was a muffled ringtone from Kyle's pocket. He studied his phone. Then looked at Natalie, "I hope you don't mind; I asked a friend to join us. He'll be here in about 10 minutes."

Natalie smiled, but inwardly her heart sank. Shortly after, the pub door opened and in stepped a 'Greek god' of a man. He glanced round the room and headed their way. Natalie's heart jumped into her mouth. As the man approached, she became aware that he wasn't looking at their table, but past it. He strolled by and she swallowed, returning her heart to its rightful place. She took a sip of her drink and sank back into her seat and waited suspiciously for what fate had in store for her. When Kyle's friend turned up, a little later than expected, she was however, pleasantly surprised. He was no Adonis, but he had a reasonable physique and there wasn't anything objectionable about his face. She wouldn't feel uncomfortable to be seen out with him. Kyle introduced him as Toby.

Toby stuck out his hand, first to Zoe and then to Natalie. As his fingers closed round Natalie's hand, he looked directly at her and beamed. His eyes crinkled at the corners, his lips parted slightly revealing perfectly even white teeth, and to Natalie, his whole face was transformed. It was the most wonderful face she had ever seen. As she beamed back, a warm glow spreading throughout her being, she had a strong sense of, yes, desire, but also familiarity. She felt she knew him already. She knew nothing about him but his first name and yet, she knew the heart of him. When he let go of her hand, offering to go and get drinks, she felt sure that the electricity between the two of them would have been visible to Zoe and Kyle, but the pair seemed oblivious. When Toby returned, he placed the glasses on the table, moving his chair nearer to Natalie with his leg. Then he sat down next to her, their legs touching. It took a whole lot of concentration, not to put her hand on that knee and explore that sturdy thigh.

The evening passed quickly. At some point the subject of Zoe's inheritance had come up and lots of advice had been offered as to how to go about taking on and managing the hotel. Zoe seemed disinterested in the business side and patently saw ownership as more of a party asset. Kyle was keen to take a look at the building and advise on any work that was needed. He was a little horrified when Zoe stated that the whole lot needed work as it was very old fashioned.

"It is art deco," he blurted. "I haven't seen the inside since my cousin's 21st but there are some fabulous pieces in there." Seeing her disgust he added, "It probably just needs a spruce up and a way of showing it to its best advantage. People love art deco."

Chapter Six

When she finally got to bed, Natalie couldn't sleep. Her mind was busy with all sorts of possibilities. She and Toby had talked and talked. At some point their hands had connected beneath the table and, as they sat side by side, he had explored her fingers. Turning her hand over, he had traced the lines on her palm and then slowly run his index finger up to the crook of her elbow and back again. Then he had just held her hand and leant against her; the two of them sitting as one. She didn't think she would ever forget that moment. She could have stayed there forever. Maybe, spiritually, she always would.

Lost in intimate thoughts, all her senses heightened, Natalie suddenly became aware of something beyond her room. A soft sound had set off a little alarm bell. She wanted to ignore it but a subsequent click from the direction of the apartment door got her scrambling for her dressing gown. Putting on the light and opening her room door, she saw that the apartment door was ajar. Zoe's bedroom door was wide open. Stepping out into the hall she headed down the stairs, and into the hotel. It wasn't difficult to follow Zoe as the hotel's motion-sensor lighting lit the way.

By the time Natalie had caught up, Zoe had reached the kitchen. Natalie was about to ask her what she was doing but now, it didn't seem too unreasonable that Zoe simply wanted something to eat, and it was her hotel, after all. However, Zoe seemed oblivious to Natalie's presence. Tentatively, Natalie approached. As she stepped round the side of her friend she froze. She recognised that look. That was the look that Zoe had had on her face after she had fallen out of the window.

"Zoe, what are you doing? What is going on?" There was no response. Zoe wasn't even looking at her but scanning the wall of cupboards. Then she grasped at a door handle and tried to pull it. The lock held fast.

"Zoe, what are you doing?" Still no response, just a continued tugging of the door handle. Natalie took hold of Zoe by the shoulders and turned her round. "What are you doing? Look at me. Tell me what you are doing. What are you looking for?" Zoe looked frantic. She whipped herself round, out of Natalie's grip and threw herself at the cupboard door. Natalie screamed at her, "Zoe, stop it." She grabbed her again and shook her, "Zoe, you're scaring me. Please stop. Look at me. LOOK...AT...ME!" She took Zoe's head in her hands, their noses practically touching, and stared into Zoe's eyes. There was a brief moment of recognition, then bewilderment. Zoe muttered, "Meg, Meg, Meg" like a mantra before starting to shake. Natalie held her then started to silently cry.

She felt helpless. She didn't understand and she was scared.

Back in the apartment Natalie made them both a cup of tea, in silence. She had so many questions but didn't know where to start. She also didn't expect to get any answers. Although staring into space, Zoe did seem to be sharing the same universe again, but she was pale and slightly clammy: the blankets Natalie had wrapped her in, seeming to have made no difference. However, she did start to take sips of tea and worked her way through a full packet of chocolate chunk biscuits, providing Natalie with relief and annoyance in equal measure.

The pair of them sat and dozed until it came light. After a sleep Zoe appeared a bit more like her old self and suggested that they head down to the hotel for breakfast. She ordered a full-English and tucked in with gusto, then said brightly, "Let's take the lift down to the beach and have a walk along the shore.

"Oh!" said Natalie. "I really think that we should get you back to the hospital. I am worried about you. Something isn't right."

"What? I'm fine."

"No, Zoe, you're not. You are introverted. You won't talk to me. And, as for last night... you have never sleepwalked before – or whatever that was. This just isn't you. Something is wrong. It needs checking out, and me, I'd never forgive myself if something happened to you. I need to know that I have done what I can to look after you. Zoe, please!"

To her surprise Zoe caved, and by mid-morning Natalie was once again sitting alone in a corridor whilst Zoe was elsewhere undergoing tests. Natalie had talked to a doctor and done her best to explain what had happened, but now, in daylight, it all seemed a little lame. Again, the hospital could find nothing wrong, but Zoe was given an appointment with a Clinical Psychologist for a fortnight's time. Another could be arranged back home if they were no longer in the area.

Back at the hotel, they had some lunch and Natalie suggested that they talk to Karen about looking at the books, but Zoe insisted there was time, right now she wanted to check out the beach.

They headed out into the grounds. A woman in dungarees and a checked shirt, her hair bundled into a knot on the top of her head, was standing, leaning on a pair of 'loppers', studying the remains of the topiary dolphin. Sadly, it now bore a greater resemblance to a kraken. Natalie briefly considered 'The Kraken Hotel and Lido'; it could draw a completely new range of clientele. With this thought train chugging round in her brain, she followed Zoe over and smiled as introductions were made. The woman hefted the loppers, giving them a couple of test clips with strong tanned hands, the odd liver spot visible.

She gave them a non-committal nod and besides saying her name, Ruth, tactfully kept her thoughts to herself.

"Do you think it can be saved?" asked Zoe. "I really hope it can. The hotel would not be the same without it. That dolphin means a lot to the family."

"It means a lot to me too," said the gardener, pointedly. "I'll do what I can."

"Please, it's important," said Zoe and noticing that Natalie was giving her an odd look, added, "It probably saved my life."

Leaving the woman to get on with her miracle they made their way towards the edge of the cliff and a metal walkway which extended beyond it. At the end was a glass and metal structure, housing a lift. Obviously built in the 1920's its much painted door had a 2020's stainless steel swipe card box attached. Retrieving a swipe card from the depths of her bag Zoe opened the door. They stepped inside, closed the door, and pushed a large red button labelled 'down'. There was an alarming jolt and a grinding noise, then, they smoothly began to descend. Any noise from the mechanism was quickly lost in a maelstrom of screeching white. Between gulls they got a good view of the cliff face and several seagull nests. They would have loved to have stopped the lift for a better look, but that wasn't an option. Soon they were at beach level. There was a clunk, and the door was released. Zoe pushed it open, and they stepped out onto a raised stone platform, steps leading down to an expanse of golden sand. It was a beautiful beach and right now, they had it to themselves. Taking off their trainers they dug their toes into the sand. Beneath the warm surface it was cool and damp. Leaving a trail of footprints, they headed towards the water and played tag with the waves as they built up their courage to brave the icy water. They both gasped and giggled and waded out until the water reached their knees. The pull of the waves and the visual movement of the water unbalancing them, they stopped and attempted to stand still as the water gently sucked the sand from beneath their feet. They had done it. They had paddled in the sea. They headed back and found a rock outcrop to sit on whilst their numb feet dried.

"Do you think they sell buckets and spades in the town? I'm getting the urge to build a sandcastle," said Natalie.

"Who needs a bucket and spade," said Zoe. She dove at the sand and started scooping handfuls of it into piles, patting it into turrets and ramparts. Natalie joined her and began excavating a moat: digging until she found water. A quick search and she soon had a collection of pretty, pink periwinkles and cockle shells. Together they set about decorating their fortification. Natalie was delighted. This was the Zoe she knew, fun and spontaneous. As if to confirm her thoughts Zoe sat back on her heels and looked at her hands, turning them over and back, examining them. "Well," she laughed, "there goes my 'holiday hands'. They were starting to feel smooth and soft, but now, well..."

Natalie looked at her own hands. One nail was split, and they all had sand under them. Staring at them she remembered the touch of Toby's fingers. Her heart swelled and she felt a warm glow, a grin appearing on her face, uncontrolled. She rubbed her hands together and tried to get rid of the sand. They felt rough and dry. Annoyed with herself she got to her feet and displayed her hands for Zoe to see. Zoe held out her own hands so they could compare. They looked at each other in mock horror. "We need to get back and MOISTURISE!"

Back in the apartment they took it in turns to shower. They laughed and joked. It was like old times and Natalie began to believe that things might be back to normal but, with the addition of a hotel and lido, of course. They were meeting Kyle and Toby who had offered to take them to see the latest Bond film. They would get a burger and a pint, beforehand. Standing side by side in front of a long mirror, handily positioned by the apartment door, they inspected themselves. They removed the odd bit of fluff, smoothed the odd bit of material, tweaked the odd strand of hair, performed test puckers, grinned at each other and set off.

Toby and Kyle were waiting for them outside The One-Eyed Seagull. They led the way to a small café at the other end of the town, conveniently positioned opposite the cinema. As they waited for their food the boys were eager to know what they had done with their day and if Zoe had come to a decision over keeping the hotel. They plied her with questions until it became apparent that Zoe was getting annoyed. Of course, she was keeping the hotel. It would be stupid to give it up.

"But do you know what state it is in, financially? You don't want to be responsible for something that is going to bankrupt you," said Kyle.

"It seems okay to me," she said stubbornly.

"But have you met with the accountant? Have you seen the books?"

"Yes," added Toby, "if you are going to own the place you need to understand it."

Zoe looked perplexed, "but isn't that what the accountant, and the hotel manager, Miss Hardcastle, are for?" She stood, "Hadn't we better go, we are going to miss the start." Grabbing her coat and bag she headed for the door. Natalie and the two guys looked at each other, eyebrows raised.

In the darkness of the cinema each couple got to know each other a little better: any subtleties of plot could be studied and appreciated at future viewings.

Chapter Seven

It was now Wednesday morning and Natalie had been pondering on what the boys had said and realised that she needed to get Zoe to focus and look at the reality of her situation. If she was going to take on a hotel, she needed to do so with her eyes open and not rely on other people, especially not Miss Hardcastle who patently didn't have Zoe's best interests at heart. Before Zoe woke, she phoned her parents. Zoe might listen to them.

At breakfast she announced to Zoe that her parents were coming up for the weekend and her dad was going to try to get time off work to come up sooner. "They are keen to see what you have inherited. How about we talk to Karen before they come and see what this place makes? There isn't much time before the solicitor's on Friday." Natalie noticed a slight shift in the set of Zoe's shoulders and tactfully changed tack, "Let's see if there is any spare money for that updating you were talking about."

"Yes, that entrance could certainly do with some work."

"Perhaps you could get Kyle to advise."

They found Karen in the reception office and keen to help. Anticipating what was needed she had done what she could to prepare the relevant information and had made a tentative appointment with the hotel's accountant for later that afternoon.

The girls looked at the figures and then at Karen for help. "It is really Miss Hardcastle who should tell you all this. I think the accounts are in good shape, but I am only the Duty Manager and don't deal with that side of the business."

"But is there money for doing up the place," asked Zoe.

"Again, it isn't my place to say, but I believe so. Talk to the accountant," and here she grimaced apologetically, "and Miss Hardcastle."

"Well, where is she?" asked Zoe.

"We don't know."

"What do you mean? She is supposed to be like... managing the place."

"She has been having food sent up to her apartment, but none of us has seen her since Monday."

"So, who *is* running the place?" demanded Zoe.

"I am," said Karen.

"Hadn't someone better go and see if she is alright?" said Natalie. "She scemed quite shocked at the solicitors. If no one has seen her..."

"She won't answer the door and insists that the food is left outside her apartment," said Karen. "The trays come out empty."

"Right," said Natalie, "next time her food goes up let us know and we will wait until she opens the door, and we will speak to her." Then, having glanced at Zoe, "I'll speak to her, alone."

Leaving Zoe in their apartment Natalie accompanied one of the staff up to Miss Hardcastle's door. The woman placed the tray on a hall table, rang the doorbell and then departed, ensuring that the door at the top of the stairwell closed noisily. Natalie waited, clutching the pretty bedlinen she had found in Zoe's great grandfather's apartment, which she assumed was Miss Hardcastle's. The door opened. Miss Hardcastle stared at the linen and then Natalie. Natalie feigned surprise, "I was just about to ring but don't let your lunch go cold, please..." and she stepped back allowing a confused Miss Hardcastle to collect her lunch. Without being invited, Natalie stepped in and held the door open whilst Miss Hardcastle came in with her tray. Her lank hair stuck out at an angle over her left ear. The old dressing gown she was wearing was missing a button, where it was most needed, and her glasses had a paperclip holding the left arm in place. She looked pale and flustered. Putting down the tray she did her best to close the gaping gap in her dressing gown, resorting to holding it, making her look defensive and even more ill at ease. Natalie closed the door. Without making reference to the floral bedding, she laid it on a chair and smiled. "I was worried. The staff said they hadn't seen you. How are you?"

"I am fine *thank* you."

"Good. That is such a relief. I am so glad you are okay, plus, we need you. Karen is doing a great job, but she doesn't have your expertise."

"How come Miss Spencer hasn't come to see how I am?"

"She would have but she is trying to get her head around the figures, before seeing the accountant at 2pm this afternoon. It would be helpful if you were there too."

"Why? The accountant is perfectly capable of explaining the accounts. Now, if you will excuse me, I would like to eat my lunch." With that she turned her back, sat down and started delicately slurping soup.

Natalie would have persevered but noted a tell-tale waver in Miss Hardcastle's voice. The woman was trying desperately not to cry. She decided to leave it for now. They would need to win her round. Leaving behind the bedding, there was no need to comment, both women knew that the other knew the truth about it, she let herself out, hopefully leaving Miss Hardcastle with her dignity intact. Zoe, she knew, would be unforgiving. She would need to be tactful in dealing with them both.

With the door closed Doreen dripped bitter tears into her chicken soup. She had to do something. The situation was intolerable. But what? The solicitor had made it quite clear, that if

Zoe didn't want the hotel, it *still* wasn't going to be *hers*. It could *never* be hers, but then it needn't belong to that child, either. *'No, it needn't,'* the little voice whispered in her head. *'We'll have to do something about that!'*

Over lunch Natalie told Zoe about her meeting with Miss Hardcastle. Zoe wasn't impressed.

"If she wants to continue living here then she's got to do her job. I am not having her living here being waited on. She is meant to be, well... managing. Perhaps I should promote Karen."

"Zoe, can't you see that she is deeply upset that the hotel wasn't left to her. How would you feel if it was you?"

"You would have thought that at her age she would have learnt that life can be shit!"

"Zoe! This has been her home, her whole life it seems, for years. It must have been a real shock. Have a little sympathy. I don't know what has got into you. This isn't like you. Ever since you fell out of that window it is like you are a different person..."

"Whatev's." Zoe shoved her chair back from the table and headed for the door. Natalie sighed. Maybe her parents would get through to her. Hopefully they would come before the weekend. She picked up a stray piece of lettuce and stuffed it back into her Cajun Chicken Wrap.

It now seemed dry and tasteless. Was she losing her friend?

At 1.55, with no sign of Zoe, she headed down to the main office to meet the accountant. To her surprise Zoe turned up promptly at 2pm and the pair of them went in together. The sight of Miss Hardcastle sitting beside the accountant was an even greater surprise. Natalie smiled and looked her up and down. There was a distinct difference in her appearance. She was now smartly dressed. Her face was deftly made up, but with maybe a little too much mascara: it was starting to gather distractingly in the corner of one eye. Miss Hardcastle now looked, every bit, the professional businesswoman: her appearance, her bearing, her manner all screaming power. Zoe, by contrast was dressed in jeans, trainers and a t-shirt. The t-shirt had 'Don't Label Me' in glittery bold relief across the front and 'I'm Unique!' on the back. She clearly hadn't been expecting Miss Hardcastle.

The accountant introduced himself and proceeded to explain the hotel's financial status, with Miss Hardcastle nodding knowledgeably at his side. An hour and a half of questions and answers and the girls had a reasonable idea of how the business ran, what made money and which losses were necessary evils of the hotel business, who the suppliers were, etcetera. Zoe was aghast at staff costs. One salary in particular caught her eye. She said nothing but gave Miss Hardcastle an appraising sideways glance. The accountant explained that if Zoe took on the business, she would need to decide how much to pay herself, but he would discuss that with her, at a later date, in private.

"Pay myself!" said Zoe, "but it is my business. It is my money!"

The accountant took a breath. At his side Miss Hardcastle sniffed.

"Yes and no," he said. "It is your hotel and your business but, it is a business, and the money needs to be accounted for, and optimised. It is my job to ensure that, and to show that the accounts are auditable."

She didn't like the sound of that. There was a lot to learn. Then, thinking of Miss Hardcastle's salary and assuming that she could pay herself more, it didn't sound too bad.

"But, is there money to do the place up?"

"Depending on what you want to do, yes."

So, there was money for refurbishment, but the hotel was heading for its busiest season; it would be better for work to be done in the low season and use the intervening time to plan. Natalie found this insight into hotel management interesting. There were all sorts of things she hadn't thought about before, but which obvious if you took the time: employment law, supplies, maintenance audits, COSHH, FIFO and Health and Safety. The latter she found particularly interesting and which she planned to pursue following the horrific incident with the window catch. Distracted by memory of that night she stared into space. When she refocused, she found she was looking at a guilt-framed black and white photograph. It was on the wall behind the accountant, half concealed by a pot plant, and showed a young man in military uniform.

"Zoe, is that your great grandfather?" Walking round the desk she plucked the picture off the wall and handed it to Zoe.

Zoe took it and ran her fingers over the glass. "Yes, he's grown into quite a strapping lad."

"What?" said Natalie: a slight prickly feeling, uncomfortably tickling the back of her neck.

"He was such a skinny thing as a child," she said affectionately.

"What! I didn't think you knew him."

There was a slight hesitation, and then Zoe carefully placed the picture on the desk, cleared her throat and said, "There are other pictures, upstairs."

"You didn't say anything about them before. Why didn't you tell me?"

"I only just saw them. They are on the top corridor and there are more in his apartment."

Natalie frowned. This was just weird. She knew her friend. Zoe wasn't telling her everything, and not just that, she was hiding something too.

They had had no secrets before, not that she knew, but now...

Meeting over, they headed upstairs. Dodging a couple of guests on the way, Natalie steered Zoe, keen for her to show her the pictures. Sure enough, along the top corridor were a number of black and white photographs: some, more sepia than black and white. It was mainly a collection of pictures of the hotel, but a number showed older versions of Walter Brammar, hotel owner. Natalie was relieved but still slightly puzzled. There were no pictures of him as a child. What Zoe had said of him in the office was bizarre. Young people didn't talk of older people that way, but an older person would talk of a younger one that way.

"Zoe, who is Meg?"

"She's m..." the words stuck in her throat. Zoe looked both shocked and stricken. "She's..." There was comprehension and then puzzlement: dismay and bafflement.

Natalie grasped Zoe's shoulders and looked straight into her eyes. Staring intently, she repeated, "Who is Meg?" Zoe blinked and something indefinable flashed briefly behind her eyes. Natalie saw it vanish, but had no idea what 'it' was. She could only liken it to waking from a dream and having the content slip from memory, leaving just a fading emotion that can't be recalled. But this didn't belong to her; it wasn't her loss; it was Zoe's and now Zoe was bereft and shaking; tears rolling down her cheeks. Natalie held her until she cried herself out. Then she guided her back to their apartment and sat her down. Calmer now, Zoe started apologising and insisting that she didn't know who Meg was, but she missed her. She knew she missed her. It didn't make any sense.

"When you were in the hospital the staff said that you were calling for Meg. Do you remember any more about that night, about how you came to fall out of the window?"

For a moment she thought Zoe was going to open up. She lifted her head and seemed about to speak but then she clammed up again and turned away. She looked so frail sitting there. The bubbly, gregarious individual Natalie knew, now seemed shrunken; it was like she had aged. It had only been a few days but, she now noticed, Zoe had patently lost weight. She wouldn't have thought it possible in such a short space of time. Was she ill? Should she take her back to the hospital? Something was badly wrong.

Chapter Eight

That evening Natalie, Zoe, Kyle, and Toby met at the One-Eyed Seagull. Kyle had suggested they meet at the hotel but neither Zoe nor Natalie wanted their relationships to be the subject of staff gossip. It didn't matter, but they both felt more comfortable meeting the guys elsewhere. They had a quick drink and then, at the suggestion of Kyle, headed up the High Street to the top of the town. He took them through an alleyway which led behind the buildings to a path which ran along the cliff top and up above the town. Beside the path, little brass plaques sparkled on the backs of benches that stood sentry-like, observing the horizon, and proclaimed the area to be a favourite spot of the dead, and apparently the gulls. Unable to find a clean bit of bench to sit on they stood and looked out to sea: Kyle with his arm around Zoe, and Toby with his arm around Natalie. Despite the fading light, they had a fabulous view of a rocky bay and stood for a while watching the surf, as it diligently pursued the lengthy task of turning pebbles into sand. Shouting against the wind and the gulls, Kyle pointed out various landmarks, "To our left is Toby's dad's golf course. He doesn't like to brag about it, but he does like people to know." Toby raised his eyebrows and shook his head. Kyle continued, "Down there, below the golf course is a good place to find golf balls, if you want a little extra pocket money. Over to the right, in the distance, are the docks. You will see a lot of large container ships heading in and out. The area has expanded a lot over the years with container storage and rail infra-structure dominating everything, but it must have been a really cool sight a couple o' hundred years ago when tall ships were coming and going. I would love to have seen that, but no doubt people back then thought those ships were an eyesore. Thankfully, surrounding the industrial areas, we now have a huge nature reserve." Here he pointed to the areas either side of a wide river, which ran round the back of the town and out to sea. "Below us is the town, and, of course, The Dolphin Hotel."

It was by far, the largest and most extensive property in town. The girls were surprised. With its street frontage it hadn't been apparent how much of it there was. From the High Street the building fanned out slightly and then the grounds not only extended out to the cliff but behind a number of the adjacent buildings.

"Wow, I hadn't realised how big the hotel is," said Zoe.

"Yes," said Kyle, "that is chiefly why I wanted you to come up here to let you see just what it is you are taking on. That hotel has been there a long time. It has a fascinating history. Parts of the building are a good 400 years old, and more. It has been altered and added to over the years but has essentially been the heart and soul of this town since, who knows? It is probably the oldest surviving building we have."

"You should work for the tourist board," said Natalie, laughing, "You are so, like, formal! What happened there?" she said, pointing at a section of cliff, at the nearer edge of the property. It had obviously, at some time in the past, fallen into the sea. It looked like it had taken a sizeable chunk of the Dolphin Hotel's grounds with it. In the gap, small shrubs and grasses were valiantly clinging to the sides demonstrating that with time, nature would turn the collapse to her advantage.

"Oh, that. The Luftwaffe did that. A couple of stray bombs took out the cliff and part of the back of the hotel. They were aiming for the docks. But then," looking at Zoe, "you would probably know all about that, being your family history."

The girls stared at him.

"Yes, didn't you know? A number of people were killed. It was all in the papers at the time. If you go to the library..."

She ran at the cliff top. It wasn't there anymore: bits still crumbling and sliding away; large chunks disintegrating and disappearing into the dark. She threw herself at the ground, grasping anything she could. A sucking, dry sigh, as more earth and rock fell away. Beneath her outstretched hands the ground tilted slightly.

Flat to the grass she crabbed herself backwards and rolled and kept rolling until she reached the wall of a raised flower bed. Even the solid ground felt unsafe. As the enormity of what had happened began to sink in, she looked around. Could he have survived? Could he have escaped? It didn't seem possible. He had been right underneath it. An area the size of a tennis court had disappeared into the sea. Senses heightened, she listened desperately for sounds of life. Instead, she heard only the sounds of the waves below and the drone of bombers above. Down the coast she could see a distant inferno: hazy black silhouettes of ships and warehouses shimmering in the blaze. Even at a few miles distance she could detect a stinging, acrid smell in the air. She looked upwards at the sound of yet another bomber going overhead. Horrified, she could see light shining from a room at the top of the hotel: the blast had taken out the glass and a torn curtain was flapping wildly in the wind. Wet and muddy she scrambled to her feet. Slipping and falling and clawing her way she ran for the door. She had to extinguish that light.

"Zoe, Zoe. Stop. Please stop." Kyle was trying desperately to hold her. She fought, equally desperate to get away. Lashing out wildly she caught Toby a glancing blow as he tried to grab an arm. Stunned, he staggered away. As she lashed out again Kyle grabbed her in a bear hug from behind. Natalie, fearful and exasperated, slapped her across the face. Zoe and Kyle fell backwards and sat in a heap on the floor. The slap seemed to have done the trick. Zoe stopped struggling.

It was a while before anyone spoke. No-one knew what to make of what had just happened. Kyle had been explaining that after the war the back half of the hotel had been rebuilt. The local community had worked together to get the hotel up and running again. Then, all of a sudden, Zoe had thrown herself at the ground, started rolling and screaming and then run at the cliff edge. Kyle had only just stopped her from going over. With the help of Natalie and Toby he had managed to pull her away and drag her back from the lip but, until Natalie slapped her, she seemed intent on going over the edge.

With the light fading Toby insisted that they head up to the golf club. It wasn't far and quicker than heading back into town. He could borrow a car from his dad and together they would take Zoe back to the hospital.

At the golf club Toby went off in search of his father. The others found seats in the bar. Toby quickly returned to say that his dad wasn't there but should be back soon. He produced a round of drinks and handed them out. Zoe sat quietly whilst Natalie related everything that had happened since they arrived at The Dolphin. She went on at some length. It was such a relief to talk to someone about it all. She told them how worried she was and how baffled. None of it made sense. Zoe had never behaved like this before. It was like she was a different person half the time.

Whereas Natalie had been reluctant to push Zoe, afraid of upsetting her, the boys had no hesitation. They fired questions at her. Why had she run at the cliff? What did she think she was doing? Was it related to what Kyle had said? What? When? Why?

Cornered, she finally blurted out, "I don't know. I...the light. I had to put out the light. Yes, I had to put out the light."

"What light?"

She stared, "I don't know. Things are so real, so vivid. Then they fade. I need to find..." Here she looked at a loss again: wrapped her arms round herself and started rocking. "To help her."

"Meg? Is it Meg? You kept saying her name," said Natalie.

"Meg?" Zoe looked puzzled.

"Yes, in the hospital and then in the kitchen you kept saying Meg."

"Yes, I've got to find Meg." Zoe kind of disappeared inside herself, then, looked wildly at Natalie, "Do you know where she is?"

"No, of course I don't know. I don't know who she is, let alone where. Do you know who she is?"

With all 3 staring at her, Zoe said, "She. She's ...my daughter."

After the meeting with the accountant Doreen had decided that she needed a plan. Right now, the best thing she could do was bide her time. She didn't know what she was going to do. She didn't even know what she wanted for herself. She just knew that if she couldn't have the hotel then she didn't want that infant to have it either. *'No, that won't do,'* said the voice, *'We must stop her.'* The rational part of her knew that the sensible thing to do was to get to know Zoe and work with her to make the hotel a continued success. It was in both their interests. She knew that, but the irrational part of her wanted Zoe to fail, and the hotel to be run into the ground. The latter however, she couldn't tolerate. The hotel had been her baby for so long. She had taken over the reins when Walter became ill. She had picked it up and dusted it down and slowly helped it grow. It was now a mature and healthy business, and it was all down to her. No, she would bide her time. *'But not for long...'*

To Natalie's surprise Toby drove them up the coast to a small cottage hospital. When Natalie protested, he explained that Zoe would be seen much quicker than at the General. He was right. It had a small minor injuries unit and there were just 3 other people in the waiting room. Within 15 minutes the four of them were talking to a doctor who was able to access Zoe's notes online from the hospital she had been taken to previously. A subdued Zoe sat forlornly on a plastic chair, whilst Natalie related all that had happened since they arrived at the hotel. Then Kyle and Toby chipped in to emphasise the struggle they had had with her on the cliff top and explain the slightly purple hand shape on her left cheek. Another doctor was called. Zoe was seen on her own. Then the first doctor came to tell them that they would like to keep her in over night for observation.

Leaving Zoe behind and not knowing what else to do they decided to get something to eat, which had been their intention all along. They took the car back to the golf club and Toby got a couple of menus from the bar. The ensuing food conversation returned some sense of normality to the group. Natalie chose a quiche salad, Kyle the shepherd's pie and Toby, beer battered cod and chips. Whilst they waited for their food a large bowl of salt and vinegar crisps was placed on their table shortly followed by a plate of heavily buttered, sliced white bread. Kyle and Toby grinned at Natalie who was looking questioningly at the bowl and plate. The lads took a slice of bread each and proceeded to pile crisps on top. Then they folded the slice in two, encasing the crisps with a satisfying crunch, and took a noisy bite. Thinking that she would never manage to eat her quiche Natalie took a slice anyway, plus a handful of crisps and made her own crisp butty.

As she sank her teeth into the soft white bread tiny bursts of flavour exploded in her mouth. As she chewed, the cold, silky soft butter contrasted beautifully with the vinegar on the crisps. If only Zoe was enjoying this with them.

Chapter Nine

When Natalie woke, she made herself a cup of tea in the apartment kitchen and then went and sat outside on the roof terrace cocooned in a duvet. There was surprisingly little wind, but the sun had yet to reach the metal chair, and she was glad of the duvet's insulation. Sitting in the lee of the building and the head-height trellis, which separated Walter's apartment from that of Miss Hardcastle's, was tolerable. She sipped and watched as the sun crept up to the horizon, its silver rays like the radials of a glistening spider's web in the fresh morning air. She squinted, then looked away as the first brilliant beams crested the horizon.

She needed to think. Zoe was in no fit state to make a decision about the hotel. It was Thursday already, and the solicitor was expecting a decision in the morning and the paperwork signing. Checking her phone, it didn't look like her parents were going to make it before the weekend. Until they had known that Zoe's inheritance was the hotel, the two girls had simply planned to enjoy a few days away and then take the train home. They hadn't discussed staying, but that was the logical thing to do. Perhaps the solicitor would allow them to postpone the meeting for a few days.

She stood and walked to the edge of the terrace and admired the view. No, Zoe couldn't possibly give up on this place. It was just too awesome.

Further along the terrace, beyond the dividing wall, a lace curtain twitched. So, just that Natalie; it looked like that little slut Zoe had stayed out all night. *'Yes, having fun. I used to have fun. She hated me for that – such a prig!'* The security camera feed to her apartment, fitted when she had taken over managing the hotel, showed the entrance hall and reception desk, as well as other parts of the hotel. Doreen had seen Natalie return, but not Zoe.

At 9am Natalie phoned the solicitor and explained that Zoe wasn't well. She didn't go into detail but explained that they were planning on staying and hoping to meet with him some time next week. She would get Zoe to call him when she was better. That done she made herself another drink and some toast and phoned the hospital. Once again, they couldn't find anything wrong with Zoe, but wanted to keep her for further assessment. Natalie was told she may visit in the afternoon.

With nothing else to do she started idly wandering around the apartment. The kitchen area was clean. Miss Hardcastle had obviously kept on top of that, especially as she had anticipated moving in. There was nothing nasty in the fridge and nothing out of date in the cupboards. She washed her plate and cup, dried them and put them away. In the living room she plumped the odd cushion, but there really wasn't anything that needed attention. She went into Zoe's room and gathered a few items to take to the hospital, stuffing them in a carrier-bag. The room was much larger than hers and square. The main window looked out at the sea but looking through the side window she could see over the rooftops of the adjacent buildings and up towards the golf club. It was a much nicer room than hers which had one window overlooking the High Street and a sky light. She stood at the window and traced the path up the cliff to where they had all stood the previous night. From this vantage point she could see the cliff, edge on. Zoe would not have survived that drop. Turning away she focussed on things nearer to hand. It was strange being surrounded by someone else's possessions. Walter's belongings were everywhere. There were a couple of cardboard boxes in a corner of the room, into which someone had folded his clothes and placed them neatly inside. A big bin bag held shoes, all well polished. A couple of flat caps and a trilby sat on a chair, a scarf draped over its back. Natalie ran her hand over it, as if that would help give her a sense of the man. She picked it up and held it.

There was a faint smell of biscuits and maybe tobacco. She put it back on the chair.

On the wall over the bed was a large seascape painting in oil. She smiled. Kyle would love this. Three ships with masts were depicted heading out of a harbour, which she could only assume was the one down the coast, as it would have been, many years ago. On the opposite wall, was a bookcase with a selection of novels, dictionary and thesaurus, and a row of Dolphin Hotel diaries. On the wall above, a couple of framed black and white prints hung. These were obviously taken at the hotel lido and showed some very elegant young ladies, in 1920's bathing costumes, diving into the pool. In the background of one she could see a small, dolphin shaped bush. The sight of the topiary reminded her of Zoe. She realised, with sinking heart that it was unlikely that Zoe would be back in time for the staff meeting in the morning. Nothing had been said about when, but if Miss Hardcastle had arranged it, she would need to cancel it. Zoe certainly wouldn't have time to prepare, let alone be ready mentally, to address the staff. She washed and dressed and went downstairs in the hope of finding Karen.

A young man was standing at the reception desk. Natalie had a vague memory of him amongst the faces at the staff meeting. He smiled.

"Good morning, Miss Walker. How may I help you?"

"Hello. What is your name please?"

"Carl."

"Morning, Carl. Is Karen here?"

"No Miss Walker. She isn't on duty until 2pm. Is there anything I can do?"

"Has the staff meeting been arranged for tomorrow? We need to move it to next week. Zoe, Miss Spencer, wants to see the solicitor first. Would you pass that on please?"

"Yes, certainly."

"Thank you. We will let you know when to rearrange it."

As Natalie headed back upstairs, Carl stuck his head into the back office. Miss Hardcastle looked up from her desk and nodded. Yes, she'd heard. As he returned to the front desk, she pursed her lips, lost in thought. What did that mean? And, 'next week'! So, they were staying.

Natalie, with nothing better to do, headed out into the hotel grounds. She stopped by the topiary dolphin. A sturdy forked branch had been stuck into the earth to support the dolphin's head, giving it back its basic shape. However, individual branches were showing unhealthy signs of damage. Some had been cut back to aid its recovery, but it would be a long time before it grew back to its original shape, if what was left survived. Silently she thanked the bush for its sacrifice; it had saved Zoe's life. Natalie looked up at the window, from which Zoe had fallen. Then she stepped round to the side, puzzled. The bush wasn't directly under the window, it was a good 6 metres away. How? She stepped backwards to better judge the angle. Even taking a running jump it would be difficult to clear that distance.

"Quite a leap!"

Natalie jumped and turned to find Ruth, the gardener, standing next to her. She smiled ruefully, "Do you think it will survive?"

"Some of it will. Whether it will ever look like a dolphin again, only time will tell. How is she?"

"Oh!" Natalie turned and studied the woman. Did she know Zoe was in the hospital again? "Nothing broken."

"She must have been quite shaken though..."

"Yes." Natalie involuntarily looked up at the window and her eyes tracked the distance to the dolphin.

The gardener followed her gaze and waited.

"I just don't see how she could have reached the bush. I don't even know why she opened the window."

"Maybe she couldn't *help* herself..."

"What do you mean?"

"Obviously sensitive, like her mother."

Natalie stared at her. "You knew Zoe's mother?"

"*She* didn't stay long. Best *Zoe* leaves too." With that she turned and headed round the side of the building leaving Natalie staring after her, as rooted to the spot as the bedraggled dolphin. Was that a threat, or just advice? The delivery had been deadpan. Either way it was alarming. Later, she wondered why she hadn't run after her, demanded to know what she meant, demanded the woman explain. Deep inside she knew why. She just didn't want to acknowledge it: to acknowledge that she was afraid. She had seen the answer in Zoe's eyes, more than once. Maybe the gardener was right. Maybe she did need to get Zoe away from this place.

Deep in thought she made her way to the cliff lift and swiped her card. As the metal frame groaned, her mind whirled as the seagulls swirled around her. She tried to plan all the things that Zoe needed to consider, in order to take on the hotel. If she gathered the right information, she could present it to Zoe when she was in a fit state to take it all in: if she ever was. To the smell of old oil, the lift slowed and lurched to a halt. With a heavy clunk, the door freed itself. She pushed it open and stepped out. Running her hands through her hair she secured it behind her ears. Head down, she set off along a well-worn path beneath the cliff, following it as it skirted large boulders. After about 100 metres she found herself beside the collapsed area of cliff. What had fallen was quite significant. Despite the passage of time the scar was quite fresh, the exposed earth and rock markedly different from the weathered cliffs either side. Water lapped at large boulders heaped at its base, and it looked as if there had been a cove here before the earth had buried it.

Natalie examined the strata and marvelled at this wedge of time. She wished she understood, from a geological point of view, what she was seeing. Zoe would know. Zoe would be busy, following the folds of the rock, counting the layers, climbing up and picking at loose bits, identifying and ageing it all. Would she be able to finish her degree?

"Frightening, what one bomb can do, isn't it?"

Natalie whipped round. A grey-haired lady with a weather-beaten face was beaming at her. She was dressed in jeans and a smock top. On her head sat a blue beret which appeared to be struggling to keep her hair under control. The woman hitched the wicker pannier she was carrying, higher onto her shoulder, and bent to ruffle the head of a stiff furred mongrel, which bounced at her side. As Natalie's gaze moved from dog to pannier, the woman said succinctly, "Driftwood,"

"Oh," said Natalie.

"I make stuff from it, to sell. You may have seen some of it in the town shops."

"Maybe," muttered Natalie.

"I haven't seen you about before…"

"No, I haven't been here long. Tell me about the bomb!"

"Oh, that was towards the end of World War Two. The Germans liked to get rid of any unused bombs before returning home, after bombing the docks," and she pointed down the coast, shielding her eyes. "One took out the cliff and another took off the back of the hotel, killing the owner and her two children. Well, the boy died in the sea, with his girlfriend, so they say. His body was found, but not hers. Such a tragedy. The older son went off to war and came home without a scratch, and all those who stayed home died. Dreadful. The town helped him rebuild after the war. Where are you staying?"

"At the hotel."

"Oh, you aren't the new owner, by any chance?"

Natalie hesitated, there was something in the tone of the question, the phrasing and emphasis; it was 'loaded' in some way. The woman smiled, maybe she was wrong. "No," said Natalie, not sure how much she wanted to reveal to this woman, not sure why she was reluctant to confide. "No, not me. Why?"

"Oh, Nothing." A whole fleet of emotions sailed across her face. "Staring at the rock-fall like that, I just thought that you might be *her*."

Natalie crouched down and fondled the dog's ears, "What's *your* name?"

"That's 'Hobnail'. Tough as old boots." She hitched her pannier again. "I'm Lianne, by the way, and you are?"

"Natalie."

"So, what have you got planned for the day?"

"I'm not sure yet. Just having a wander, and you?"

"Well, I need to get this lot back and see what I can make from it. Anyway, nice meeting you. Perhaps see you around." She threw a ball, and Hobnail tore into the surf after it. Before she'd gone 10 metres the dog was back. He dropped the ball at her feet and shook sea water all over her. The woman picked up the ball and deftly hurled it along the shore, raising cartwheels of sand. Hobnail caught it mid-air on the third bounce and came bounding back, sand and water flying, firing rays of coloured light. Natalie sat on a rock and watched them go. When the pair were just dots, she stood and massaged some feeling back into her bottom. She took another look at the fallen cliff, then slowly headed back to the lift.

As she rose up the cliff face, she decided that she would find the gardener and ask her what she knew about Zoe's mother. Back in the hotel grounds she wandered around all the likely places, in search of the gardener. Having exhausted the garden, she headed for the various outbuildings and found a greenhouse tucked away in a corner at the side of the hotel. A quick glance told her that there was no-one in there. At the back of the greenhouse was a shed. She knocked. Then she tried the door. It was locked. Disappointed, she headed back to the hotel.

Chapter Ten

At the hospital Zoe seemed more like the Zoe Natalie knew. She gratefully looked through the clothes that Natalie had taken for her and looked a little puzzled by the toiletries. When she asked about Kyle, and Natalie said that she would bring him with her that evening, Zoe appeared to have no idea that the hospital expected her to stay another night.

"Why? I am perfectly alright."

"Do you not remember what you did yesterday? Is that normal?"

"I, I..."

"You tried to jump off a cliff top!" Natalie almost screamed at her.

"No, I... it wasn't a cliff top!"

"What!"

"It was the light. I had to put out the light."

There it was again. It was in Zoe's eyes, but not Zoe's eyes; they were someone else's. Natalie ran for a nurse. By the time she had found, explained to, and persuaded one to come back with her it was Zoe's eyes they looked into. Following a brief conversation, the nurse left. Shortly after, Natalie left too and almost ran out of the building. She had to get away.

Sitting on a bench outside the hospital, waiting for a taxi, Natalie took a call from her mother. Her father couldn't get time off work, but they would drive halfway up Friday evening and stay somewhere overnight. They would be there sometime late Saturday morning. Saturday seemed an awfully long time away.

The chatty taxi driver was really getting on her nerves. By the time she reached the hotel she felt like screaming. She thrust money at him and leapt out slamming the door. Not wanting to engage with anyone else, she turned away from the hotel and headed up the High Street but soon found herself sat on a bar stool inside The One-Eyed Seagull. As the barman placed a pint of some local craft beer in front of her, she took out her phone and found she had no signal. Frustrated she stuffed it back in her bag as the barman gave her a sympathetic shrug. Tipping nuts into a bowl, he slid it along the counter to her, then busied himself emptying the dishwasher. He wasn't going to bother her. She was grateful.

In the corner of the room a group of three elderly men sat playing dominoes. She watched them for a while until one of them noticed. "Want a game luv?"

"No, no thankyou."

"Aw, come on, luv. Don't sit there on your own." A chair was dragged into the space left, as they all shuffled their chairs round.

"No. Thankyou."

One of the men grabbed a beer mat from another table and another of the men started dealing out the dominoes for another game.

"I don't know how to play," she protested, but she sat down anyway.

"Its easy. We'll show you. Pete will go first. By the time its your go you'll have got the idea."

Pete, a skinny individual, laid a double six in the middle of the table. The next man, Sean, laid a six/five tile against the first. Then John, the man who had invited her to join them added a five/one. Natalie hesitated then laid a one/six.

"You got it. Reduce your high tiles but hang on to a variety so you can always go. If you can't then you need to pick up tiles until you can. First to get rid of all their tiles wins. There are points involved but you'll learn that as we play."

As play continued Pete tapped one of his tiles on the table, "I'm knockin'."

"He means he can't go and there are none left to pick up," explained John.

After a couple more games Natalie felt that she knew what she was doing. Another pint was placed at her side and, as she took a cool sip, she realised that for the past hour she hadn't thought about Zoe, or the hospital, or the hotel, at all. She thoughtfully placed her next tile and listened to the banter between the men, all of them old enough to be her grandfather.

"Have you seen our Milly, since she had her lips done?"

"That is Sean's niece's daughter," explained John.

"Aye. I did. If it were reconstructive surgery, it would be really impressive. Did you tell 'er to wear a seatbelt in future?"

"She wants 'er bum done next."

"Well, she'd get through doorways easier," said Pete.

"No, no! That is what I thought, but she wants it lifting."

"What is she going to sit on?"

"I'm knocking," said Natalie, stupidly pleased that she got to tap her tile on the table. The sound, acting like a gavel, successfully disrupted the conversational flow. Checking her watch, she was surprised at the time. "I really must go. Thank you. I really enjoyed that."

"You are welcome. Anytime. We are here most afternoons," said Pete.

"Never underestimate the power of pals and a pint," said John with a wink.

"Yes, you take care," added Sean.

As she pulled open the pub's heavy door and stepped on to the street she smiled. They had noticed that she was upset and worried, yet none of them had pried. They just let her share their company and it had helped: it had really helped.

She picked up a 'meal deal' on her way back to the hotel. Karen was bent over a map giving directions to a couple of hotel guests and Natalie was glad that she was able to sneak past. In the apartment she kicked off her shoes and ran a bath.

At 7pm the apartment phone rang. Natalie was relieved that this call didn't come transferred from reception; Mr Brammar, naturally, had had his own line. The boys were outside, ready to visit Zoe. She smiled at one of the staff as she skipped down the stairs, nodded at reception staff and stepped out into the street before anyone could speak to her.

In the sanctuary of the car she relaxed, "I really hope Zoe gets back soon. I am sick of avoiding staff questions. They must be wondering what has happened to her, and I just don't know what to tell them."

"I have lots to tell you both," said Kyle, waving a folder. I have been doing some research. I believe I have found out who Meg is, well, was."

"Oh? Who is, was she?"

"Walter Brammar's sister. He had a younger brother called Jack and an older sister called Megan. They both died in 1944 when the hotel was bombed, along with Mary their mother. All three are buried up in St James' Cemetery. Walter was the only one of the family to survive. He was away fighting."

"Mam, I have to go. I'll miss my train," he said hovering on the step.

"Here, take these," she said, holding out a brown paper parcel.

"Mam, don't fuss."

"Just some ham sandwiches and a lump of cheese."

Gratefully he clasped her outstretched hands, squeezed them, then took the package. She picked a piece of imaginary fluff off his shoulder and smoothed down his sleeves, running her hands over his sergeant's stripes, "They suit you," she said, and kissed him on the cheek.

"Love you, mam," he said as he kissed her back. "Love to Meg and Jack." Then, he was gone, striding up the street, hitching his kit bag.

"Walter, you take care, luv," she yelled. Closing the door, she turned and gave a wan smile to the receptionist who was busying herself, trying not to intrude on the intimate moment, trying to ignore the slight glisten in her employer's eyes.

Mary dove through the office door and closed it. He was so young. There was barely anything of him. He was tall, but so slim, yet he seemed strong. He stood erect and proud, and she was proud of him. She wished so much that his father had lived to see the man he had become. A man, but still a boy. His body may be grown and his face mature, sadly much older than his years, but she still saw the boy in his eyes. Her little boy.

She looked at the clock on the wall, stuffed her handkerchief back in her sleeve, ran her fingers through her hair and stepped out into the hotel.

"Madam, two gents are coming up from London on Friday. They will be staying a couple of nights. It sounded 'official'. Shall I get the 'Sea View' rooms ready?"

"Two gents? Who are they?"

"I don't know. The lady wouldn't say and said we were to keep the visit quiet, War Work!"

"It's always War Work. Okay, Alice, if you find out anymore let me know."

"No, that can't be Zoe's Meg. Why would Zoe be looking for that Meg. It doesn't make any sense," but little things that Zoe had said swarmed about Natalie's head. She tried to swat them away but gradually they settled and there was no ignoring the mound of evidence. She tried to deny it, but was it possible that Zoe believed she was Mary, and Mary was desperately trying to find her daughter Meg? Kyle was talking.

"I'm sorry," said Natalie, "What did you say?"

"I said, we should go and see the graves. I've got a lot more info here too about the bombing. It seems that Mary didn't die immediately, but some time later, from her injuries."

As they walked through the hospital they speculated on events, piecing together the little things that Zoe had said and all the things she had done. As they approached the nurses' station, they hesitated. The staff were behaving a little oddly. As they went to walk past, one of the nurses asked them to wait, whilst she went to get the nurse in charge. Puzzled, and growing a little alarmed, they stood and waited, whilst idly examining the scrapes along the wall's trolley-height scuff boards. When she arrived, the nurse in charge led them into her office and asked them to sit.

"We tried to phone you, to come and collect her when the doctors cleared her for discharge. Then, when one of the nurses went to ask her how she was getting home, did she need a bag for her things, etc. she wasn't there. She left everything behind. We looked for her, got the porters to search the grounds, but CCTV shows her walking out the front door."

"Have you called the Police?" asked Kyle.

"No, she was cleared for discharge. We couldn't find anything wrong with her."

"Well, there clearly is," blurted Natalie. "She had no money, well, not enough to get a taxi, and she knew we were coming in the evening. Did she leave her phone?"

The nurse reached behind her and picked up a plastic bag. She searched through it, "Yes, it is here. She left everything,"

Kyle swore, and said, "You reckon that is normal behaviour. When did anyone last see her?"

"About an hour ago. I am sorry, but she was free to leave."

Outside they split up and walked the streets round the hospital, meeting up 20 minutes later. "Where would she go, she doesn't know the area," said Toby. "Let's drive back to the hotel, maybe she is walking that way, she probably remembers the route and she only needs to follow the coast."

"It is going dark," said Natalie, "It isn't that warm either..."

"We'll find her," said Toby.

"If we don't find her on the way and she isn't back at the hotel, I'm calling the Police," said Kyle. It took a while to get back. They slowed and checked every time they passed someone, getting alarmed looks from some. They were nearly back at the hotel when they spotted a young woman, no coat, walking along the pavement. Natalie breathed a sigh of relief. As they pulled up alongside and Kyle wound his window down the woman turned and backed away from the kerb.

"Sorry," said Kyle, "We thought that you were someone else."

Back at the hotel, Natalie was beyond caring what the staff thought. Karen looked up as the three came through the door. "Is Zoe here?" asked Natalie.

"No, well, I haven't seen her. Is something wrong?"

"Let me know if you see her."

Leaving a puzzled Karen, the two lads followed Natalie upstairs.

The apartment was empty, as Natalie knew it would be. Kyle phoned the Police and Toby put the kettle on, finding what he needed to make them all a drink. Kyle provided a string of answers, referred to Natalie from time to time, argued, explained, explained again. When he finally put down the phone he was frowning, "They are putting out her general description but, as she obviously left of her own accord, they aren't going to '*alert Interpol*'!" As the others smiled ruefully, he added, "We are to let them know when she turns up. There was no 'if'."

As Toby handed Natalie a cup of tea she burst into tears, "I don't think I can take any more of this." Gently, he sat down beside her and put his arm round her shoulders. She barely noticed his presence.

Kyle paced the room, "I'm going to the Police Station, talk to them, make sure they are looking. I have a photo on my phone, hopefully that will help."

"We should all go. If we take 2 cars, we can search more area. The hotel can let us know if she turns up here," said Toby.

"The hotel staff don't know what is going on. They don't know she was in hospital," said Natalie.

"Why ever not?"

"Well, I..."

The young men stared at her.

"I suppose I could tell Karen, the lady on reception."

Kyle picked up the phone and said for Karen to come up to the apartment.

"Are there any maps here?" asked Toby. "We can divide the area." A quick search of the bookshelves, and Toby was soon spreading out an O.S. map on the dining table.

Karen arrived and was let in. She took one look at Natalie and went straight to her, noting the absence of Zoe she was all questions, "What's wrong? Where is Zoe? Has something happened to her," and spotting the map, "Is she missing?"

It took a while for Natalie to explain, choosing her words carefully. Karen had her back to the boys who patently thought that Natalie should tell her everything, but she limited the information to the fact that she had had to take Zoe back to the hospital for a third time, as she wasn't 'right' after the fall from the window, but that the hospitals couldn't find anything wrong and now Zoe had just walked out and they didn't know where she was.

"Have you called the Police?"

"Yes," said Toby, "but as she left voluntarily, they think it is too soon to be concerned."

"I'll make them concerned," added Kyle. "We need to go." He addressed Karen, "If she turns up here will you take care of her and let us know she is back?"

"And don't let the rest of the staff know, please," begged Natalie, "she is mortified enough by all that has happened without this too."

Doreen flicked between monitors and followed the groups departure. So, who were the two boys and why had they all been speaking to Karen? She pushed her glasses back up her nose and rapped her fingers on the desk. Still no Zoe, and that Natalie looked upset. If only there was a monitor in Walter's apartment. Sound, sound would have been good! Something twitched in the back of her mind. *'Maybe they killed the bitch'.* Inadvertently, Doreen smiled.

At the Police Station, at Kyle's insistence, they were taken into a side room and allowed to tell their story and express their concerns. It may have helped that the desk sergeant was a member of the golf club and knew Toby's father. Zoe's photo was distributed to those on duty. To their dismay there were only two officers patrolling what was a large rural area, plus a couple manning the station. Natalie was suddenly struck by how much Kyle cared for Zoe, he seemed more frantic than she was. She turned her attention to Toby. He was sitting next to her, leaning into her, shoulders touching. He was right there, holding her hand. Up to this point she had been more or less oblivious to his presence: so intent was she on finding her friend. He squeezed her hand and held her gaze, "We'll find her."

At 10pm, having driven round every road more than once, they dropped Natalie back at the hotel. Karen was due off duty and Natalie didn't want to involve any of the other staff. Kyle and Toby drove round some more but, unable to see anything that wasn't on the road, they called off their search until daylight.

Natalie paced the apartment, then sat in a chair clutching a cup of tea. She tried watching TV for a while but had no idea what was going on or even what she was watching. At some point she must have dozed off. She shot bolt upright at the sound of the phone. Rising, she nearly fell full length, scuffing a shin on the coffee table. Regaining her feet, she shot across the room. Blinking madly, in an effort to focus, she grabbed the receiver, "Yes?"

"Miss Walker, sorry to disturb you but would you come down to the kitchen please, Miss

Spencer is here and behaving most oddly. We..."
but Natalie was already on her way.

At the bottom of the stairs, she was met by
the receptionist who escorted her through to the
kitchen, babbling, "We don't know what to do.
She is..., well... you'll see."

Natalie saw. She stopped in the kitchen
doorway, shocked to her core. The duty chef was
shouting and desperately trying to appease the
figure that was Zoe. Dishevelled, pale and wearing
only one shoe Zoe tugged wildly at the shelving in
one of the floor-to-ceiling wall cupboards. Pans
and oven trays were scattered across the floor.
Natalie took a couple of steps into the kitchen,
sidestepping a mucky red footprint smudged
across the tiles. At her approach, the duty chef
backed away, glad to be relieved of responsibility.

"Zoe. Zoe! What are you doing? Zoe!"
Ignored, Natalie moved nearer. "Zoe, please stop.
STOP IT!" she screamed, but Zoe continued, the
rattling growing in force and volume. She seemed
completely oblivious to Natalie. The other two
women stared, aghast. Tentatively, Natalie
reached out and placed a hand over Zoe's bare
arm. It was cold. So cold. If it wasn't for the flexing
muscles tugging at the door, Natalie would have
thought she was touching a corpse. Unable to
stop her, Natalie turned to the other two women
for help. Together, the three of them managed to
prise her hands from the doorknob and
manhandle her through to a staff room at the side

of the kitchen. More compliant now, they were able to sit her in a chair. Natalie knelt in front of Zoe and took her head in her hands, forcing Zoe to face her. The reception phone rang, and the receptionist went to answer it, and the duty chef took the opportunity to sneak back to the kitchen. The sound of pans and baking trays being gathered and returned to the cupboard, followed. Alone, Natalie looked into Zoe's eyes. She recognised the same far away look that Zoe had worn on the night that she had fallen out of the window, on her previous night-time visit to the kitchen, and when she had attempted to run off the cliff. She thought about what Kyle had said about Meg. Shaking and uncertain, knowing she was about to cross a line, but compelled, she whispered, "Mary," and waited. "Mary?" Did she imagine it? Or, had something about Zoe changed. Was that a fractional pupil dilation or realigning of iris pigmentation? Natalie didn't know, but something had shifted, something ethereal rather than temporal. "Mary?" Yes, there was interest, "Mary, are you looking for Meg?" She held her breath. The eyes looked directly at her, penetrating and questioning, and she felt it. She felt the hope. Not sure how to proceed but knowing it was vital that she did, she said, "I know where she is. We can go in the morning." Natalie saw relief, and gratitude. She looked into the woman's eyes and knew Mary. She knew the woman whose eyes looked out of the photograph on the stairs. Humbled, she gently wiped a tear from the corner of the woman's eye, with her thumb, and said, "Can I speak to Zoe now?"

As she continued to hold Mary's head, the eyes slowly refocused. It took a while but eventually Zoe looked back, slightly quizzically at first, then bemused. When Natalie let go, Zoe sat back, events tumbling through her brain as she processed what had happened. When she visibly crumpled, Natalie took her in her arms and held her tight.

Before heading back to the apartment, Natalie had a word with the receptionist and the duty chef, swearing them to secrecy over the night's events. She didn't believe for a minute that they would keep it to themselves, but she just hoped that they valued their jobs.

Chapter Eleven

The phone was answered almost immediately. The relief in Kyle's voice as she told him that Zoe was back, and asleep in bed, made Natalie quite emotional. He was eager to know everything that had happened.

"Kyle, can I tell you in the morning? I'm shattered. Yes, please let Toby know."

She dragged a couple of thick rugs into Zoe's bedroom, and some bedding and placed them in front of the window. Then she got a collection of tins from the kitchen and stacked them in front of the bedroom door, as a crude alarm. Hopeful, that Zoe couldn't leave without her knowing, she soon fell asleep.

When she woke, it was light, and Zoe was still sleeping soundly. So, Natalie got herself a cup of coffee and a slice of toast and took her duvet out to the terrace. Her mind spinning, she pondered on the events of the night. Had she done the right thing? Had she actually spoken to Mary? Had that helped, or had it been a dangerous thing to do? Was that really Mary, or part of Zoe's personality that thought she was Mary? Did Zoe need a psychiatrist or a medium? Last night, she had been certain that she had been speaking to Mary, and that her promise to take her to Meg in the morning had provided relief and allowed her to retreat, and Zoe to resurface. What was going to happen when they took Mary to Meg's grave? Natalie had never had to break the news of a death before. She hadn't been there when Zoe was told that there had been a car accident and that both her parents and her grandmother had died, but she had seen the aftermath. She had seen the shock, the horror, the bewilderment, the utter despair. Could she do that to Zoe again? She had no idea what to say or what to do. She had no idea what the reaction might be. Now she felt that she had been stupid to say what she said to Mary. How would she react if she understood that Meg was dead? What effect would it have on Zoe?

A bell rang. Natalie's toast folded in her hand and fell between her fingers, landing jam side down on her duvet. Cursing she laid the sticky bundle carefully on the chair as she stood and headed for the door. Clutching her dressing gown, at the neck, she peered through the spyhole in the apartment door. It was Kyle and Toby. She took a quick glance at the wall clock as she opened the door. It was 9.15am.

The two men bubbled with relief, Kyle firing question after question. Slowly she worked her way through the events of the night.

"Have you let the Police know that she is back?" asked Toby.

"Er, no. I..."

As Kyle continued to pump her with questions Toby phoned the station. "*Now* they are sending someone round!"

"What! Whatever for?"

"They want to check she is okay for their report."

Whilst Natalie got dressed the men helped themselves to coffee. She was just combing her hair when the phone rang. It was Reception to say that there was a Police Officer to see Miss Spencer.

"I'll go get him," said Kyle.

"I'll go see if she's awake, and like, you know, herself!" She held crossed fingers in the air and disappeared into Zoe's room.

Zoe was sprawled across the bed, not a care in the world. Natalie grasped her by the shoulders and shook her.

"What, what's going on? Huh? Is everything okay?"

"Yes, get dressed."

"Why, what day is it?" Zoe sat up and scanned the room, as if seeing it for the first time.

"How are you feeling?"

"Okay, why?"

"What do you remember about yesterday?"

Zoe stared.

"You were in the hospital, and you just walked out. No-one knew where you were until you turned up here at 2am."

Zoe screwed up her face and looked puzzled, but Natalie knew her too well. "Don't behave like you haven't a clue," she snapped. "We were all worried sick. Why did you just walk out? Why didn't you wait for us to come get you?" She was on the verge of screaming. "There is a Police Officer on his way up to see you."

"A Police Officer! Why?"

Natalie crouched in front of Zoe and stared her in the eyes. Yes, it was Zoe she was speaking to, a Zoe who was now looking, well, vaguely scared, but herself. Hearing a door click and voices in the living room Natalie lowered hers, "*because*, we called the Police when we couldn't find you. We searched all over even after it had gone dark."

There was a knock on the door. "Look," whispered Natalie, "just say you are fine, you are really sorry for causing any bother, but you were annoyed at having to wait. You couldn't wait to get out of the hospital. He just wants to check that you are okay. Then hopefully he'll leave." Then, loudly, "She's just getting dressed." Natalie flung a selection of clothes at Zoe, crawled under the bed for a pair of shoes, and then ran a comb through Zoe's hair as Zoe did her best to straighten the jumper she had pulled on, tugging it down over her jeans. Natalie then handed her a pair of socks to cover the dressing on her right foot, that she had applied from a hotel first aid box, before leaving the kitchen the previous night. Zoe pushed her feet into the shoes and winced, but seeing how fraught and exasperated her friend was, she forced them on and stood. She was about to go into the living room when Natalie grabbed her, "Your jumper is on inside out."

Once the jumper was on correctly, she gave Zoe a once over, "Go wash your face, and your hands, you can have a shower afterwards. I have no idea what that smell is, but I suggest keeping your distance from people.

The Zoe that emerged from the en-suite and strolled into the living room was bright and charming and oozing apologies, and Natalie wanted to slap her. Kyle ran to Zoe and hugged her and was patently so glad to see her that Natalie thought for a moment that he was going to propose. After all the trouble that Zoe had caused, Natalie marvelled that he could be so forgiving, and so nasally tolerant, which made her want to slap him, too. However, Zoe's charm offensive even worked on the Police Officer, who turned out to be female. Soon Zoe had delivered all the required answers, in a convincingly calm and rational manner. The officer was suitably content and left. Even Natalie felt reassured, until she thought about their pending trip to the graveyard.

Leaving Kyle and Zoe together, Natalie and Toby went out to the terrace. Putting his hands on her shoulders he looked her in the eyes and asked, "How are you?"

"I am so sorry about all this. Nothing like this has ever happened before. She is normally bubbly and a bit scatty but never anything like this. She is basically a sensible human being. She..."

"No. Forget Zoe. I am asking how you are. Talk to me."

"I... I... I'm..."

"Come here." He folded his arms around her and pulled her close. She rested her head against his neck, and he leant his head on top of hers, burying his nose in her hair. He inhaled deeply and hugged her tighter. Noticing a tiny trickle on his neck, and a stifled sniffle, he stroked her hair and kissed her parting. Then he opened his jacket and wrapped her inside it. All the time he spoke soft words into her ear, so softly that she could barely make them out. The words didn't matter, didn't matter at all; the intonation and sentiment meant everything. She could feel his heart beating and felt his chest rise and fall, and gradually her heart rate dropped to match his. His jacket smelt vaguely of dog, but he smelt of soap, and ginger spice. As she gently inhaled, she wanted desperately to look up and seek out the lips that were still murmuring soothing words, but she didn't want to break the spell and the timing was wrong. Instead, she savoured the moment a little longer, dried her eyes and then leaned back, held in his embrace. He winked at her. Then laughed, as if he'd known exactly what she was thinking.

"Shall we rejoin the others; see what further dramas your friend can come up with?"

"Yes," she said, then cleared her throat, turning a little pink.

In the living room Kyle and Zoe were chatting animatedly and getting on splendidly. Natalie was sceptical that all was well, but it seemed that Kyle had broached the subject of taking 'Mary' to see Meg's grave and Zoe was eager to get going. How he had achieved this Natalie didn't know but it seemed that Zoe was keen to please him. How much comprehension she had of this bizarre situation she also didn't know. Was it just a trip to see where her ancestors were buried or, did she understand that 'she' was visiting her 'daughter's grave'?

"Toby and I will pick up the pair of you in the morning, then we can perhaps all go out to lunch together. I know a lovely little place just up the coast that does some fabulous crab, and," seeing Zoe's face, "cod."

"Can we not go *today*," asked Natalie, alarmed that the visit was to be postponed and that she would have to spend another night with Zoe and possibly 'Mary'.

"We're working. In fact, I, at least, must get going. I'm late as it is," said Kyle. "Do you want to meet this evening? Say, 7.30 in The One-Eyed Seagull?"

When the men left, Zoe's sparkle, it seemed, went with them. When Natalie placed a plate of toast on the coffee table, she found Zoe, one foot folded up on her opposite leg, picking at the plaster on her foot. It took a while, but she succeeded in removing it. She then neatly folded it and placed it on the table next to the toast.

"Zoe! Nooo... that's disgusting! Look, go and have a shower, and take that with you. Then I want to talk to you about the hotel."

"There's grit in it," she said, nipping the sole of her foot in an effort to elevate the offending skin and make it pickable. "Have you got any tweezers?"

"No."

"Yes, you do they're in your toilet bag."

"You're not using those."

"Why not?" asked Zoe.

"Use your own."

"But, you never use yours! You really ought to."

Eventually, Zoe emerged from the bathroom, clean and smelling fresh. She was smartly dressed and her make-up flawless.

Natalie sighed. She wished she felt as bright and relaxed as Zoe looked. However, if Zoe's outer appearance was at all a reflection of her inner being, best Natalie seize the moment. She desperately wanted to talk about Mary and the recent events, but she was also scared to broach that subject, and the more pressing matter was the hotel, and what Zoe planned to do.

"So, what do you fancy doing today?" she asked, in an effort to judge Zoe's mental state.

"I don't know."

"I had a walk down on the shore yesterday and met a woman who makes things to sell, out of driftwood. She had a lovely little dog called Hobnail with her. Perhaps we could have a walk down there together, and we haven't like, seen all the garden yet and the Lido."

Gaining neither agreement nor objection Natalie put on a jumper and got her jacket. She was relieved, when Zoe did the same.

At reception they asked if the Lido was open. It wasn't, but they were given a key.

When they passed the topiary dolphin, they were saddened to see that more of it had been chopped; it obviously wasn't doing too well. The head part still looked to have life in it; the prop that the gardener had put in place to support it, appeared to be working. There was no sign of the gardener.

As they approached the Lido, a weak sun gave a slight luminescence to the blue and cream tiles that adorned the entrance. An arch with 'Dolphin Lido', picked out in gold lettering, welcomed guests to the inferred luxury beyond. On top of the arch a grinning blue and white dolphin leapt from white waves, one crystal eye twinkling whilst the other winked cheekily. Zoe led the way, unlocking the gate and holding it open for Natalie.

They frowned at the leaf strewn pool, glad that the gate was kept locked, hiding the area from guests. They walked round the pool's edge and tried to imagine what it looked like full of water. With a good clean, the blue and cream tiles would probably look bright and cheerful, and on a hot day the water would be inviting. However, the place just looked grim, cold, and miserable. They headed for the changing rooms and Zoe unlocked the door. The interior needed a good airing. Cobwebs laced each window. Drifts of dead bluebottles lay on the windowsills. The wooden benches, which ran along the outer walls, were dusty and strewn with tiny flakes of plaster. Beyond the entrance hall the building was split into two, male changing rooms on the left and female on the right. They strolled into the male area, just because they could, noting the uninviting urinals, a couple of toilet stalls and some very large square sinks with big brass taps. At one end there was a curtainless curtain rail and a row of showerheads. There were navy tiles on the bottom half of the walls with a thicker navy tile on top and cream tiles above. They all needed a good clean.

They moved back into the entrance and through to the ladies' changing area. This was a little brighter with burgundy and cream tiles. Natalie did a circuit of the room, pushing open a couple of the toilet stall doors and wrinkling her nose. A clean at the end of the season would help as well as, presumably, one at the start. Letting the last cubicle door close, she walked across the room and turned on a tap, leaping backwards; the water pressure was more than adequate. Then she joined Zoe who was sitting on the wooden bench that ran along one of the walls, a row of hooks above. She froze. Zoe was staring at the ceiling light. Natalie knew that look.

The light burned deep into her retina. Still, she continued to hang onto its glow, the pain a distraction from the rest of her body: the pain keeping her in the present, keeping her tethered to life. She coughed, sporadically, but with each successive gasp she inhaled more fluid. Hands rolled her onto her side. She winced, but with her next breath she was able to clear a little of the fluid and get a little more air into her lungs. Grateful for the minor relief she relaxed a little, but the light was no longer there. She needed the light, she needed to hold on, she needed to tell them, to let them know. Hands on her back, hands on her shoulder, someone was speaking, "Mary? Mary? Are you okay? Mary, talk to me. Tell me what's wrong?"

Someone was talking to her; someone was trying to listen to her. She needed to make them understand. The person was squeezing her hand, looking into her eyes. She tried to focus: her pupils slow to react, the fading image of the ceiling light, multicoloured, obscuring the woman's face. She tried to form words, but the sound wouldn't come. An agonising cough and she forced air through her vocal cords, "Meg," she croaked, "Meg... is in the...sheese store."

"The 'what' store?" The person was staring at her: staring at her down a long dark echoey tunnel. The woman didn't seem to understand.

It was getting darker: the light just a pinpoint, the face, just a blur. She felt the hand squeezing hers, caring and pleading, conveying trust. "The cheeeeese store." She could barely see; vision gone completely on her left side. The hand shook her. She rasped in more air, "Meg is in the cellar. Find her. Please, find her."

"Mary, I'll find her for you. I'll find her," said the woman. She squeezed her hand and caressed her shoulder, "I will find her for you," she repeated, committing to her promise, as Mary faded deep into the darkness.

"Zoe, Zoe, look at me. Zoe…" Once more Natalie took Zoe's head in her hands and turned it. Once again, she stared deep into her eyes. It took longer this time. Longer for 'Mary' to let go and Zoe to surface. Gradually Zoe looked out. Finally, she spoke.

"I died here."

"What?"

"I died here. This is where I died. In this room. I remember the light. That light," and she pointed at the ceiling.

Natalie turned and looked. Then she looked back at Zoe. "Do you remember anything else?"

"Er, yes, trying… to make them understand, to look for Meg."

"What else? Where is the cheese store?"

Zoe frowned, "In the cellar," as if she was surprised that she knew the answer.

"Come on, lets get you out of here. Perhaps go find some lunch."

A compliant Zoe followed her out.

Chapter Twelve

Exiting via the back garden gate they strolled along the cliff top in silence and found a back way into one of the High Street cafés. They seated themselves in the window so that they had a view of the sea. Whilst Zoe studied the menu Natalie studied Zoe. She seemed more together now. Something had changed. Hopefully the incident at the Lido had, in some way, improved things. Zoe appeared more centred, grounded somehow, more here, in the present. She seemed brighter. Whilst they waited for their food Natalie broached the subject of the hotel and what Zoe planned to do about it.

"Keep it of course!"

"So, what do you plan to do with it?"

"Well, the accounts look healthy and if we can do something about the décor, the place will be awesome."

"Have you thought about when you will talk to the staff and what you are going to say?"

"Yes, I had some time to think whilst I was in the hospital. It has been running fine up to now, no reason it can't continue. Everyone just needs to continue doing what they are doing until I learn how to run the place. Then I can think about any changes I want to make. Simple!"

"Oh, Wow! That's great."

"Yes, first I want to get to know all the staff, keep them on board. Might have to get rid of Miss Hardcastle though."

"You can't do that. Where would she go? What would she do?"

"That isn't my problem."

Natalie gaped. "You can't be that heartless. She's an old lady."

"A nasty old lady."

"Zoe!"

"Whatev's."

They sat in silence until their food arrived, Natalie at a loss for what to say: angry at Zoe. Zoe, not interested it seemed in making amends, studied her phone. Initially irritated by this social exclusion, Natalie silently fumed. Then she gave in and took out her own phone whilst she had a signal available. She scrolled through the myriad of emails and text messages, tapped out replies to some, and marked others for dealing with later.

Soon, plates appeared. Natalie made space on the table and requested some ketchup as Zoe continued to tap into her phone; the only acknowledgment of the waitress being to hold her phone to one side.

Natalie tore the corner off her ketchup sachet and squeezed the contents onto her plate, then licked her finger. These rapid mood swings of Zoe's were draining. Natalie didn't know who she was looking at across the table. Was this friend

Zoe, traumatized Zoe, or Mary? She didn't know and there was no-one she could turn to for help. No, that wasn't true; there was Kyle, and Toby, but it seemed an awfully long time until 7.30pm.

"Zoe, how about we have a look round the shops for some clothes?" Zoe raised her head, so Natalie continued, "I wasn't expecting to stay here so long. I could do with some better shoes to wear on the beach."

"We need to try the washing machine too. I don't remember seeing any washing powder," said Zoe, "Do you?"

"Er, no." Natalie guessed she was talking to friend Zoe.

"Do you want anything else, or shall we go?"

So, they spent the afternoon wandering round the shops. With two cheap pairs of trainers, a sparkly top and a packet of soap powder swinging in carrier bags, they returned to the hotel.

Karen was on the reception desk and Zoe stopped to ask her to please let the staff know that she would speak to them all at 10 am on Monday morning, in the Conference Room. Natalie followed her up the stairs, bemused by this change, but with a niggling doubt playing with a thread of her hope.

That evening, when they entered the One-Eyed Seagull, they found the lads waiting for them. Kyle had a stack of papers in front of him. He was eagerly sorting and grouping them. Toby looked up and beckoned them over, pulling out a chair.

"I have lots to show you," said Kyle. "I've printed this lot off. Articles from the local papers about the bombing of the hotel." He placed a sheet in front of Zoe, and she started to read, Natalie leaning in and scanning the articles.

Hun flattens local landmark

Tragedy struck the Dolphin Hotel on Monday night when one of three stray bombs destroyed the back of the hotel, killing landlady Mrs Mary Brammar. Rescuers are still searching for Meg Brammar, aged 18, and Jack Brammar, aged 15. Jack's sweetheart, Edna Green, aged 18, is also missing. The eldest son, newly promoted Sergeant Walter Brammar, had left that morning to return to his unit.

Mrs Brammar was found in the grounds at the back of the hotel which had completely collapsed. She died several hours later from her injuries.

Body in water

A body discovered floating in the sea has been identified as that of Jack Brammar, aged 15 years. The remains of his boat were also found along with a scarf belonging to missing Miss Edna Green, aged 18 years. Jack was the youngest son of Mrs Mary Brammar, who died after a German bomb destroyed the back of The Dolphin Hotel and Lido on Monday.

Body found in remains of Dolphin Hotel

A body found in the remains of the Dolphin Hotel has been identified as that of Megan Brammar, aged 18 years. Rescuers retrieved the remains from the cellar of The Dolphin Hotel which had collapsed when struck by a German bomb on Monday.

Miss Edna Green remains missing.

"So," said Kyle, "those are the pertinent ones. There is more detail. You can have this lot," and he pushed the stack of papers across the table. "Hopefully, visiting the grave tomorrow will help."

They all looked at Zoe, who was staring into space, but she looked at each of them when she realised the attention was on her. "I don't know why I wasn't taken to a hospital."

"What? You were..." blurted Natalie as the boys stared open-mouthed.

"Don't you remember?" said Kyle, taking her hand. "Three times!"

"No, I remember that. I mean Mary. Why wasn't Mary taken to a hospital?"

There was silence for a while and then Kyle said, "There were 3 bombs. One took out the cliff, one hit the hotel, and the last one took out the road. If the tide was in, then there would have been no way out of the town."

"Yes, the tide was definitely in," said Zoe.

"How do you know?"

"I just do."

Before they could question her further, there was a bit of a commotion as chairs were pushed aside, and an elderly gentleman tapped Natalie on the shoulder, "Hi love, so you know young Toby, do you?"

"Oh, hi Sean."

"You two have met?" queried Toby.

"Ay, we had a fine game o' Dominoes yesterday afternoon. Nice to see you again lass," and gave Natalie a wink. "Gosh, what you got there? Is that about the bombing? Say, you aren't the new owner, are you?"

"No, that would be Zoe."

"So, you're old Walter's great-granddaughter, are you? Pleased to meet ya lass. A fine establishment you got there."

"You knew him?" asked Zoe.

"Yeah, he came in here regular, back in the day. He liked to get away from the hotel. He were older than me like, so we didn't have much to do with each other, but he were a nice chap. I were only a nipper when The Dolphin was bombed but folks talked about it for years. Still do, and, what 'appened to your mum, that were awful too. Well," he said looking up, "Pete's here. I'll leave you be. Nice meeting you lasses."

The rest of the evening passed quickly, and Toby and Kyle escorted Zoe and Natalie back to the hotel, arranging to meet at 10am, the following morning, to walk to the cemetery together.

At the top of the hotel Doreen observed as the girls climbed the stairs, counting their steps, the little voice in her ear, *'with those silly shoes, it wouldn't take much...'*

Chapter Thirteen

Natalie pulled on her gloves and stuffed her left hand in her pocket. Her right hand she linked through Toby's arm, leaning-in to him as they headed up the High Street. "Are you sure you want to do this today? It is freezing," said Toby.

"Not really, a nice roaring fire would suit me better, but I want to get this over with. Hopefully it will help. I don't think I can take much more of this. I've been awake most of the night, listening. She was talking in her sleep. Well mumbling. I couldn't make out what she was saying but at least she stayed in her room and as far as I could tell, in bed."

"Kyle and I could do a shift, if you like."

"Thanks, but no. The staff have enough to gossip about without you two staying the night. Besides, my parents will be arriving today. Oh! Big yikes! I haven't booked them a room!" She checked her phone, but there was no signal. The others checked theirs.

"We won't be long. It isn't much further," said Kyle. "Then we can head back and get some lunch."

At the end of the village, they forked left following the main road which took them away from the coast and round the back of the headland. It was a bit of an uphill drag, but it wasn't long before they reached a pair of imposing wrought iron gates. Kyle led the way through and stopped by a wooden framed notice board. Pulling a piece of paper from his pocket he glanced at it and then gave his attention to the board. A large map of the cemetery was displayed behind a glass door. He ran his finger up one of the rows and along another. At the far back of the cemetery was grave M35. "This way," he said and set off, an arm tucked through Zoe's. Natalie and Toby followed behind, Natalie watching her friend closely.

At the top of the cemetery, on the crest of the hill, beneath a row of hunkering hawthorns was a set of matching headstones.

"Right, we're here," said Kyle pointing. "This one is Mary's grave."

"Oh," gasped Natalie. It hadn't occurred to her that Mary's grave would be here too, or how 'Mary' would react, seeing her own grave. Scanning the headstones Natalie saw that Megan and Jack were there. At the end of the row was a much newer plot strewn with polythene wrapped flowers and a temporary plaque stating 'Walter Brammar'.

"It doesn't look like they ever found Edna Green. I haven't been able to find a grave for her," said Kyle, "but then, she could be buried elsewhere. I need to do more digging." No one laughed.

Kyle led Zoe along the row, talking softly to her as he did so, clutching her arm and holding her hand. Natalie and Toby followed slowly along behind, Natalie watching Zoe. Was that a slight hitch of her shoulders, a slight falter in her step. She seemed slightly hunched and, 'old'. Yes, old. Was this Mary she was watching: a mother seeing her children's graves? By Jack's grave Zoe stopped and gently removed her arm from Kyle's. Then she walked between the graves and crouched by Megan's, transfixed it seemed, by the headstone.

"No, no, oh no," mumbled Zoe, agitated. "NO...!" Suddenly she grabbed a stone from the ground and leaning her full weight against it, slashed a great scratch across Megan's name. The granite squealed and tiny chips flew. All three lunged at her. Before one of them could stop her, she had made several more. Together they dragged her away and hung onto her whilst they stared at the headstone. The scratches weren't deep, mainly marks in the lichen, but there was definite damage. The name 'Megan' was now barely legible.

All three started talking at once, demanding to know what Zoe thought she was doing. Natalie was practically hysterical. Despite her misgivings, she had been hoping for some closure from this visit, but now... she wanted to slap Zoe again, and slap her hard. She couldn't take this. She felt so helpless. Not being able to trust someone, was wounding. She ached, with despair. Toby was holding her, whispering words in her ear, kissing her hair, wrapping her in his arms and holding her tight. "I think you need to get her away from here. You say your parents are coming. Get them to take you both home." Natalie's head snapped up and her eyes met Toby's. His pupils widened as they met hers and he gave her a rueful smile. "I don't want you to go, but we both know that it is the right, possibly only, thing to do." As a tear formed in the corner of her eye, he wiped it away, then gently pressed her head into his neck, wrapped his arms round her again and rocked her slowly.

Kyle had been holding Zoe, trying to reason with her, not knowing if he was talking to Zoe or Mary. He tipped her head, getting her to look at him, to make eye contact, to get her to see sense. She looked at him, but what he saw, wasn't Zoe. There was a depth to her eyes. A depth, behind a film. A haze that shifted, drifted and swirled. A haze that was compelling and knowing, but the pupils were dilated, like those of a corpse. With a jolt he let go and stepped back, gravel crunching. Released, Mary turned on her heels and started running down the path to the gate.

Natalie set off, with Toby close behind. Kyle stood rooted to the spot, cold to his core. Up until now there had been an acceptance, but not really the belief. Now, he had no doubt, no 'get out clauses', no excuses, no 'yes buts'. This was another being that had taken over Zoe, and he was not just scared for her, but of her. He wanted to run, to be far away, to be rid of this fear that was creeping through him. It was like being a child again, afraid of the monster under the bed. BUT this terror was real, tangible, intense. This time his parents wouldn't come running and comfort him. Instead, heart thumping, he set off; shaky legs stumbling down the path.

Before Natalie reached the gates, Toby overtook her, but before either of them reached the road, there was a squeal of brakes and a screaming horn. Toby was first through the gates. He skidded to a halt, scanning the scene. A silver BMW was stopped at an angle; smoke seething from its brakes, dark tyre marks scarring the tar. Natalie ran into Toby, unable to stop, shoving him forward and into the gutter. Together they scanned the scene, scanned the ground, scanned the tarmac, dropped to their knees and looked under the car. Then to their relief the car set off, its horn blaring madly at a figure running into the distance. Toby turned and gathered Natalie into his arms, kissing the top of her head.

Doreen had been idly watching the monitor. A middle-aged couple had just turned up at reception and appeared to be remonstrating with the receptionist, who was now picking up the phone. She waited for her phone to ring, but it didn't. Then, through the wall she heard the faint sound of ringing from Walter's apartment. She still thought of it as Walter's Apartment; she couldn't bring herself to refer to it as anything else. She was just considering the implications of this call when a dishevelled Zoe came running across the screen. The couple and the receptionist all looked stunned, but the couple obviously knew Zoe and were calling after her. Then all three followed her, and reception was left unattended, the scene static. *'Better go see'.* Doreen put on her suit jacket and headed for the door. *'Better find out what is happening. She shouldn't get away with it. She's just as responsible...'*

When Natalie and Toby stepped into reception, they were surprised to find the reception desk unmanned. Then, from somewhere in the depths of the hotel they heard voices, agitated, raised. As Kyle joined them, they followed the sound, which was coming from the kitchen.

"That's my parents," said Natalie. "What..." and she broke into a trot. The others set off after her. As they stepped into the kitchen all three stopped. Across the room, her father was trying to pull Zoe away from the cupboard that she had been trying to get into on the night Natalie had found her in there. Her mother was in tears, pleading with Zoe. The kitchen staff and receptionist were all standing about looking bemused and helpless. On the floor lay the cupboard contents, pans, tin trays, dishes, and a sack of flour, split and scattered across the tiles: numerous footprints adding to the mess. The cupboard continued to rattle.

The air changed: a subtle alteration of temperature that was sensed rather than felt, a static with its own adrenaline. Natalie felt the hairs on the back of her neck stand erect. A prickling, an awareness of something other. The skin of her back knew, it crawled. Her head reasoned that if she couldn't see it, she could deny it existed. Deep down she knew this to be illogical, but she clung to it like the red fluffy comfort blanket she had as a child. Then, by the cupboard, Zoe stopped struggling. The room fell silent. One by one their attention shifted. One by one they stared at the door. The kitchen staff huddled together, each trying to hide behind the other. Kyle and Toby whipped round and faced the door, backing away. Afraid, but compelled, Natalie slowly turned. She had no idea what she was expecting. She just knew that she didn't want to see, but couldn't, not look. What she saw was initially reassuring. It was just Doreen, a human being. Then she looked at the eyes. The figure in the doorway was human, but not. It looked like Doreen, but it wasn't.

"Do you want to go down to the cellar?" said the figure, looking slightly coy and taunting. It held aloft a large brown metal key, dangling it like a child might do before snatching it out of reach.

As the others froze, Zoe stepped forward. Her eyes on the key, she followed, never taking her eyes from it as the cellar door was unlocked. The figure stepped inside the door and held it open, wide. Silently Zoe drifted across the kitchen, through the door and past the figure into the darkness. Once she crossed the threshold the door slammed shut. The frame rattled and plaster fell from the wall at its edges; tiny flakes that floated and fell, larger pieces that dropped with a thud, shattering into dust. Then silence. Flour swirled and settled on the floor. There was an audible gasp as the tension snapped.

"Zoeeee...," Kyle leapt at the door and flung it open. Slapping his hand against the wall he found the light switch. As light weakly illuminated the cellar below there was a scream and muffled thudding. Something, or someone was falling down the steps. Kyle disappeared, his feet pounding on the stone. "She pushed her. She pushed her down the steps," yelled Kyle.

Toby was the next to follow him, with Natalie and her parents bringing up the rear. Someone found the bottom light switch and switched it on. The first thing Natalie saw was Kyle bear-hugging Doreen and dragging her away from a prone Zoe who was whimpering and holding her arm. It looked like Doreen had been kicking Zoe, but Natalie was uncertain what she had seen as her view on the way down the stairs had been obscured by Toby. It made no sense for Doreen to have pushed her. Natalie knelt by Zoe as her parents crouched beside them. "Her head's bleeding," said her father, "I'm calling an ambulance."

"I'll do that," said Toby, "you stay with Zoe, Mr Walker," and he headed up to the kitchen.

"Help. Somebody help me," called Kyle, "I can't hold her much longer." Doreen had her feet off the ground and was wriggling and kicking at Kyle's shins. He held her fast in a bear-hug, but she was slipping down, and he was struggling to keep her contained. She was glowering at Zoe and growling threats: her vitriol so intense and high-pitched that it was impossible to understand what she was saying.

Zoe looked up, and at Doreen. Doreen looked at Zoe. Natalie saw something pass between them, a fleeting acknowledgement of something shared. Then it was gone, and Zoe was looking at her wrist and whimpering again, cradling it and rocking.

Mr Walker started to get to his feet but, before he could help, Doreen had put her feet on the floor and jerked her head back into Kyle's face, sending him staggering backwards. She then dodged past Mr Walker, as he got to his feet, and ran for the stairs.

Zoe was now sitting and clutching her arm, in between inspecting her knees, and giving her hips and shoulders a flex. Thankfully, she appeared to be herself again. She winced as she moved. Then, as Natalie moved to one side allowing the light from the single bulb to illuminate Zoe's arm, Zoe looked at it and dry retched. Her arm now resembled a fork. There was a distinct 'step', just before her wrist. Natalie too, felt sick and looked away.

Toby came clattering down the steps, "There's an ambulance on its way, and the Police."

The Police arrived first, shortly followed by the Paramedics. Mrs Walker went in the ambulance with Zoe, and Mr Walker and Natalie followed in his car. Kyle and Toby gave brief statements to the Police, corroborating what Zoe had said, that she had been pushed and then kicked as she lay on the floor. Doreen was found in her apartment, arrested, and taken away.

Natalie was looking at her phone and getting an intermittent signal, when her father suddenly gasped and put his foot down. Sound pierced her ears, and she looked up to see the ambulance rapidly disappearing into the distance, its blue lights now flashing and its siren blaring. "Don't lose it, I don't know where its going. That isn't the way to the General."

The drive seemed an eternity. On the outskirts of the city the lights were against them, and Natalie frantically searched her phone for the nearest hospital in the hope that it would be the right one.

"There", he said, pointing at a big red road sign with 'Hospital A & E department' emblazoned across it. Several more signs, braking, signalling, honking of horns and weaving, and the building appeared. After a desperate 10 minutes parking and paying, and language Natalie had never heard from her father before, they were heading through the doors of the hospital. Inside, an array of bewildering signs and a strong smell of disinfectant and desperation greeted them. Sounds echoed round the large entrance hall and brightly coloured corridors led off to colour coded parts of the enormous medical maze. Natalie dragged her father over to the reception desk and elbowed a couple out of the way. Irate, the man was about to complain, but fell silent when he saw Natalie's ashen face.

The receptionist was unable to tell them anything, she didn't have a Zoe Spencer registered on the system, but directed them to Accident and Emergency. They set off. Someone in their wisdom had chosen red for the A & E department and a red line on the floor led them along corridor after corridor, to the other end of the hospital, where red protective bumper bars panelled the walls like thick dado rails. Anywhere else it would have been cheerful.

Mr Walker stopped a harassed looking nurse who was carefully carrying something in gloved hands, the contents of which were covered in paper, and was directed to the A & E reception desk, where there was a queue. In rows of seats, sat the dripping and distressed. Natalie searched the faces but there was no sign of Zoe, or her mother. The queue moved surprisingly quickly and soon Natalie and her father were answering questions and then told to sit, someone would be with them soon. They had barely sat down when they were called. A nurse in dark blue led them to a small room in a quieter part of the department. After a tearful greeting with her mother the nurse sat them down and explained that Zoe had lost consciousness in the ambulance, that she was being assessed and prepped for surgery; it looked like she had a fractured skull and pressure on her brain from bleeding. Shocked, they all sat and waited whilst an indifferent clock ticked ever slower on the wall. When the door opened, they all leapt and then showed visible disappointment when Kyle and Toby were let in.

"Sorry," said Natalie, "We were hoping for some news". Quickly, she explained, then asked how the boys had found them.

"We went to the minor injuries' unit, but you weren't there. When we explained she had been pushed down stone steps and kicked, they said she had probably been brought here."

Medical explanations and consent forms, cups of tea and a change of rooms followed, and the day wore on. At some point Toby went and bought some sandwiches, which sat mainly uneaten amongst a collection of cold tea and coffee cups. Eventually they were told that Zoe was out of surgery and was being moved to Intensive Care. The surgery had gone well but she would need careful monitoring for the next few hours. She was sedated and ventilated. As well as the extradural haematoma she had several fractured ribs, broken radius and ulna, and extensive bruising. They could see her briefly, but then they may as well go home. If her condition changed, they would be notified.

Doreen was no longer weeping. She had no tears left to cry. When they brought her a drink of water, she drank it down in one go. The voice in her head had gone, seemingly satisfied. She had a vague memory of events. She remembered her actions, but her motives were an alarming mystery to her. She remembered being angry, so angry, but didn't know why. She remembered the exhilaration of the push and the glee of the kicks; the thought of it now, an addictive thrill. Alone, in the over-heated cell she had time to analyse events. Mrs Brammar? Not Walter's wife, surely. Why would she be angry at her? She was angry at Zoe, but she would never, ever go so far as to try and hurt her. Yet she had. She had enjoyed it. She had put all her strength into those kicks and felt powerful. How could she have done that? Why would she?

Whenever, someone came to her, she asked them about Zoe, but they would tell her nothing, their demeanour ominous. Did she want a solicitor? Yes, yes. She gave them the only name she knew, George Titherington.

Zoe looked so small, and fragile, lying there with a shaved, bandaged head, tubes attached feeding in fluids, monitor leads, and a plastered wrist. Her naturally fair complexion seemed stark against the head dressing. The lack of make-up and false lashes made her look about 12 years old. This wasn't the lively bubbly Zoe they all knew. This was a vulnerable, very human and mortal being. A nurse gave them an explanation of what they could see and reassured them that Zoe was doing well. It didn't look like it; the complete lack of expression on her normally animated face shocked them.

'She looks so peaceful', thought Natalie, but then realised, that was what people often said about the dead.

From the back-office Mary could hear the receptionist, a slightly obstructive tone to her voice. Stepping out into reception Mary pulled up short. "Oh, good morning."

"Morning, is Jack in?" A young woman was standing fingering a red knitted scarf which was wrapped round her neck. Irritatingly it matched her lipstick, exactly.

With a sigh Mary replied, "Yes, Edna, he is fixing chairs in the dining room."

The young woman beamed and disappeared down the corridor to the back of the hotel, calf length skirt swishing, heels clomping, perfectly straight line drawn up each bare calf. Mary wasn't certain what it was about the girl that irked her. It wasn't just that she was too old for her son; in a few years time the 2-year 3-month gap wouldn't matter. The girl was just, brazen! She, Mary, had never been like that, and thankfully her daughter Megan wasn't either. Having been at school together, the two girls were the same age. With their long, dark brown hair rolled at the sides and pinned up, they were similar in appearance, yet their mannerisms and behaviour so different. She finished the letter she was writing and popped it in an envelope. Once sealed and stamped, she placed it on the reception desk. Then she followed the trail of scent down the corridor to the dining room. Incongruously, it smelled red. She had never associated a colour with a smell before, but the thought was inescapable. Before she reached the dining room, she became aware of raised voices: two female voices.

"I told you not to sit on it, he hasn't fixed that one yet. And who let you in here anyway? It might be a hotel, but you can't just walk in like you own the place."

"Your mother let me in!"

Mary stepped through the double doors and surveyed the scene. Jack was on his knees quietly screwing a leg back onto a chair, taking no part in the argument going on over his head. The two young women were facing each other; no love lost between the two of them.

"He doesn't need a scarf. He has plenty."

"Ah, but this one, has my perfume on it." *With that, Edna took off the scarf and draped it round Jack's neck. He coughed. "See you later," she said, planting a bright red kiss on his surprised lips and turning just in time not to bump into Mary in the doorway.*

Kyle didn't want to leave, but the others shepherded him away. Outside it was dark, streetlamps and headlights a stark contrast, apathetic drizzle doing nothing to help their mood; relief that she seemed to be doing okay but a nagging fear that things could still go wrong.

Doreen sat bolt upright as the little hatch in her cell door was opened. An eye peered through the gap before it was clanged shut and her cell door unlocked. Her heart beat a little faster as she was taken down the corridor and told that her solicitor had arrived. She dabbed the corners of her eyes and blinked a few times. Then she ran her fingers through her hair and cleared her throat. The lighting in the room, to which she was taken, was a little stark. She blinked again as she sat down on the lightweight plastic chair and hitched it up to the table. At the other side sat George Titherington. She felt awkward; the last time they had met she had been openly hostile to him. Now, she regretted her behaviour. It wasn't his fault that Walter had left the hotel to that Zoe. She tried a weak smile, "Thank you for coming."

"So," said Mr Titherington, "I understand that you have been arrested for assault – grievous bodily harm. Is that right?" He opened up his laptop and switched it on.

"Yes."

"Would you like to tell me what happened?"

At first, she said nothing, struggling to find the words, then, surprising even herself, she just blurted out, "I pushed Zoe down the cellar steps."

"Zoe? Zoe ... Spencer? Walter Brammar's great granddaughter?"

"Yes!" and she burst into tears.

"Oh! Then, I'm sorry, but I can't represent you. I am Zoe's solicitor. It would be a conflict of interest. Look, unless you know another solicitor, I suggest that you see the duty solicitor."

Back at the hotel, they were greeted by an anxious Karen who berated them for not letting the staff know what was happening. She then apologised, acknowledging that caring, didn't give her the 'right to know'; she was just an employee after all.

"I am so sorry," said Natalie, "We were so worried that it never even entered my head, that you would be worried too."

"That is okay."

"No, it's not," said Natalie. "I should have thought to let you know. We are so grateful to you for all you do here. In fact, and I know I can't officially do this, but I am sure Zoe will agree, I am promoting you to temporary Hotel Manager, effective immediately. Please say yes, we really need you to take charge," and she burst into tears.

Chapter Fourteen

As soon as she woke, Natalie phoned the hospital. Zoe had had a good night and was stable. The staff were pleased with her. She remained sedated and was showing no adverse signs. At breakfast, Natalie found that her parents had phoned too, as had Kyle and Toby, who surprised them by appearing in the dining room.

After some initial awkwardness, Toby took the initiative and, to Mr Walker's amusement, formally introduced himself and Kyle. The day before, he and Kyle had just been there, as part of the scene and been accepted as such, no questions asked. When he stumbled over his explanation of their relationship with Zoe and Natalie, he turned slightly pink as he looked at Natalie. They hadn't discussed their relationship; it had no named status and he suddenly realised he shouldn't be stating it out loud, to her parents, without discussing it with her first.

"Good friends?" suggested Mr Walker.

"Yes," said Toby and Natalie, in unison and too quickly.

"Please, call me David. Would you like some coffee?" he said, raising his hand and waving over one of the staff.

"And, I'm Sharon," said Mrs Walker.

Coffee arrived and after some initial throat clearing Toby said, "I would like to invite you all to the golf club for lunch. Kyle and I have discussed this, and there is something that we need to talk about." He lowered his voice and added, "away from here. I have invited Karen to join us too. She should know the extent of what we are dealing with here. We should all know everything that has happened regarding Zoe, and now Miss Hardcastle."

Natalie frowned, there was something else, something that she didn't know. "Miss Hardcastle hasn't been released, has she?" Natalie looked at Toby, who shook his head, then at Kyle. Neither would look her in the eye. As her bacon grew cold, she listened to the others' inane talk filling the time. Zoe was doing okay; she had spoken to the hospital herself and Miss Hardcastle was in police custody. So, what now?

More coffee arrived; the staff appearing to loiter. Was it curiosity, or merely attentiveness to the new owner's family? Natalie grew increasingly annoyed. The head waiter, who had previously made a point of sitting her and Zoe at the table overlooking the topiary dolphin, was now irritatingly obsequious. Scrunching her napkin and flinging it on the table she announced that she was going for a walk.

Toby caught her on the landing as she let herself into the apartment for her coat. "Are you okay?"

"I thought I was, but now I'm not sure. Should I be, or is there something I ought to worry about, besides being worried sick about Zoe?"

"That depends. Sorry. I'll explain later. Come here," and he wrapped his arms around her and pulled her close. She tucked her head into his neck and sighed, enjoying the warmth, the closeness of another human being, simply being cared for. Then she looked up at him and their eyes met. He cupped the back of her head with his hand and looked deep into her eyes. Tiny flecks of gold sparkled in his brown irises as his pupils dilated, letting her in. Little dimples appeared at the sides of his mouth, just before it met hers. With his left foot he closed the door.

Doreen dripped tears into her mince and mash. The duty solicitor had listened and made notes and now she was to see a doctor. She couldn't decide if this was a good thing or a bad thing. There was a subtle change in the behaviour of the staff. The person who had brought her dinner had seemed less dismissive, or maybe she had imagined it. Maybe the man was just different to those on the earlier shift. He brought her a couple of paper napkins. Was this for her tears? Or, were they an accompaniment to the meal, that he had missed? She didn't know, but she was grateful, her sleeve was quite damp.

Late morning the five of them arrived at the hospital and were let in to see Zoe, two at a time. Natalie and her mother went in first. There was no apparent change and although the staff encouraged them to talk to Zoe, there was nothing to say, and Natalie left to let her father in whilst her mother sat holding Zoe's hand. Then her father came out, looking close to tears and sent Kyle in. The staff reported that Zoe was making reasonable progress, and they would aim to wake her up in a day or two. Natalie wondered when 'good' had gone to 'reasonable' but said nothing. It was explained that Zoe had a probe monitoring her intracranial pressure, which needed to remain stable and within normal limits before they could wake her.

They didn't like leaving her, but it was a relief to leave the hospital and step into the fresh air. At the golf club Toby led them to a private room, once again overlooking the sea. When Karen turned up, introductions were made, and food ordered. Toby took a sip of his drink and, with a glance at Kyle, cleared his throat.

"Sorry for all the mystery but Kyle told me something in the car last night that the rest of you should know. First, I think we need to run through everything that has happened since Natalie and Zoe arrived in the hotel. Natalie, I think you should tell your parents and Karen, everything."

So, hesitantly at first, Natalie began to run through how she woke in the night to find that Zoe had fallen out of the window, despite the child locks. She told them how scared she had been by the look in Zoe's eyes. She told them that, despite falling 3 floors, Zoe had no injuries but appeared not to be able to hear. She went into every little detail of how Zoe had behaved and what she had said. She related Zoe's trips down to the kitchen in the middle of the night and how she nearly ran off the cliff top, and the incident in the lido. She told them about how, most of the time, Zoe did not seem herself; it was as if someone else was looking out of her eyes. Finally, she told her parents, and Karen, that she believed that Zoe's ancestor, her great great grandmother was the one looking back. Finally, she said it out loud. She believed Zoe to be possessed by Mary Brammar who was trying to find her daughter, Megan, in the bombed out remains of the Dolphin Hotel. Food arrived and Natalie fell silent as the others absorbed this.

Food delivered and staff gone, she expected her parents and Karen to fire questions at her, to dispute what she had said. Instead, they remained quiet, lost in their own thoughts, bizarrely accepting.

Toby did a recap of events in the cemetery and the lead up to the confrontation with Doreen, in the cellar. Then he looked expectantly at Kyle, who picked up the story.

"When I went through the cellar door, Zoe was three or four steps down and Miss Hardcastle more or less jumped down the steps behind her. For a woman of her age, I could not believe how agile she was. With one hand on the handrail, she put her other in the middle of Zoe's back, and pushed her, hard. It wasn't a trip, an attempt to stop herself falling, it was a deliberate shove. Then she ran down the steps after Zoe and began kicking her. When I grabbed her and pulled her away, she began to squirm and kick…"

The others waited, and Toby looked at Natalie. This is what she needed to hear. This was the bit she didn't know, and she knew that she didn't want to, but had to know. Breath caught in her throat, she sat motionless, mouth dry, all senses focussed on what Kyle was about to say.

"All the time I was holding her she was screaming and yelling."

"Yes," said David, "We heard her. It was ear-piercing. Horrific!"

"Did you hear what she was saying?"

"No, I doubt dogs could have!"

"I could. She was screaming abuse at Mrs Brammar. She was referring to Zoe as Mrs Brammar." All but Toby stared. "Other than Walter Brammar's wife, Elizabeth, there is only one other Mrs Brammar, that fits: Zoe's great great grandmother, Mary. She was shouting at Mary Brammar."

Whilst everyone was still pondering the implications of what Kyle had said, Karen took a deep breath, "Well, there is something else.

Something that none of you are aware of." She looked at Natalie. "It is something that happened whilst you and Zoe were moving into the flat, just after Zoe had challenged the kitchen staff about the cellar key..."

"Yes," said Natalie.

"Well, when I got back downstairs Doreen emerged from the office with a key. I guess she had got a spare out of the safe. She made me follow her into the kitchen, where she unlocked the cellar door. Together we went down the steps. She seemed oblivious, but there was something down there. I don't know how to explain it. It was like something out of a horror movie. You know, when you are watching and wanting to yell at the actors - don't be stupid - don't just stand there - get out - run! Stuff I've laughed at before. Stuff that, well ... there was a kind of energy. Something lurking, prowling, building in... malevolence. All this time Doreen was searching the shelves: searching the floor. I don't know why. I don't know what she was looking for, but she seemed totally unaware of the atmosphere. Then, a mug flew across the cellar. It flew with such force, such violence. Then another flew and smashed one of the ceiling lights. At first, I was rooted to the spot. I couldn't move my legs. I felt I couldn't breathe. Then the energy seemed to gather in the centre of the room, circling Doreen. I couldn't help myself. I ran up the steps, leaving her down there."

The others waited.

"The kitchen staff, stared at me, then turned their attention to the open cellar door. The air at the top of the cellar steps appeared to pulse, distorting the wall behind it. Then there was a kind of sigh, and it ceased. Then we heard footsteps coming steadily up the steps and Doreen emerged."

Now she looked at Natalie again, "You noted how I looked when you and Zoe came down to go out, asked me if I was alright, said I looked like I'd seen a ghost! Well, Doreen didn't look any different, maybe just a new, sparkle to her eyes. We were all amazed, and I felt such a fool. Since, I've even wondered if I'd imagined it. Not anymore. I guess it wasn't just a sparkle. I guess, she wasn't alone."

In the evening, they went back to visit Zoe. Nothing had changed. They took it in turns to sit for a while, holding her hand.

Mary watched her go, making sure she left, hating the girl and unable to fathom why. Was it because she was so different to herself? Was it because she was so blatant in her flirtation or was it simply that the woman had got her claws into her son, her youngest son. She looked at him now, knelt on the floor, stuffing the ends of the scarlet scarf inside his jumper, apparently unaware of the emotions conflicting his mother. He picked up the screwdriver and resumed mending the chair, seemingly oblivious to the implications of the scarf and the possessive red stain on his lips.

"Jack, we need to move the stuff tonight. We have government guests arriving tomorrow. I don't know who they are, but we will need to get the staff back in whilst they are here. Can you do it?"

He sat back on his haunches and considered, "If the swell isn't too great, I'll manage. Tide should turn about nine."

Then she looked at her daughter, "We'll 'ave to manage on our own. I don't like it, but Pete won't be able to get here in time."

"It'll take me longer on me own," said Jack, "but the new crates are smaller. If you can take 'em up two at a time it should be okay."

"It is a shame Walter had to leave," said Megan.

"No, I don't want him to know anything about this. He has enough to worry about without worrying about us. We'll manage."

Chapter Fifteen

At 8am Natalie went and spoke to the staff. She guessed that they would already know, as most of them had been there on Saturday, but she needed to talk to them, in an official capacity. She didn't know if they would listen to her. After all, she wasn't the owner, but someone needed to tell them that Karen was now their new boss.

She got Karen to gather the staff, who gave her their full attention. It appeared that after the events of Saturday night they were all eager to hear what Natalie had to say. Briefly she ran through what had happened, limiting events to the push, Zoe's condition, and Miss Hardcastle's arrest. She did not wish to create, or add to, any speculation as to why Miss Hardcastle had done what she had done, and she certainly had no intention of talking about 'possession'.

"As you are no doubt aware, Miss Hardcastle was arrested on Saturday night, for pushing Miss Spencer down the cellar steps. Zoe is in hospital and has undergone surgery. She is expected to make a full recovery but until she regains consciousness we can't know for sure. In the absence of Miss Hardcastle and Zoe, I have promoted your Deputy Manager, Karen Johnson, to temporary Hotel Manager. You will now take your instruction from her," having completed her rehearsed statement she breathed a sigh and waited to see what they had to say.

Two of them stepped forward and congratulated Karen. Then the rest gathered round, nodding, and smiling. It seemed she was a popular choice. Relieved, Natalie slipped away and left Karen to take over, Natalie knowing that Karen's first intention was to promote one of the others to Deputy Manager.

Just as Natalie and her parents were about to leave for the hospital Karen found them. She was going to need the key to the office safe.

"Oh, Doreen must have it. She either had it on her when she was arrested, or it is in her apartment. Zoe certainly never had it."

They all looked at one another. Did they have the right to go into her rooms? Equally, if it was at the Police Station would the Police just hand it over? Presumably they would need Doreen's permission, and would she give it?

"I need to see about paying the staff and getting my name on the accounts," said Karen.

"Won't the accountant have access to that?" said Natalie.

"Probably but I still need access to the safe, because it has all the spare keys, and, I believe, a couple of guests' passports."

Natalie turned on her heels and headed for the stairs, "Come on, we'll go in together."

Fingers crossed, Natalie tried Doreen's door. It opened. Natalie looked at Karen and they both breathed a sigh of relief. A quick glance round and they spotted a large mahogany desk over by the window. On it was a monitor and keyboard, assorted papers, pens etc. As she moved the stacks of papers she knocked a mouse, one of two. Light now drew her attention to a second screen, mounted on the wall above the desk. Natalie stared at it aghast. The screen was live and split into six images. It was possible to observe most parts of the hotel. Doreen would have been able to see all who came and went in the reception area, what went on in the bar, the dining room, the conference room, various parts of the grounds. Natalie took hold of the mouse and clicked between the screens. There were 16 different camera feeds in total, and she quickly found that it was possible to rotate them and zoom in and out.

"This needs moving out of here and into Zoe's apartment," said Natalie. "Anyway, that can wait, we need to find the safe key."

They took a set of drawers each, there being one at each side of the desk, and started working their way through the contents.

"Ah, here," said Karen. "This looks like it," and she held aloft a chunky Chubb key.

"Right, is there anything else here that you think you will need?"

By the time they left, they each had armfuls of notebooks and ring-binder folders containing hotel documents and other items with hotel logos. The desk and adjacent shelves didn't appear to have any items personal to Doreen.

"It is going to take me some time to get to grips with this lot," said Karen.

"Well, let me know if I can help," said Natalie. "I think it is going to be a while before Zoe is of any use. My parents will no doubt help too, whilst they are here."

Back in reception they found Kyle sitting on the stairs, with notebook and tape measure. "I thought I would see what I could come up with that Zoe might like. The features here are just amazing. Those columns and those carved panels of swimsuit clad divers entwined with dolphins - they really need to stay, but the wood could do with a clean, take it back to its original shade. The geometrical relief on the ceiling needs a refresh and maybe a change of colour to brighten the place and give it a modern appeal. I hope that it is okay. I am just making notes and sketching some ideas. I won't do any work without her approval."

Natalie looked over his shoulder, "Wow, that is lush. So good. You can really draw. I am sure Zoe will be delighted but, shouldn't you be at work?"

"Yes, but I had to do something. I can't make her better, so this... well..."

Leaving him to his task Natalie and Karen took their haul through to the back office and plonked the items on the desk and the floor. Then Karen tried the key in the enormous floor-mounted green metal safe. Using both hands she rotated it. With a heavy clunk it turned, and the door swung open. "I was right, there are a couple of passports in here. Glad we were able to get at those! What else have we got?" She pulled out a stack of old envelopes and some old hotel diaries.

"I'll leave you to it," said Natalie, "I need to talk to the solicitor, let him know that Zoe is in no fit state to sign anything yet."

"Yes, I'll speak to the accountant and see what I need to do about paying the staff," said Karen, replacing the items in the safe and locking it.

When Natalie phoned the solicitors office she was surprised to be put straight through to Mr Titherington.

"Hello, if you hadn't called me," he said, "I would have called you. Yes, I heard about Zoe. How is she doing?"

"They say she is doing as well as can be expected. We are hopeful that she will make a full recovery, but she won't be ready to sign any papers for a while. I hope it is okay, but I have promoted the Deputy Manager to Hotel Manager.

She is now running the hotel, and I will do what I can."

"Okay, keep me updated."

When her parents appeared, she suggested that they went out for a walk, thinking that it would do them all good to have a bit of fresh air. She was also eager to show them the grounds and surrounding area. Their first stop was the topiary dolphin, which Natalie was pleased to see didn't look any worse. The propped branches remained green and did not appear to be drooping. Her mother gave the bush a closer inspection and said that she had hope for it surviving. Her father stood off to one side inspecting the drop from the highest window. He traced the fall and the necessary trajectory for Zoe to have hit the hedge, and just shook his head. Natalie moved to his side and followed his gaze. "I know. It doesn't seem possible," she said. In the distance, a movement caught her eye. Someone had come round the side of one of the greenhouses and was walking, pushing a wheelbarrow. Natalie set off running, apologising to her parents as she went. Ahead, the gardener disappeared inside one of the greenhouses.

It was larger than the rest and full, floor to ceiling, with plants and small trees. There were three beds separated by two concrete paths running the length of the building. Natalie took the left one, listening and glancing through the foliage to make sure she didn't miss the woman. Somewhere amongst the foliage a couple of birds trilled. She hoped they weren't trapped in there. Then from the far corner came the sound of running water. Rounding the corner she could see, leaning over a stone trough, the gardener rinsing a stack of pots. She didn't hear Natalie approach, water splashing fiercely out of an old brass tap, and she jumped at the sound of her name.

"Hello Ruth, remember me?"

The woman turned off the tap and wiped her hands on her canvas apron. She then tucked them inside the waist-high front pocket, braced and defensive. "Yes, what can I do for you?"

"What did you mean, when you said Zoe was like her mother, and that *she* didn't stay long, either?"

"Sensitive."

"How do you mean?"

"Strange. She shouldn't have come here. *Her* mother were just the same. Left as soon as she could. Now, I must get on. If you'll excuse me." She turned and switched on the tap again.

"No," said Natalie. "Tell me what you mean by that."

The gardener glowered and began scrubbing the pots, clattering them together as the bristles of her brush splattered water. Natalie stepped backwards.

"Please."

This time, without turning off the tap, she said, and Natalie could barely hear her, "Strange, the both of them. Mr Brammar had little patience for their wild ramblings."

"What wild ramblings? What did they say?"

"Not my place. I'm just the gardener. You need to find someone who worked here when Mrs Brammar was alive. All the staff changed after the deaths."

"Deaths? What deaths?"

"His daughter, and granddaughter and her husband. The car accident. Now, I must get on. Good day." She turned off the tap, turned on her heel and let herself out of a side door, closing it deftly, behind her. Natalie stood and stared at the island of terracotta, suds bursting and sliding into the water that was still sloshing about the sink. Her father arrived by her side. Then her mother joined them. She turned to her parents and repeated what the gardener had said. Neither parent spoke but she sensed some subtle communication pass between them.

"What?" said Natalie.

"Oh, nothing," said Sharon. "It is just strange. I wonder what she could have meant."

Deep in thought Natalie led them to the lido, then remembered she didn't have the key. Instead, she took them to the lift and down to the shore, her father marvelling at the engineering, and how it was still in good working order after all

174

those years. Natalie just thought its age alarming. As they stepped out at the bottom David gave the door a caress. Mother and daughter raised their eyebrows. A few steps up the beach and they looked behind. He was standing back, shielding his eye, looking up at the lift shaft and the large pulley-wheels at the top.

"Come on, he knows which way we've gone," said Sharon as she looped her arm through her daughter's. So, how are you doing? Are you okay?"

"I am so glad you are here. If it hadn't been for Toby and Kyle, I really don't think I could have coped."

"So, tell me about Toby..."

"Well, we met not long after we arrived, and he has been so helpful. They both have."

"I meant, well, you seem to be getting along very well..."

"Er, yes. Its weird. We haven't known each other long but it is like we have known each other for ever. If I said that he was just 'there' that would sound really stupid, but it is like he is where he is meant to be. He always just 'fits in', does the right thing. He knows what to do, what to say... he... I..."

"Love..."

"I, don't know..."

"Love, just take your time. As you say, you have only just met. For what its worth... your dad likes him."

"I like who?"

Sharon turned to her husband, "Her young man, Toby."

"Yes, sensible that one. Not like that Angst you found last year, with the bleached mullet and toe ring!"

"Angus!" said Sharon.

"If you say so."

"David, stop it," she said. "I know for a fact that my parents didn't like your earring and tattoo, although I am not sure how they knew about the latter. I certainly never told them."

"Tattoo?" exclaimed Natalie, "Hah! You've got a tattoo, Dad?"

"Yes, I do. No further questions as no further answers will be given. So, this is where the cliff came down, is it?" He stood, hands on hips squinting upwards.

"Really! You've got a tattoo," said Natalie, looking from parent to parent for clues. "Go on. What and where?"

"None of your business."

"No, you can't leave it like that. Just wait 'til I tell Zoe..."

The three of them walked on in silence for a while, lost in their own thoughts. After about 20 minutes Natalie stopped and pointed upwards. "This is where she tried to run off the cliff. She would never have survived that drop. Anyway, we'd best get back; the tide is turning."

As they passed through reception Karen called them into the office. She had taken a phone call to say that Doreen had been transferred to a psychiatric unit and was needing some more clothes.

Natalie didn't like that. The implications were huge and varied. She wasn't certain what to think. Was this a good thing or a bad one? Did it mean she wasn't going to be charged? Did it mean she would be back at the hotel at some point? On the one hand Natalie thought Doreen no more guilty than Zoe, as neither had been 'themselves', but on the other hand Zoe had been seriously injured. Doreen had been no fan of Zoe's. How much of the push had been real animosity?

"I can take them if you like," said Karen, "but I'd like someone to come into her flat with me, always best to have a witness."

"Okay. Can we do it later, we're just going out to get some lunch."

She led her parents up the street to The One-Eyed Seagull. She sat them at a corner table by the window where they could look out onto the road, and went to the bar for drinks and a menu.

"How is Zoe doing?" asked the barman. "Don't look so surprised, Wanton Ness is a small town, word gets round very quickly."

"She is still in hospital but hopefully she'll be okay." She gathered the three drinks between her hands, and was about to carry them away, when she stopped. "You don't happen to know where I can find any of the staff who worked at The Dolphin in the time, before Mrs Brammar died, do you?"

"Julie, our Sous Chef used to work there, but she is away on holiday at the moment. I'd try The Crab and Shrimp, if I were you. I think they took a couple of the Dolphin's kitchen staff."

When their ham and cheese toasties arrived, they tucked in. Between mouthfuls, each had plenty to say. Managing a hotel was a big new venture, but without Zoe, nothing could be done. All they could do was to encourage Karen and the staff to keep running it, successfully, as they had been doing prior to Mr Brammar's death, but only time would tell if they could do that without the steerage of Miss Hardcastle?

"This is all very well," said Natalie, "but I don't think Zoe can live there. As soon as she is better, we need to get her away from here."

David and Sharon looked at each other but said nothing. Natalie looked on expectantly, "What, you think she should stay here!"

"Well," said David, but stopped as his wife put her hand on his.

"Let's see how she is when she wakes up."

"What! She is obsessed with going down into the cellar." Natalie lowered her voice. "We've got two 'entities' here and we don't know what they are capable of. Apart from the 'push' we've had mugs thrown, not to mention what happened on the first night with her flying out of the window, and you are talking about her staying here."

"She may want to stay," said Sharon.

"Yes, added David, "She is an adult. We can't make her go home."

Natalie was trying to get her head round this when the door opened and in walked John, one of the men with whom she'd played Dominoes.

"Hello, lass. We'll be starting up a game when the others arrive. You and your friends are welcome to join us."

Natalie introduced him to her parents.

"Really sorry about your friend. I hope she makes a good recovery. She's the new hotel owner, isn't she?"

Natalie nodded. Did the entire town know?

"Strange goings on. You don't know what to believe. Cursed that hotel. Cursed."

The door was shoved open and in hobbled Pete, removing his cap, "Big bugger that." He then stood to one side and held open the door, chuckling. Sean came slowly into view, attempting to remove his coat. "Bleeding gulls," he said, turning sideways to reveal a huge grey-white slick, flowing lava-like down his back.

"More like a bloody albatross, mate," said John. "Nooo! Don't shake it."

Sharon leapt to her feet, "Wait, wait. Let me," and she carefully removed Sean's coat, folding the offensive area to the inside. "It's a mac. It will be waterproof. I'll take it to the ladies and rinse it off."

"No, I'll do it," said Sean snatching it back.

"Let the lady do it. She'll do a much better job than you."

"No," he said marching off with Pete in tow, jacket held at arms length. Lowering his voice he muttered, "I don't want her going through my pockets."

"What, why would she?" said Pete. "What have you got in there?"

Sean scowled and kept on walking.

"Really, at your age!"

John watched the two men disappear into the toilets and raised his eyes to the ceiling. He made his excuses and left them, to take up station at their usual table at the far end of the room.

Again, at the hospital, there was no change with Zoe. This, they were told, was a good thing. It didn't seem like it. It was all taking too long. In between talking to each other they related what was happening at the hotel, in case Zoe could understand. They said that Kyle was working on plans to modernise the entrance hall and make it more appealing. Natalie said what a good artist he was and wished that Zoe would soon be able to see what he had sketched.

With no guests, Mary told the receptionist to finish up, then go home. Leaving the woman to finalise the duty roster and leave notes for the morning stating which rooms to make up for their government guests, she went through to the kitchen and down to the cellar. It was a large oblong room with a recessed area at the far end. The walls were all covered in shelves. Prior to the war, these had been stocked floor to ceiling with jars and bottles and sacks of varying sizes, all full of food and drink and cooking ingredients. Now they were practically bare.

"Has Margaret gone home yet?" asked Megan emerging from the recess.

"Not yet, but she won't be long. I'll go check in a minute."

"Ma, we need to get ready. Jack won't have much time."

"I know."

Together they moved a barrel to one side and then Mary went back up to check on the receptionist. She'd gone. Reception was empty and silent. So, Mary stepped through the inner door to where she could bolt the outer door. She heard something. Not sure what, she stood, rooted to the spot, and listened. Still not sure, but concern rising, she flung open the outer door and stepped into the street. Now it was distinct. Now she was certain.

"Close that door," yelled a voice from the darkness. Looking, she could just make out the dark figure of a man in a long coat with a tin helmet: A.R.P. stencilled in white on the front. Her heart racing, she shut and bolted the door. Then closed the inner door. Somewhere, in the distance, she heard a loud 'boom': felt it through her feet. Using her hands, to fend herself off the walls, she ran for the cellar.

Chapter Sixteen

As soon as she woke Natalie phoned the hospital. It took a while for anyone to answer, then a while to get an answer to her questions. Depending on Zoe's condition, it was likely that the doctors would attempt to start waking her up.

Natalie went straight to her parents to let them know.

"Can we go see her? Should we be there?" asked her mother.

"No. They will just reduce her sedation and monitor her response. It is likely that they will need to sedate her again," explained Natalie.

"So, what do we do?" said David. "I can't sit around here all day doing nothing."

At reception Natalie stopped and spoke to the young man at the desk. Carl, the newly appointed Deputy Hotel Manager smiled attentively.

"Good morning, Carl," said Natalie. "Is there anything that you need help with?"

"No, I think I am okay. I've taken a couple of bookings for the weekend and got the plumber to see to a tap in 46. Two of the house staff have phoned in sick. I've managed to cover one of their shifts but, if I haven't managed to sort the rest, Karen will be in at 2pm. I'll ask her what to do."

"Well, it sounds like you have everything under control. Karen made a good choice in appointing you. We are just off to The Crab and Shrimp, should you need to track us down."

Halfway down the street, Natalie unbuttoned her coat. The sun was bouncing off the walls and windows opposite, and with no breeze it was warmer than she had expected. The Crab and Shrimp wasn't the easiest place to find, despite it being clearly marked on the printed street map she'd picked up from The Dolphin reception desk. With her father itching to wrest the map from her, she led them through a maze of streets and alleys to the lower end of the town. Here the buildings were less uniform and less grand. These buildings were pre-Victorian, smaller and functional; built by, and for, fishermen and their families. When she passed the for-sale sign on a delightful little white painted cottage, with pale blue window and door frames, she felt sorry for any removal men. No cars made it down these narrow passages. The front door, opening directly onto the street, was newly painted in a bright red. The sellers were obviously keen to show it in its best light. Pots of primroses sat on the window ledge, held in place by a thin metal bar. No doubt it would be bought as a holiday cottage. Most of the other properties in the row had 'vacancy' signs in their windows.

At the end of the lane Natalie turned left, and there, facing the sea, was The Crab and

Shrimp. At some point in the past, it had obviously been a couple of double fronted cottages. Now it was one, surprisingly wide, restaurant. Across from it, on a strip of grass, were tables and benches. A group of walkers sat sipping at mugs, admiring the sea view; walking sticks and rucksacks strewn at their feet; an attentive dog hoping for scraps, running back and forth.

"Right," said David, pushing open the front door. "What can I get you both?"

Inside was surprisingly light and bright. White-washed lime walls bounced the light around and recessed fluorescent strips bathed the ceiling in ever-changing pastel colours. Glass ornaments sparkled with tiny prisms, giving the entire space a fairy grotto feel. It was both cheesy and elegant. Love it or hate it, thought Natalie, it couldn't help lifting one's spirits. The complete absence of anything sea or beach related was a surprise. The art on the walls was abstract and contemporary and chosen to enhance the lighting effects. Between the glass ornaments sat intricately carved and highly polished wooden pieces, their abstract forms hinting at shapes, but left to the viewers imagination.

At the bar Natalie made her own enquiries whilst David got them all drinks. When she explained that she was trying to track down ex-staff of The Dolphin Hotel the manager was initially a little wary. Once she explained that she had no intention of trying to poach them back to

The Dolphin, he was keen to help. He disappeared through a door at the back of the bar. It was a while, but when he finally returned, he apologised, "I'm sorry, but I can't get her to come and talk to you. I don't know why. She won't say."

"What about the other member of staff? I understand that two came to work here."

"Oh, there was, but she didn't last long, had some kind of a break down. I don't know what happened to her. Sorry," he shrugged his shoulders and switched his attention to a group of people who had just come through the door.

Natalie joined her mother and father and took a sip of her coffee. Peering over the rim of her mug her eyes came to rest on one of the wooden items on the windowsill. She was admiring the smoothness of the wood and the form of the shape, trying to decide what it reminded her of, when she spotted the label at its base. It was handwritten and stated, Lianne Crosby, local artist. The name rang a bell. Lianne, Lianne! Could this be the work of the lady she had met on the beach? The lady with the dog, Hobnail. She reached over and picked up the piece. It was beautifully tactile and reminded her of so many things but at the same time looked like nothing in particular. She looked at its base, £65. She looked at her parents, who were watching her, then gave it one last caress and placed it back on the windowsill with a sigh.

"Anyone want a sandwich? I'm starving," said David. Orders taken; he went off to the bar again.

Natalie started wondering. Perhaps she could track down Lianne and see if she knew anything about The Dolphin's history. It wasn't what she had said. In fact, she hadn't *said* anything at all. It was more what she hadn't said. Natalie, however, didn't want to add to the gossip in the town, by asking too many questions, but they really needed to know what had happened in the past. Something had, she was certain.

"Dad, do you think you could try talking to the gardener, see if she'll talk to you, she's more your age."

"I can try, but I don't know what I am going to say. Your mother would probably do better, she's had more practice at prising information out of people. She is very good at coming up with open questions and not being put off by people being evasive."

"You mean she's nosey," said Natalie.

"I never said *that*," said her father, as he took a jab in the ribs from his wife.

"Well, hopefully Kyle and Toby will be able to find something out. Their families were both living here then, and it isn't that long ago. There must have been *some* gossip.

David went to the bar to pay. When he returned, Natalie and her mother stood to leave. "Don't forget your wooden thing," he said. Natalie stared as he waved a receipt. His eyes directed hers to the windowsill. "It's yours, love."

"What! It isn't my birthday!"

"No, but you looked so happy, holding it, and I haven't seen that look on your face, all the time we've been here," and he quickly turned away. When Natalie and her mother caught up, he was standing looking out to sea, blinking into the wind.

Halfway down the cellar steps Mary met Megan running up, screaming incoherently. Mary grabbed her daughter by the shoulders and shook her. Her back to the light, Mary couldn't see her face.

"It's collapsed. The ceiling. The far end, over the sea. It's come down. Its all come down."

She swung Megan round to the light. She was white as a sheet. Dark, wide pupils stared back under dusty white lashes. Tears spilled over, leaving clown-like streaks down her cheeks. Beneath Mary's hands, Megan shook.

"I can't hear him anymore."

"Go back down. See if you can see him. I'll go up and look."

Megan turned and ran back down, screaming, "Jack, Jack!"

Mary ran blindly through the hotel, not bothering to switch on the lights as she went. A corridor chair went flying, thudding into the plasterwork. She didn't care. Her feet slid on the highly polished wood floor. She staggered and slid again. Catching her heel on a rug, she fell, full length. She crawled and scrambled to her feet, desperate to keep going. Dark objects loomed, vague shadows formed her world, but she made it to the back door. Trembling, she fumbled with the catch, then stepped out into the wind.

At 2pm Natalie and her parents quick marched through the hospital eager to get to Zoe. As they approached her bed it was obvious that she wasn't awake. A nurse was pushing buttons on one of the machines by her bed. She turned and smiled. "It is going to be a little while longer before we can wake her up. When we reduced her sedation, she got quite agitated. So, we had to increase the sedation again."

With sinking hearts Natalie and her mother sat, but her father turned and walked heavily out of the ward.

Natalie talked inanely, updating Zoe on what she and her parents, Kyle, and Toby, had been up to. There didn't seem much to tell but she carried on anyway; sitting in silence was soul-destroying. Sharon did her best to add to the flow of chatter, adding an awkward, 'yes', and 'that's right' and 'mmm' and 'uhaa', until Natalie got irritated and snapped at her. Then they both burst into tears, with Natalie attempting to keep talking and hide her distress.

The door slamming behind her, Mary leant into the wind. Buffeted from side to side she ran down the steps and across the lawn, across flower beds and through a small privet hedge. She ran at the cliff top. It wasn't there anymore: bits still crumbling and sliding away; large chunks disintegrating and disappearing into the dark. She threw herself at the ground, grasping anything she could. A sucking, dry sigh, as more earth and rock fell away. Beneath her outstretched hands the ground tilted slightly. Flat to the grass she crabbed herself backwards and rolled and kept rolling until she reached the wall of a raised flower bed. Even the solid ground felt unsafe. As the enormity of what had happened began to sink in, she looked around. Could he have survived? Could he have escaped? It didn't seem possible. He had been right underneath it. An area the size of a tennis court had disappeared into the sea. Senses heightened, she listened desperately for sounds of life. Instead, she heard only the sounds of the waves below and the drone of bombers above. Down the coast she could see a distant inferno: hazy black silhouettes of ships and warehouses shimmering in the blaze. Even at a few miles distant she could detect a stinging, acrid smell in the air. She looked upwards at the sound of yet another bomber going overhead. She couldn't see the bomber, but what she did see filled her with horror. Light was shining from a room at the top of the hotel: the blast had taken out the glass and a torn curtain was flapping wildly in the wind. Stupefied, she clutched the grass. Every nerve fizzed, primed against threat. Threat all around, threat from above, threat from the very ground beneath her body. With no place of safety, nowhere to run, she cowered, absorbing sights and sounds and smells: the approaching drone of another wave of aircraft; the distant siren, sickening in its intensity; the smell of burning chemicals and the visual rearrangement of the familiar landscape, and the wild, wet, wind.

Then the screeching gulls galvanised her into action. Wet and muddy, shins bleeding, she scrambled to her feet. Slipping and falling and clawing her way, she ran for the door. She had to extinguish that light.

When they got back to the hotel Karen was eagerly waiting for Natalie to accompany her up to Doreen's apartment, to get the clothes to take to the psychiatric unit. They let themselves in and both automatically drifted over to the window to look at the view, despite it being almost identical to the view from Walter's apartment. Natalie tried the door to the terrace. It opened and she stepped out. There were a few pots containing sad looking shrubs and a table and chair in the lee of the dividing partition between Doreen and Walter's terrace. At the other end of the terrace was a raised decked area, giving an elevated view. On closer inspection it looked like this was the original home of the table and chair; tell-tale marks on the weatherbeaten boarding.

"I reckon they've been recently moved," said Karen, coming to stand beside Natalie.

"Yes," said Natalie. "She's been eavesdropping through the trellis; not that Zoe and I have spent much time out there together. She couldn't have heard much. Come on, let's get her stuff."

Inside, Natalie moved the mouse on the security cameras. "I bet she spent ages sitting watching this."

Karen found a bag and gathered some clothes as Natalie continued to scroll through the images. "Karen, are these cameras recorded?"

"I don't know. I suppose so."

"Would they go back a couple of weeks?"

Karen shrugged, and went to look over Natalie's shoulder, "What are you thinking? Oh..."

"Exactly." Together they stared at a view of the topiary dolphin.

That evening, whilst David and Sharon went to visit Zoe, Natalie got picked up by Toby and taken out for dinner. At first, she had protested, saying that she needed to see her, that it wouldn't be right not to visit. It took a while to persuade her, both parents insisting that she needed a break; something to take her mind off Zoe, with Toby pleading and pointing out that Kyle was going and that Zoe would probably rather have him visit. Eventually she conceded that he had a point.

So, she'd put on her best outfit, done her hair, and then diligently used the tweezers that Zoe had been so scathing about, wondering what Zoe thought she had been doing wrong, before applying her make-up. Toby too, had made an effort; smart, but expensively casual. He always managed to look smart even when unshaved and in his work clothes, which varied depending on what he had been doing at the golf course, that day.

So, she thought, this is a date then.

He drove them away from the coast and up into the hills. The restaurant was set amongst trees, on the side of a hill. Below it, the ground levelled to accommodate a small lake, then dropped affording a view of the valley. Chippings crunched as he brought the car to a halt. They hurried towards the entrance porch, glad to step into the warmth. A huge fire gave a welcoming glow to the room, and they wasted no time removing their coats.

"Your table is ready, sir, but would you care for a drink at the bar first?" said the waiter.

Toby looked at Natalie, who just shrugged. Then she heard Toby's stomach rumble and laughed, "Let's eat."

It soon became apparent that Toby knew the staff, and that the waiter was an old friend. When she commented, he said that having lived in the area all his life, and with his family being in the catering business, there were few places with people that he didn't know. Unless, she wanted to drive a good 50 miles from the coast.

"So, you haven't told me what you do at the golf club. I assume that it is more than washing dishes or carrying people's golf clubs."

"I do a bit of everything, including washing dishes if need be and, for some of our more 'influential' golfers, caddy, although that mainly consists of driving the golf cart. I also work in the office, helping my dad manage the place. Some day it will all be mine," he said with a grin.

"What, no siblings?"

"Nope. Only child."

"Me too, until Zoe..."

Toby reached across the table and took her hand. "Hey, look at me..." Slowly she raised her head. His was on one side, looking quizzically at her. She felt him squeeze her hand. It was warm and strong and comforting. "If I said don't worry, she's going to be fine, you'd only say, 'you don't know that'. Well, I don't, I can't know. But, I am going to be *here,* for *you*, no matter what happens. The hospital seems optimistic. There has been no 'preparing us for the worst'. So that is good. Yes?" He took her other hand and squeezed that too. "She is so lucky to have you, and your family. Your parents seem to really care for her. Your dad is quite cut-up about it all."

A waiter arrived at her side, and Toby let go of her hands. She felt their loss acutely as a plate was placed in front of her. Then, under the table, his ankle brushed hers, and she felt complete once more.

"Tell me about *you*. Tell me about *Natalie*."

"Oh..."

"What do you like to do," he prompted.

It took her more than a couple of heart beats to internalise and think about herself, then ponder on the fact that it had been some time since she had done that. "I like to sing..."

"Really, what do you sing?"

"Well... stuff that I've written."

"You are a song writer. That is awesome. Do you perform? I'd love to hear you."

"No, its just for me. I'm not that good and it is kind of part of my degree."

"Of course, Art and Music History, right? I'd still love to hear it and I bet you are better than you say. Wow!"

"I doubt that. What about you? What do you like to do?"

"Me, I like to rock climb. That's my thing. I'd love to climb El Capitan."

"Isn't that that huge rockface in Yosemite that people sleep over night, hanging from, whilst climbing it?"

"Yes, that's the one."

As the evening wore on, they discovered a shared interest in horror movies, but agreed that they may now both be shying away from those. They also both enjoyed camping and fancied walking The Inca Trail, in Peru. "We must do that. We must totally do that," said Toby.

When he dropped her off at the hotel, she grinned at the receptionist, taking the woman completely by surprise. Puzzled, she watched bemused as Natalie disappeared up the stairs, apparently humming to herself.

Chapter Seventeen

For the first time in nearly two weeks, Natalie slept. She woke to rapid knocking. She shrugged on her dressing gown and, bleary-eyed, went and opened the door.

"We were worried something had happened. It's nearly 11 o'clock," said her mother pushing her way in.

Natalie watched as her mother strolled about the apartment. Was she checking to see that Toby wasn't there? She fumed silently but said nothing. Apparently satisfied, Sharon filled the kettle and switched it on. "We need to get going. Your father wants to go to the library." Natalie wondered why but was too irritated to ask. She simply said that she was going for a shower.

Once dressed she put a couple of slices in the toaster and poured boiling water over a teabag. Finally, she had to ask, "Dad, why do you want to go to the library?"

He looked up from his newspaper, "To look at old records for the hotel. I want to know why Zoe was trying to get into that cupboard."

Natalie frowned. It wasn't like her father to read The Times. "Is Karen on this morning?"

"Yes, she's having a look through the office, but the library will probably have all the old newspapers on file too."

"You two go to the library. I'm going to ask about the town, try and track down Lianne that I told you about. And, Dad, put that newspaper back in reception."

It didn't take Natalie long to make her way down to 'The Crab and Shrimp'. The barman recognised her and was again happy to answer her questions. He didn't know where Lianne lived, but a lot of her work was in two of the shops, part way up the hill, at the start of the High Street. They may be able to tell her. Armed with her street map she quickly found the first of the shops. The window had a variety of wooden items, including those, the style of which Natalie recognised as matching the piece her father had kindly bought her. To an electronic chime, she stepped inside. This was an expensive shop. It had few items on display and few customers. She didn't need to look at the price tags, to know. Not that there were any price tags visible. The display work and lighting weren't set up for bargain hunters or the holiday souvenir seekers. As an assistant approached, she felt distinctly underdressed. She felt awkward and vaguely guilty, which she knew was ridiculous.

"How may I be of assistance?"

"Hello. I am trying to find the artist, Lianne Crosby. You appear to have some of her work here. So, I thought that you may know."

"May I ask why?"

"It, is a personal matter."

"Are you a friend?"

Natalie was beginning to get irritated. The mild frostiness of the first question could have been a misinterpretation on her own part, but the raised eyebrow and implication that if Natalie was a friend, then how come she didn't know the woman's address, really riled. However, retaliating would be unlikely to gain the woman's help. "Sort of. We met on the beach and got chatting. She asked me a question that I couldn't answer at the time."

The woman said nothing, but Natalie sensed a slight shift in her attitude. "Please, I'd really like to talk to her again and I believe that she would want to hear what I have to say."

"Okay, if you let me have your contact details, I will let her know you called."

"Oh, thank you. My name is Natalie. You might want to remind her that we met on the beach. Thank you."

Outside the shop, Natalie heard a text arrive on her phone. It was Kyle. He had phoned the hospital and was lucky to have spoken to one of the nurses who knew him from his visits. She was therefore willing to give him more information than he would otherwise have got. The hospital was again reducing Zoe's sedation to see how she responded.

Limping down the hall, oblivious to the loss of a shoe, light suddenly illuminated her world. Blinded, she did not see Megan charging out of the kitchen, switching on lights as she ran.

"Mam," Megan cried, stopping short and staring at her mother. Mary was wet through and caked in mud. Her dress was torn and marked with green stains. Her legs were bleeding, and her bare left foot was deep purple and swollen.

"Did you see him? Did you see Jack?" asked Mary.

"No, but Edna's here," said Megan studying her mother's face, searching the depth of her eyes, reading the fear and the shock. "She found her way down. I had to lock her in."

"What?"

"I had no choice. She's seen everything. I didn't know what to do."

"How did she get in?"

"I don't know; Margaret, must have let her in, before she went home."

"Go let her out but keep her here. There is a light showing upstairs. I'll be back down in a minute."

"What are we going to do?"

"I don't know. I... I... won't be long. Go..."

Megan disappeared and Mary headed up the stairs, heart pounding in her ears. Edna: she didn't need this. That girl was nothing but trouble. She'd never keep her mouth shut. If she talked...

When Natalie reached the second shop, she hesitated before going in, as she had hopefully achieved her mission. Then, she realised that it wouldn't hurt to have two people contact Lianne and it might speed things up a little. Her only other solution was to stalk the beach. However, the shop assistant didn't have any responsibility for buying stock and said that she didn't know Lianne.

When she got back to the hotel, Carl called her over. There had been a complaint from one of the guests. Apparently, the bedsheets were 'itchy'. He had spoken to housekeeping who were adamant that all the sheets were the same. They said they would change them but couldn't see that it would make any difference.

Natalie just shrugged. She had no idea what to do.

"Should I phone the laundry company," said Carl, "and see if they have different powders for people with allergies?"

"Yes, good idea. Let me know what happens. If they can supply different sheets that would be brilliant. At least it will look to the guests like we are trying to help. Well done."

Leaving a happy Carl, she went up to the apartment.

Mr and Mrs Walker arrived soon after, laden with carrier bags. Without even asking Natalie, Sharon set about making sandwiches for them all, whilst David put the kettle on, eager it seemed to get some lunch before setting off to see Zoe. Plates and mugs were got out and soon Natalie was sinking her teeth into a ham, cheese and chutney bap.

"So, what did you find out at the library?"

"Well, they had lots of pictures and newspaper articles, most of which we could only look at, but we did get these," said David and he spread out a collection of photocopies. Some of the pictures were black and white but a couple were coloured, typical of the 1930's early Kodachrome photographs. It took Natalie a while to work out what she was looking at. It was the back of the hotel, but she struggled to make sense of it. The topiary dolphin was there, naturally smaller, but what was behind it bore no resemblance to her present memory. Then her father showed her another photograph, taken from farther away. Putting two and two together she realised that the back of the hotel, did not come out as far and the dolphin was off to one side. At the time of the bomb, there would have been a flat roof over the current position of the dolphin.

"Do you see," said her father, "the hotel was extended when it was rebuilt. If Zoe's Great-

great grandmother got blasted out of a top room she would have landed on the roof of the ballroom, which collapsed. See, it says here that Mrs Mary Brammar was pulled alive from the rubble of the ballroom."

Natalie looked. Despite the colour the picture was mainly black and white. In the foreground a huge heap of rubble sprawled, surrounded by tiny hints of green, where the rain had washed the foliage; nature reasserting itself. It must have been horrendous. Had Zoe experienced that?

At the hospital they were again disappointed. Despite expecting it, as the hospital hadn't contacted them, they had still been hopeful that Zoe may be awake. This time one of the doctors came to see them. Although her condition was stable, he told them that she had became agitated when the sedation had been reduced, and it was important not to risk raising her intracranial pressure. The bleed hadn't been severe as they had been able to operate quickly. They were a little puzzled as to what was causing her agitation. All her vital signs were within normal limits, and she was receiving more than adequate pain relief. She should be awake by now and talking to them. They would keep trying to wake her, but the family should be aware that should she deteriorate, it may be necessary to operate again.

They sat for a while, talking about anything they could think of. Some of it consisted of their research, but they didn't know if it was a good idea to share this with Zoe, even if she could comprehend. Natalie reminisced. She talked about their beach holiday when the girls had been 15 years old, about waterslides and whirlpools and an impossible 'surf rider pool' that neither of them could stay stood up on for more than 2 seconds. She talked of how they had counted their bruises, competing to see who had the most. Natalie forced a laugh as she told it, but Zoe remained impassive.

On the drive back to the hotel, Natalie again raised the idea of taking Zoe home, as soon as she was well enough to travel. Again, her mother mystified her by being resistant. Exasperated and baffled, Natalie demanded to know why. It made no sense.

"She shouldn't have come, but now she is here, she should stay," said Sharon, looking at her husband for apparent support.

"What do you mean, she shouldn't have come!"

David and Sharon looked at one another. Natalie sat in the back of the car, looking at one parent, then the other. What didn't she know? What weren't they telling her?

"Did you know this was going to happen?"
Silence.
"What? Tell me!"

"Love… leave it!" said her father.

"What? Leave what? I don't believe this."

"We've got to tell her…"

"Please," said Natalie. "You can't leave it like this."

David pulled the car over and stopped. Then he swivelled round in his seat, and Sharon did the same.

"Okay. When Zoe's great grandmother died and her parents and grandmother came up here for the funeral, Zoe stayed with us."

"Yes, I know that."

"Yes, but what you don't know is that her grandmother was insistent that she stayed with us. She didn't want her to come up here."

Natalie waited, now realising that it was a little odd that Zoe had been stopped from attending her great grandmother's funeral. She was 14 at the time, it would have been expected that she attended.

"Her grandmother insisted that she stay; she effectively paid us to keep her away. That trip to Alton Towers was paid for by her grandmother and we were told to say to her parents, that it had been arranged in advance of the death. It hadn't. It had been arranged because of…"

"One has to wonder why. Did her grandmother expect something like this to happen?" added her father.

When they returned to the hotel, Karen gestured for them to wait, whilst she finished dealing with a guest. It soon became apparent that this could take some time. They went and sat in the corner of reception and waited. The seats were comfortable and, all in all, it was a pleasant place to sit. Natalie cast her eye over the décor and tried to see what Kyle saw. Despite her love of art, it really wasn't her style, but she could appreciate the skill that had gone into the mouldings and carved woodwork. The staircase had a sweeping elegance to it, and she had a sudden vision of herself in a flapper dress, swanning majestically down, flipping a feather boa over her shoulder. She looked forward to seeing Kyle's vision. Her parents sat on the edges of their seats, thinking their own thoughts. Her mother picked up, and flicked idly through a magazine, but her father just sat, staring into space.

Free, at last, Karen told them that she had taken the clothes to the hospital for Doreen, but Doreen had refused to see her. She said that she had explained in vain that she was the nearest Doreen had to family, but the staff refused to tell her anything. She planned to go again in the hope that repeated visits would gain the hospital's trust, especially as she was the only one visiting or enquiring.

Chapter Eighteen

Before getting breakfast for herself, Natalie phoned the hospital. She was told that Zoe was stable and that they were again going to try to wake her. She said a silent prayer and went to find her parents.

She hauled herself up the four flights of stairs and launched herself at the door of the offending room. It flew open and she dived at the standard lamp, the only light lit in the room, and nearly pulled the flex from its plug. Plunged into darkness, she stopped and drew breath. Then she walked to the window, desperate for a view of the cliff. She pushed aside the tattered blackout curtain. The wind howled through the hole. Rain lashed her face.

There was nothing to see; there was nothing there. The grounds ended, where they shouldn't. In the distance sirens moaned. She glanced in their direction and saw a red glow. The docks were ablaze. Alarmed seagulls darted and whirled, crying out into the night. She turned away, heading for the door.

There was a gasp. A void opened. It sucked everything to the centre of the room, taking all sound with it. She went forwards, then backwards, blasted through the air like a rag doll. A silent wave of pressure propelling all...

She fell. Lurching, falling, grasping at air, finding only dust: choking, blinding dust. With sickening solidity, she landed and lay, unmoving, her mind numb with disbelief, her body numb with shock. Dispassionately, she examined the experience: comprehension beyond her grasp: fear scratching, clawing. There was a shuddering, and she dropped again, half rotating, falling, bouncing. Through it all she was aware of the silence, an oppressive silence with an energy all of its own. Unable to control her limbs she felt the pain as they flailed through the tumbling debris. It seemed an eternity, then merciful oblivion.

There was a hand on her face: its touch clumsy, abrasive; fingers in her mouth, poking, gouging, and clearing. She gasped for air, inhaling brick dust. She coughed uncontrollably, in spasms, unable to get enough air. Pain racked her chest, her arms, her legs. Briefly she felt relief as something heavy was lifted off her. Then the return of sickening pain and heart-thumping panic. She blinked against the grit in her eyes, desperate to see and make sense of it all. The silence persisted: surreal and enveloping and then, blessed oblivion again.

As the sun was shining, they decided to go for a walk and Natalie suggested going down to the shore again in the hope of bumping into Lianne and Hobnail.

In the grounds it seemed they weren't the only ones enjoying the fresh air, several guests were exploring. Irritatingly they had to queue for the lift down to the shore. However, it was interesting listening to the guests talk, completely unaware that Natalie and her parents were related to the owner. The main topic of conversation was the watery coffee served at breakfast. It seemed to be a cause for concern for most of the queue. Apparently, it was even worse than earlier in the week. The marmalade was appreciated, and Natalie wondered what was so special about it but determined to remember to tell Karen.

Being crammed in the lift with six others wasn't as pleasant as being on their own, but soon they were out on the beach. The guests dispersed leaving Natalie and her parents to wander on alone. The tide was out, and the golden sand stretched into the distance. This time they walked south, away from the collapsed cliff. A runner passed by at the water's edge leaving a trail of dark prints. As water seeped into the indentations, they turned shiny; multi-coloured rays bouncing brightly. In the distance three dogs could be seen but none looked like Hobnail. On the horizon, a tanker went silently left to right heading for the docks. Above, gulls circled and screeched, making themselves heard over the rolling shush of the waves at the water's edge.

They walked as far as the harbour wall and then, their way blocked, they turned and headed back. Soon they reached the base of the steep, zigzagging walkway, leading to the top of the cliff. Part way up they paused at one of the benches, ostensibly to admire the view, each silently glad of the rest. Sharon managed to find a clean area of seat. David and Natalie stood.

"Come on," said David, "I fancy an ice cream."

As they passed the bench that she had sat on with Zoe, Natalie couldn't believe that over a week had passed. So much had happened: so much that would have seemed ridiculous before then, so much that had changed; her beliefs, her trust in what was, even her confidence. In some respects, she felt like a little child again. Her parents were there, her comfort, her everything. Once. Now, they seemed like children too. She knew that they were no more confident or capable than she was. She had believed that she was an adult, her life under control. She believed that she could solve anything, just by applying herself. Now, they were all children. All they could do, was share their fear and be each others' comfort blanket.

Natalie followed her father up the path, her mother trailing behind. Then her father stopped and waited. When she caught up, he put an arm round her. "Come on love, it'll be alright. Let me buy my big girl an ice cream. Would you like a flake in it?" He knew her so well. Humbled, she tucked her arm through his. She looked back and waited until her mother caught up and linked arms. Together they trudged up to the promenade.

Opposite the steps stood a green and cream painted kiosk. David sauntered up to it, fishing his wallet out of his trousers, whilst his wife and daughter found a seat in one of the green and cream painted shelters, facing the sea. It wasn't long before he arrived with a clutch of ice cream cones, a flake sticking out of the top of each one. He handed them out and then went over to the promenade rail, where he leant scanning the horizon. He placed his tongue on the ice cream and rotated the cone, leaving a swirl round the flake. Ice cream! It had been a while since he had eaten a cone. In fact, he couldn't remember the last time. He rotated the cone again, checking for errant ice cream. There was a weight on his right shoulder. It felt like he had been grabbed from behind. Before he could react, his assailant pushed off, wings flapping, and he watched as his chocolate flake flew up and away, crumbling and dropping. He turned swiftly, following its direction and splattered ice cream over his sleeve.

As Natalie and her mother failed to stifle their amusement he stomped over to the ice cream kiosk, muttering. When he explained why he was back for more ice cream, the salesman replied, 'Yes, the gulls are my best customers.'

Back at the hotel Toby was eagerly waiting for them. "If I can get into the system, it shouldn't be too difficult to scroll back. From what you and Karen have said, it sounds similar to the security system at the golf club. I've brought a USB so we can save what we want."

Natalie led the way, and they let themselves into Doreen's apartment. Toby settled himself at the computer and nudged the mouse. Then he reached up and did a quick search of the contents of a shelf above. He took down a couple of notebooks, flicked through them and then put them back. Then he spotted a smaller notebook and inspected that. He turned the pages back and forth and then spread it flat on the table. Carefully he typed in a word and gained access to the camera controls.

Sharon, who had been wandering round the apartment sniffing and wrinkling her nose, stopped and joined the others as they peered over Toby's shoulder. On screen was a view from the side of the hotel. It looked down on the topiary dolphin and the back entrance to the hotel. They waited whilst Toby rewound the recording to the night of the girls' arrival at the hotel. Natalie breathed a sigh of relief: the recording went back far enough. He wound it forward, at double speed, from midnight. There was little to see; a mostly black and white night-vision image that was static, apart from blurred white streaks of gulls arriving and departing from window ledges. At 01.06, there was a flash and brief colour, then the picture reverted to its former scene. Toby rewound and then played it forward at normal speed. They all gasped, in disbelief. Then he rewound it again and played it forward, slowly.

Initially the whole screen went white. Then it resolved to indeterminate dark shapes flying through the air. The objects began to spin and tumble. Orange light illuminated them from behind. Splinters of wood, chunks of brick and plaster, shiny, reflective pieces all flying through the air, then dropping. Rubble and dust. In the centre of the debris, a body, rotating, flailing, dropping. It landed, immobile, dust settling on it. Then, there was an implosion and it dropped, disappearing into a cloud. Toby froze the image and zoomed in. Then he zoomed out again and rewound, catching the body mid-air. Natalie gasped as her mother whimpered.

"That isn't Zoe. Zoe was wearing pyjamas. That must be Mary."

The others stared at the image. A knee-length dress was clearly visible, ballooning in the blast.

"Look, look," said Toby, and he pointed to the background of the image.

Slowly, it dawned on the others what they were seeing. The distant lights weren't those of the docks. They weren't large, powerful lights on gantries illuminating containers. They weren't 100ft cranes with red aircraft warning lights on the top. They weren't yellow streetlights or car head lights. These lights were pointing at the sky. These lights were moving, searching the sky, searching the sky for culprits responsible for the enormous red glow surrounding them. The docks were ablaze, peppered with bright explosions.

When they had recovered from the shock and could think again, Toby, deep in thought, took a copy of the recording to see if he could get some separate images. He was puzzled. Ignoring the implications of what they had seen happening, he didn't think the recording was possible. The camera had appeared to combine day and night vision capabilities, and it wasn't even a new system.

"Well," said David, "that confirms my theory about the footprint of the building being changed, and the dolphin being moved."

Back in the apartment, the phone was ringing, and a green message light was flashing. Natalie leapt at it and picked it up.

"Hello, yes. Yes, it is.... Really! Oh, my goodness. Thank you. Yes, we're on our way." She slammed the phone back into its cradle. "She's awake and she seems okay." A tear spilled over and ran down her cheek.

At the hospital, they couldn't find Zoe. Then they were told that as she was awake, she had been moved to a single room. The staff were amazed at how well she was. The family were pleased and relieved, but they needed to see for themselves.

When they walked through the door, Zoe closed her magazine and put it to one side. It slid to the floor. Natalie and her father dived at it, crashing their heads together. Zoe sniggered. It was the best sound. No response, to all the 'how are you?'s, could have been more reassuring.

"Does your head hurt?" asked Sharon studying the encircling bandage.

"Not really, but it does feel a little odd."

"And, you? What about the rest of you?"

"My ribs are sore and my arm aches and everywhere feels bruised. How is the hotel?"

So, they gave her a censored version of what had happened since her fall. When they said that Doreen had been moved to a secure unit, she scowled slightly but made no comment. They didn't stay long, not wanting to overwhelm her. Before leaving, they told her that Kyle would visit her that evening.

As they left the hospital, Natalie again raised the issue of getting Zoe home, realising that her parents hadn't explained why they seemed so against it. After all, it had been Zoe's grandmother who hadn't wanted her to come.

"As we said before, maybe her grandmother expected something like this."

"But that doesn't explain why we shouldn't *now* get her away..."

"Okay," said David, "but promise you won't tell Zoe, at least not yet. Not until she's fully recovered."

"The Police didn't tell Zoe, and when we found out, we thought it best she didn't know," said Sharon.

"*Know what*?"

"The car crash..., wasn't an accident," said David.

"It wasn't! What do you mean?"

"No, love. It was Mrs Spencer's *fault*". He waited a while for this to sink in. "She was the only one in the car not wearing a seat belt. The people in the car behind said she was trying to push the door open. They were doing 65 miles per hour. It is believed that she unfastened her seatbelt and tried to get out. Mr Spencer lost control, and the car overturned in a ditch."

Natalie was sickened. Why would Zoe's mother do such a thing? It made no sense. Mrs Spencer had been a sensible rational human being... No...! Noooo!

Later that evening, Sharon cooked a pasta bake in the apartment. She had invited Toby to join them. They would dine about 8pm. She sprinkled grated cheese on top of the pasta and asked Natalie to put it in the oven when it reached temperature. Then she announced that she was going to Miss Hardcastle's apartment to clear out her fridge.

"What? Now?" said David.

"Yes, something is smelling in there".

As the door closed David turned to Natalie and asked her how she was. He would have to go back to work soon, and she needed to go back to university for the start of next week. What were they going to do?

Yes, he was right. That hadn't entered Natalie's head. It was Thursday already. Her entire world had shifted to the here and now. It was as if her former life just didn't exist, but it did. Soon, she was going to have to address it.

"You must go back to university, Natalie. You must finish your degree."

Must she? It no longer seemed important. Logically she should finish it. What would she do without it? *She* didn't have a hotel.

"I know you've got Toby here, love, but if 'it is meant to be' you'll make it work."

There was a beep. She put the pasta dish in the oven, conveniently turning her back on her father. Yes, Toby. She couldn't leave him. The thought of leaving here without him just wasn't an option.

When Sharon returned, she was clutching a bin bag. We need to get rid of this in the morning. It is disgusting.

Toby arrived and handed David a bottle of red wine, "To celebrate. When we get Zoe back there will be a bottle of fizz, provided that she is allowed to drink."

David took the bottle and rummaged in the kitchen drawers until he found a corkscrew. They talked, each expressing their relief. The wine slowly added to their joy and soon they were laughing and joking and talking about the future. Sharon produced a cheesecake from the fridge and sliced it into four. Then it wasn't long before they were clearing the table and stacking the dishes. Toby rolled his sleeves up and started washing up. David raised his eyebrows, then gave Natalie a wink.

To everyone's surprise, Sharon suddenly announced that she was going to clean Miss Hardcastle's fridge.

"Now?" said David. "It's nearly 10 o'clock."

"Yes, if I don't do it now, I'll forget," and she disappeared clutching a disinfectant spray and a kitchen roll.

Natalie and her father picked up tea-towels and started drying. They had almost finished when the door burst open, and Sharon ran in, startling them. Sharon never ran.

"Zoe's here."

"What?"

"She's here. I just saw her on the security camera."

"No!"

"Are you sure you didn't see a re-run of last week?" suggested Toby.

"She wouldn't have a clue how to do that," said David, but his wife was already out of the door and heading for the stairs. Half-way down the second flight of stairs she elbowed a couple of startled guests out of the way. Natalie, David, and Toby passed them by muttering apologies. When they reached the lobby, reception was unmanned. They turned towards the kitchen.

The way to the cellar was wide open and the light on. The receptionist and kitchen staff were all stopped mid-action looking into the yawning doorway.

Chapter Nineteen

David was the first down the steps. The single working ceiling light cast a pale and inadequate glow, barely reaching the sides of even the narrow part of the cellar.

"Zoe. Zoe."

"Zoe...!"

There was no sign of her.

"Get some light."

From the floor at the bottom of the stairs Toby retrieved a torch, abandoned when the ambulance crew took Zoe away the previous Saturday night. Handing it to David, he pulled out his phone and switched on its light. As the beam shone wildly round the underground space, bouncing off spilled sacks of flour, old tins and bottles, it alighted on an area of wall that didn't reflect. Toby walked towards it, bits of broken glass, crunched under foot. As he drew nearer, he heard a sound.

"Shush..."

They all stood still and fell silent. Something was rattling. Then there was a slight whimper, and a grunt.

"Zoe?"

Shining his light in an arc he saw that the wall had a recess. Reaching it, he shone the beam inside, probing its depth. As the others gathered behind him, his light rested on a figure in the corner, back turned, intent on some task. As David joined him, the two lights illuminated Zoe. They called her name.

There was no response. She neither answered nor acknowledged their presence.

"Zoe," yelled Sharon. "What are you doing? Stop it. Come away from there."

"I don't think she can hear you," said Natalie. "I don't think that is *Zoe*."

She stepped to the figure's side. Heart pounding in her ears, she said quietly, "Mary, how can we help you?"

"It won't open."

"What won't open?" replied Natalie. "There is nothing there."

"Megan!"

Behind them, a clatter of steel-toed boots descended the cellar steps and Kyle arrived at their side, "Zoe. Zoe."

Natalie held him back. "No, Kyle. This is Mary."

"When I left her at the hospital, she was fine, perfectly normal. She was sleeping when I left. Then the hospital texted to say she'd gone. They'd been ringing your mobile!"

The shelving in the corner of the alcove rattled again. Toby was now shining his torch into the corner in front of Zoe and talking quietly to her. Then he played it round all the shelves lining the alcove. Kyle took David's torch and did the same. It was just shelving, older than the rest of the cellar, the walls behind panelled with vertical planking. The rattling came again and the same whimpering, grunting despair.

Kyle shone his torch on Zoe's hands. Her right index finger looked to be stuck through a knot hole. As she moved her finger, there was a clicking sound, and a scraping as the plaster cast on her arm scraped on the wood. Once more he ran the torch beam around the shelving, inspecting the joints. They looked loose, warped, forced. Then he turned back to Zoe.

"Mary, is there a door here? Is that the catch? Let me see," and he gently moved her out of the way. She stood meekly to one side, but appeared coiled, waiting.

Kyle inserted his finger into the knot hole and felt around. There was a metal bar. He moved his finger up and felt the bar lift. He leant against the shelves and pushed. There was a slight, barely perceptible 'give'. He tried again. The wood groaned and there was a little more movement. He handed his torch to Natalie, as did Toby. Then they put their shoulders to the panel, counted to three and threw their combined weight against it. The whole shelving unit swung grittily backwards, crunching on debris on the stone floor beneath. There was an atmospheric 'gasp'. Swirling dust. Stale and rank. An indistinct assault on the nostrils, a sting to the eyes.

Beyond the shelving was a gaping, echoey, void.

All sound died, then dropped to another level: a total absence of sound. When the boys stepped out of the hole, instinctively moving away to stand beside the others, no-one heard a thing. Kyle put a protective arm around Zoe and drew her close. Initially puzzled, he moved his fingers around, probing, checking texture, checking form. In place of the fleece she was wearing, he felt a wet woollen coat. Under the layers of clothing he felt a stocky frame, slightly hunched. In his nostrils not the vague smell of antiseptic and bandages that he'd smelt at the hospital, but an unidentifiable scent, wet wool, and stale sweat. His arm dropped. He stepped away, fearful, backing until he bumped into Toby and the others, clustered together, making themselves small.

Beyond the gap in the shelving, something was happening. Something was building. They sensed rather than heard it. The wildly flickering torch beams, shaking in someone's hands, played with the darkness through the gap, revealing nothing. They waited, incapable of any other action.

Then Mary stepped towards the hole. "ME... GAAAANNNNNN...!" Shards of silence flew, ear-splitting and electrically shocking. Hair stood on end; every nerve painfully firing, burning through muscle, and searing brain. It grated and screamed. The sound echoing balefully round the cellar, bouncing and scratching, then finally dying.

In front of them, Mary stood trembling, arms outstretched, silent now. The void again sucking sound.

Sometimes a rip appears in the veil separating the living from the dead.
Sometimes the dead can't rest in peace.

Down in the depths of the hole, the something was stirring. It began as a breath, a gentle sigh. It started to hum and throb, a beat gathering tempo, pulsing, and driving. Bit by bit it drew energy, gathering it like flowers, collecting it in bunches, arranging and displaying it, sparking light and colour.

"MEG... AAAANN!"

Mary stepped into the gap; her arms outstretched. In the hole a bubble of light was now visible, stretched, taut, filling the space. Mary reached out. She placed her hands on its iridescent surface. It flexed. Colours swirled. She palpated it, moving with its rhythm, caressing its form. Then, she closed her hands, and dug in her nails. The membrane stretched and squeaked. There was a tearing ripping sound, its edges crackling. Mary staggered backwards, carried by a colourful blast as it burst forth from the hole. It enveloped her and held her upright. Lifted her off her feet. Held her there. Suspended. Then, her outstretched arms crumpled in on themselves, grasping the light, embracing it. Mary and the light became one, a blurred glow, that swirled and clung, fused, and throbbed. Then it expanded filling the cellar, seeking out the corners and dark recesses, enveloping them all with a calm serenity. Sadness and joy intermingled, forcing hearts to swell and eyes to spill their tears.

Natalie felt Toby's arms surround her, protective and tender. She leant into him. Felt warmth and love, comfort and peace. Then he gently kissed the top of her head.

The glow fused and moved. It swirled, centring itself in the middle of the space. A sound. A gentle hum. It began to fill the room. A soothing rocking rhythm, a mother comforting a child. The glow brightened. A luminous hot pink. The crooning sound grew. Enveloping and warm. Then the pitch rose, and the light blinded. There was a gentle pop and a brief flash, and it was gone; its earthly tether snapped.

They stood in silence, eyes still fixed on the spot in the centre of the cellar. They were alone. The energy had departed, replaced by a deep sense of calm. Beauty. Comfort. Peace.

Kyle was the first to react, diving to his knees at Zoe's side; now a crumpled form, sitting on the floor, clutching her arm. He reached out tentatively, "Zoe?"

She looked up, met his eyes.

"Are you okay? Are you hurt?"

"No, no. I'm fine. Really," she said with a smile that was bubbling with joy and tears. "We found her. We found Megan. They are together."

Chapter Twenty

As Kyle helped Zoe up the cellar steps Natalie and her parents followed. Behind them, Toby took both torches and stepped into the recess. At the top of the cellar steps Natalie realised that Toby hadn't followed them. She went back down and headed for the flickering lights in the alcove.

There was an aroma, something indefinable, a background smell, sickly sweet with a flat note. She couldn't place it. It had been there from the very moment the alcove door opened but unquestioned until now. She wrinkled her nose and stepped warily after Toby.

"Toby. Wait."

Through the hole was a set of stone steps, rough hewn in rock. The walls were initially brick: old brick, lacking uniformity: hand made. Close inspection showed they had fingerprints fired into them. Going deeper, they petered out as the walls turned to stone.

Toby waited, shining his torches on the steps, lighting her way to his side. When she reached him, he handed her one of the torches.

"You okay?" he asked, taking her hand.

"Uhu. You?"

He turned sideways on the step, his face deeply shadowed.

"To be honest, after that, I don't really know," he said and laughed. He looked into her eyes and grinned. Then he kissed her, firing waves of hormones at her already exhausted nervous system. She melted into his arms, sinking into the kiss, knees weak, heart pounding. He broke away from her mouth, kissed her cheek and her forehead. Soft lips nuzzled her neck, then nibbled her ear lobe. Strong arms encircled her waist, pulling her close, supporting her. Then she felt his breath on her ear, "I love you."

There was a gasp, and a slight pulling away. Then he laughed, "is that too soon? Sorry."

"No, its okay. I... I..."

He took a deep breath, "Come on. Let's see what is down here." He turned and pointed his torch down the steps. On shaking legs, she followed. She would follow him anywhere.

There were fourteen steps which became shallower as they reached the bottom. Side by side they stood and played their torches across the floor, up the walls and along the ceiling. The floor sloped and the ceiling height increased as it went into the distance, beyond the scope of the torches. The space where they stood at the bottom of the steps was approximately 5 metres across. It was obviously wider ahead. The walls were mainly smooth, carved by water over millennia, but some areas had been shaped by man, chisel marks scarring the rock.

Directly above their heads was a cable, consisting of two weave-wrapped wires, helically entwined, tacked to the roof. Playing a torch beam along it they saw a bare bulb, then another. The cable continued, implying more.

In the shadows, at the sides of the cave, dark shapes sat. Metal and wood chests were neatly stacked in rows, amidst other items hidden beneath tarpaulins. Toby took hold of a corner of one and lifted it. The cover was stiff, but friable. Shaped and stretched over time, the corners began to crumble. He lifted it carefully. Beneath, was a wooden crate, with a stencil stating 'Cigarettes'. Replacing the cover he inspected the other boxes. Some were labelled, others not. Further along they found racks of bottles. He took one out and wiped his sleeve along it. Brandy. Another bottle. Wine. They read a few more labels.

"This lot could be worth a fortune." The words boomed in the space, startling them both. Lowering his voice he continued. "The corks look alright, and they've been kept in a cellar. I wonder how long they've been down here."

Moving along the row they found a heap of rags, leant against the wall. Alongside was a crate with a collection of candle stubs. The smell was vaguely stronger here, wafted on the disturbed air. A crumpled stack of papers and a pencil stub lay abandoned, words scribbled long ago: an inventory possibly. Toby shone his torch on it.

Faded words were crammed onto the pages, large, then small, making best use of the available space. Not a list.

Natalie's eyes took in the scene, her brain lagging behind, reluctant; it knew but didn't want to acknowledge, to make it real, but it was. It was very real.

Natalie screamed. She stood rigid, staring in horrified fascination; her heart pounding, bile rising in her throat. Toby shone his torch at Natalie, then pointed it where she was looking, and went cold. The first thing that registered was a shoe; brown leather, with an ankle strap. It lay on one side, the tip sticking out from under a thin cotton dress. The material of which, had a faded, tiny floral pattern. It was draped in a heap with a dark wool coat, probably brown. His torch crept upwards. He knew, but he didn't want to see. He didn't want to confirm what his head was telling him. Unable to slow the advance, his beam moved upwards. Strands of brown hair reflected light back at him. Avoiding the face, he forced the beam down the other side of the body. A skinny brown-leather gloved hand, rested on a thigh. Then he realised that the hand was not wearing a glove; what he was looking at was desiccated skin.

When they reached the cellar steps, they met David coming down. Despite the minimal light in the cellar he registered the shock on the younger people's faces. At first, he thought that they were still shocked from the previous incident but soon understood it to be something else. When they told him they had found a body, he wanted to see for himself. Unable to persuade him not to go down, they handed him the torch and waited.

It was a good 5 minutes before he returned.

"I found this at the bottom of the steps," he said, holding up a square canvas covered box with a canvas strap. "It is a gas mask box. Look," and he opened it up. "It's still got its gas mask." Inside was a crumpled lump of rubber with metal and a glass eye piece. "Horrible thing. I really wouldn't have wanted to wear that. Still, better than getting gassed I expect."

They shut the cellar door and told the staff not to go down there. None of them looked to have any intention of even walking past the cellar door, even before they were told a body had been found. Some looked shocked, others as if it explained a lot. It did, however, give them all something to talk about and as Natalie, Toby and David left the kitchen it seemed that all the kitchen staff were talking at once.

In the flat David phoned the Police. They arrived swiftly, along with an ambulance, despite David telling the operator of his disappointment at not being able to put his CPR training to the test. He had put down the receiver muttering his surprise at the operator's absent sense of humour.

Natalie was delighted to see Zoe, looking, talking, and behaving like her old self. It may have been this, or the fact that they were all still high on adrenaline, but the whole atmosphere in the apartment was different now, lighter, brighter, relieved, happy. Zoe, free of Mary, and having re-united Mary with Megan, was joyous and animated, but then, she hadn't seen Megan's body. Natalie didn't have long to acknowledge this change as the hotel was quickly over-run with uniformed people.

After an initial visit to the cellar and the departure of the ambulance crew, empty handed, the police turned their attention to questioning those who had found the body. The cellar door was closed, and an officer stationed in front of it. Apparently, there was no need for blue and white tape. Those who had been in the cellar were grilled, but finally allowed to go to bed at around 5am, Toby and Kyle going to their respective homes.

Chapter Twenty-One

Zoe was the first to rise. She threw back the curtains and took in the view. She felt bright and alert, something she hadn't felt for a while. Her skull still felt vaguely odd but there was minimal pain, and the 'fuzziness' was lessening. If asked, she couldn't have said how she'd felt. She couldn't have said how much was the head injury and how much was sharing her headspace with another. Mary was gone. She was both relieved and bereft. In some respects, it was like the departure of a well-loved house guest. No matter how much you'd enjoyed their company it was a relief when they'd gone. She had many questions, things she would have loved to have asked Mary. There were things she would never forget; others she really wished that she could forget.

When Natalie rose, it was to the sound of a kettle and singing. Hit by the smell of toasting bread as she opened her bedroom door, she wrapped her dressing gown around herself and took in the scene. The table was laid with crockery and cutlery. There was cereal and marmalade, milk, and sugar on display and as she watched, Zoe placed a pot of coffee in the middle of it all. Best of all, Zoe was dressed and apparently washed: no easy task with a plaster cast. The bandage on her head was a bit skew-whiff and grimy, but the protruding hair was combed.

Natalie walked across the room and held out her arms. Zoe beamed and walked into them, wrapping her own arms round Natalie's back. Neither had any words. They just hugged silently, Natalie barely daring to squeeze her friend, until the toaster popped and burst the moment.

"So," said Zoe, "we've got a hotel to run."

"Yes, but you need to go back to the hospital, if only to get you a new bandage," she said, wrinkling her nose. "You just walked out. We need to make sure you are okay."

"I'll go, for you, but really I'm fine."

The rest of the day was taken up, talking to the Police, who'd never left, visiting the hospital, talking to the staff, and talking to the solicitor. At some point late morning, whilst the family were at the hospital getting Zoe the all-clear, the body was removed from the cave along with other items. The cellar was sealed, pending further investigations.

At 4.30pm the apartment phone rang. Sharon, who was nearest, answered it. The investigating officer wished to speak to the hotel owner. Carl, who was on reception, wanted to know if he should bring him up. Zoe shrugged and nodded. The others looked uncertain. "Yes," said Sharon.

The officer was late 50's with a receding head of grey curly hair, and a slightly stooped appearance. He introduced himself as D I Dave Bolton, took the seat offered and crossed one leg over the other.

"Would you like a tea, coffee?" asked Sharon.

"No, thank you. I won't be long."

They all breathed a silent sigh of relief.

"I just wanted to let you know that we are wrapping things up for the evening. Please don't go into the cave, or the cellar. We have sealed them off. When the pathologist reports back, we will be in touch again." Then his eyes settled on the canvas box, with its canvas strap, sitting at the end of the coffee table. "What is that? Did you find it down there?"

"Yes," said David, silently kicking himself. "It was at the bottom of the cave steps."

"Let me see it."

Opening the lid, he peered inside. Then his eyebrows went up. "This says Edna Green. I thought you said you believed the victim to be Megan Brammar."

"Yes, it is," said Zoe.

"How do you know?"

"I just do," she said defiantly.

"I need to take this with me." With a world-weary sigh he pulled a plastic bag from his pocket, unfolded it, and placed the gas mask inside.

When he'd gone Kyle said, "I think we all need to get our story straight."

"What? Why? None of us *killed* her," said Zoe.

"No, but do you want the truth to be public knowledge? Even if no-one thinks you're crazy. Especially with that wonky bandage on your head!"

"Well," it might be great publicity for the hotel, and you are forgetting one thing!" said Toby. "The hotel staff aren't going to stay quiet. Something is bound to get out. Bodies being wheeled out of a hotel kitchen tend to get noticed and commented on."

The phone rang. It was Carl, on reception. Guests were asking questions. What should he tell them?

So, a statement was written, informing guests that a body had been found in a previously sealed-off part of the cellar. It was believed that the individual had died in 1944 when the hotel was struck by a bomb dropped by the Luftwaffe. Nothing further was known at this time. The Police were investigating.

"You could do a 'piece'," suggested Toby. "Put up a series of photographs of the bomb-damaged hotel, with the newspaper clippings. All part of the rich history of The Dolphin Hotel and Lido."

The phone rang again. Mrs Walker stood with her hand over the mouthpiece; there was a

236

reporter in reception. They all looked at one-another.

"Tell Carl to read them the statement. Tell them it is now a Police matter and to talk to *them*," said David. He looked Zoe in the eye, "Do *not* go down there."

Just after 6pm Kyle and Toby left. When they got outside, and clear of the building, they phoned to say that they had been ambushed, not because their relationships to the hotel were known, but simply because they had exited the building. So far, the reporters were staying outside, but they didn't think it would be long before they ventured inside pretending to be guests.

That evening they ordered room service and planned what they were going to do, and David broached the subject of when the girls were going back to university.

"I can't leave now," said Zoe. "I've got a hotel to run!"

"She can't do that on her own," said Natalie.

"You both need to go back. The hotel can wait," said David.

An argument ensued, the girls insisting that they stay and Mr and Mrs Walker adamant that they needed to finish their degrees. Feeling that she was losing the argument Natalie blurted, "But you both said she *shouldn't* leave!"

Zoe noticed the quick glance between David and Sharon, sensed that Natalie's statement was loaded and demanded an explanation. Natalie sunk her head in her hands, realising what she had done.

"Tell me", said Zoe, looking at all three in turn.

"I'm sorry," said Natalie. "Look, with the reporters snooping around it is bound to come out. It is better she hears it from us. Don't you think?"

"Hears what?"

They looked at one another and a silent consensus was reached. It seemed the task was given to Sharon.

"Love, your parents' crash. It wasn't an accident."

Zoe sat up straight and stared at Sharon, then she looked alternately at David and Natalie.

"No, love," continued Sharon, "your father was distracted... by your mother."

Zoe frowned.

"She undid her set belt and tried to open the car door. They were doing 65 miles per hour. Your father tried to stop her, to stop the car, but in doing so he lost control, and it overturned."

"What? Why? No....."

"I don't know. The Police couldn't explain it."

Chapter Twenty-Two

Natalie woke to the scraping tap of gulls on her bedroom skylight. She got up and drew back her curtains, deliberately leaving the blind down on the skylight; she did not want a view of white splodges. She quietly opened the window, displacing a seagull, and leant out. In the street below she could see small groups of people. She could hear some of them chatting but couldn't make out what they were saying. Others were just standing staring at the hotel doors, some with cameras poised. As one looked up, she ducked back inside and hoped the gulls got them.

In the kitchen she put on the kettle and opened a packet of seeded brown bread. When Zoe joined her, they took their coffee, toast, and a blanket each, and went and sat on the terrace. It was a little chilly, but the sun was warm enough to have dried the dew off the seats. Cosily wrapped in their duvets, the fresh light breeze was tolerable. Over the sea, the sky was a clear pale blue. On the horizon, silver-white tankers ruled a line between sea and sky. Nearer, a kite surfer could be seen, bouncing over the crests, and occasionally taking off and achieving a somersault. They watched for a while, fascinated, marvelling at the skill and agility. It looked fun. It looked cold. It looked too early in the morning.

It was good to have some time; just the two of them. Zoe was glad of the quiet. She was tired but didn't want to admit it. Natalie was glad they could talk, alone. They had decisions to make, and it was easier without their parents. By the time the Walkers turned up, they had decided what they were going to do. They said nothing until it seemed that David was about to re-ignite the previous night's argument.

"We have decided," said Zoe, keen to keep the peace, "that you and Natalie should go home tomorrow, Aunt Sharon and I will stay. You need to go to work, and Natalie should go back to uni. I can get a sick note or use the coming week as reading days. It will give me more time to think what I am going to do. I want to be here. I can't leave now. You and Natalie can come back next weekend."

"Oh, okay. If, you are sure, but is it safe?"

"Yes, Mary and Megan are gone. They are at peace now, and I'll have Aunt Sharon here," said Zoe.

"And Kyle and Toby have cars so can drive them about if they need to go anywhere," added Natalie.

The phone rang. A Lianne Crosby was in reception saying that she had received a message saying that Natalie Walker wanted to speak to her.

She was invited up. On the beach she had been wearing faded jeans and a short canvas smock-top with a battered blue beret. Now, it was like a child had 'coloured-her-in'. She wore a full-length, boldly patterned floral dress under a thigh length tangerine coat. A collection of beads hung round her neck, rattling slightly each time she moved. On closer inspection the beads turned out to be small, smooth pieces of driftwood and shells. On her head was a blue silk scarf, holding back her hair. Released from the beret, she'd been wearing on the beach, streaks of pink, frothed in the grey curls. Natalie was disappointed that Hobnail hadn't come too.

Introductions were made and they all took a seat. Lianne was offered coffee but, as they didn't have any decaffeinated, she accepted a glass of orange juice. Once they were all settled, Natalie explained why she had wanted to talk to Lianne, asking her what she knew about the hotel.

"Well, I don't know what to say. There have always been rumours, talk." She looked at Zoe, "about the family, about the women."

"Go on," said Zoe. "What *about* the women?"

"Being..."

They waited... as Lianne's eyes alternated between Zoe's face and her head, its bandage being slightly askew again and not helping matters, one eye in danger of disappearing.

"Well... disturbed!"

"In what way? How?"

"I don't really know. It was said that Walter Brammar thought the women bonkers. His words, not mine. Not his wife, mind, but his daughter and granddaughter. They left as soon as they could. A lot of folks thought it was him they were trying to get away from. Everyone thought there was something odd going on. You know..."

"What do you mean?"

"Well...!"

"Well, what?"

"Well, I don't like to say..."

They all stared at her, expectantly. Lianne glanced from face to face, judging them. Then said, "You know... sex...u...al, and stuff...!"

"What?!" exploded Zoe. She winced and held her ribs.

"Sorry. Probably not my place to say, but his daughter left and rarely came back. Wouldn't bring her own daughter here. Now a body has been found in a closed off part of the cellar. It wouldn't surprise me if there aren't others."

"What! Don't be ridiculous," said Sharon.

"It would explain a lot. Guests coming and going. One or two wouldn't be missed."

"I think," said David, "that is enough. If you have finished your orange juice, I will show... you... out."

When he returned it was to say that it was chaos in the lobby. Guests and reporters were all asking questions, talking at once. Karen was doing her best to deal with the situation, but it was getting out of hand. The duty receptionist looked like she was about to burst into tears and the manager from the dining room was trying to usher 'non-guests' out of the door, but to no avail. His height and arm length made him ideal for the task but, like cats, the mob refused to be corralled. David had seen Lianne off the premises, but she had walked straight up to a group of people he believed to be reporters, and started talking. Unable to do anything about that he had gone into the kitchen. There, he had spoken to the Police Officer on duty in front of the cellar door. Hopefully, as he had 'called it in' someone would be along to help disperse the crowd.

"Zoe, you need to make Karen's promotion official, a.s.a.p. She is doing a brilliant job down there."

"Let's look," said Natalie and set off, a puzzled Zoe following closely behind. She stopped short as Natalie pushed open Doreen's apartment door. Inside, Natalie nudged the mouse on the security camera and then enlarged the image of the reception area. She didn't know what she was expecting to see but it was definitely chaos. The hall was full of people, all jostling each other, phones held aloft. There was even a selfie-stick waving crazily, like the hand of a teacher's pet.

"Someone is going to get hurt. I'm going down there," said Zoe.

"No, you've got enough injuries. I... I'll go," said Natalie.

"You!!"

"Yes."

"You, stand up and talk to a crowd! This I've got to see," and she sat down and turned to the monitor. Natalie didn't move. "Aren't you going then?!"

"Yes, I'm... just... working out what I am going to say."

The apartment door opened, and Sharon and David joined them. Zoe beckoned them over, "Come watch. Natalie is going down to make an announcement."

"Do you want me to come with you?" asked her father.

"No. I'll be fine."

"Just tell them what was said in the statement. If they persist just keep repeating 'I have nothing further to add at this time'. Do not engage with the media."

The faces on the monitor suddenly turned towards the stairs, effectively looking directly at the camera. Then, the back of Natalie's head bobbed in front of it. She stepped down a couple of steps and her arms began waving.

"Ohhh!," said Zoe, "I really must get sound for this!"

However, the facial expressions told their own story. Initially they listened attentively, showing interest and surprise. Then a microphone was held aloft. Soon there was a sea of them and mouths forming questions. Natalie was obviously saying something. They stopped speaking and listened again. A series of flashes followed, and Natalie's arms went up again. This time in front of her face. Then suddenly the crowd turned and headed for the door. They filed out quietly and were gone. The reception staff got back to whatever they needed to do, and all returned to normal, as if nothing had happened.

A little time later the door opened, and Natalie appeared, somewhat red-faced.

"What did you tell them?"

"Well, I repeated the statement. Then... they all started asking questions. I didn't know what to say. I panicked..."

"What do you mean, you panicked?" said Zoe.

"Well..."

"What did you say?"

"I... I said you'd speak to them at Twelve."

"Nooo!!!"

"Yes. I'm sorry. I didn't know what else to say."

"I can't go down there looking like this!"

The others looked at her. The bandage on her head was askew again and what hair was visible looked a greasy mess. She was also holding her ribs.

"You need a hat," said Mrs Walker. "Or, a headscarf. Come on. Let's see what we can find."

As they crossed the hall, Karen appeared, holding a hotel diary. Intent on finding something to cover Zoe's head, they didn't notice what she held.

Together they went back into Zoe's apartment. When they explained what they were doing Karen said that there may be something in lost property that would do. If not, she could go home and get a silk scarf, but, before that, she had something to show them.

"Is this one of the diaries from the hotel safe?" asked Natalie.

"Yes. There is a full set for the last 12 years. All very neatly written about the day to day running of the hotel. Some of it is fascinating. It is written in different hands, some bits easier to read than others. This bit though, you need to see. She removed a strip of paper marking a page and laid it open on the table for the others to see. The wording was neat and formal, very business like. It was a statement of fact.

Mrs Elizabeth Brammar apparently fell down the back stairs. Body found by Hotel Manager. See Accident Book.

"What, Doreen found her! You don't think!"

There was silence.

Then David said, "Elizabeth was Walter Brammar's wife. Yes?"

"Yes," said Karen.

Zoe snatched the diary. "Does it say anything else?"

"No. The rest is all business. The date of the funeral is there but then, it would affect the business. Mr Brammar, and some of the staff, would be absent for it. I looked at the accident book too, but it doesn't add anything."

"There are diaries in your bedroom," said Natalie heading for the door. "Walter's diaries."

It was missing. The one diary they wanted was not there. The year before and several years after, were all there but not the one that might have given them some more insight. The diaries were all well kept and meticulously detailed. They were neat and clear. Appointments were printed in capitals and the prose was written in beautiful scrolling long hand. However, the diary that was likely to be the most revealing was absent. Walter's words on the matter were not there!

With ten minutes to spare Zoe was washed, dressed and wearing a peach table napkin round her head. Karen had not found anything appropriate in lost property but had used her initiative. Left over from a wedding the peach napkin, deftly tied, held a dressing in place and hid all evidence of Zoe's surgery. Matched with a patterned peach top of Mrs Walkers it looked surprisingly good. It wasn't something that Zoe would have chosen to wear but she was reasonably pleased with the look. It just needed a bit of confidence to carry it off, and Zoe had that in shovelfuls.

David re-appeared from checking the monitors in Doreen's apartment and announced that the reporters were gathering in reception.

Zoe had a quick look in the full-length mirror in her room and then headed for the door. Linking an arm through Natalie's, she dragged her out of the door. "You can introduce me," she said grinning. "All you have to say is, 'Hello ladies and gentlemen. This is Zoe Spencer, the owner of the hotel.' I'll take it from there."

At the top of the reception stairs, just out of sight of the reception area, Zoe stopped. "How do I look?"

Natalie looked her up and down. "You look fine, well, awesome – as usual!"

Zoe grinned, "Go on, then. Announce me!"

Natalie slowly descended and stopped part way down, where she had stood before. Those gathered looked up and waited attentively. She stared back at them then said, "Er... Zoe," and waved an arm up the stairs.

Realising that that was going to be it, Zoe began her descent as Natalie retreated back up the stairs. Zoe took her time, partly for effect and partly because the stair rail was on the side of her broken arm and if she didn't take each step carefully the jolt hurt her ribs. Keeping her bandaged wrist hidden, she came to a halt in the spot where Natalie had been standing and cast her eyes over her subjects. Then she beamed graciously at them all. Amongst the faces she spotted Kyle, who winked at her.

"Ladies and gentlemen, thank you for coming. I am Zoe Spencer, the new owner of The Dolphin Hotel and Lido. As you are aware a body was found in a previously sealed off part of the cellar. It would appear to be the body of the former owner's sister, Megan Brammar, who died during World War Two, in an air raid. The body has been removed by the Police and the cellar sealed. Until the Police complete their investigations there is nothing further to say. Thank   you   for attending."

Microphones and phones were thrust forwards, and an assault of questions flew.

"Who found the body?"

"Are you sure there aren't any others?"

"What was the deceased wearing?"

"How come it has only just been found?"

Zoe took a deep breath. "Thank you for coming. I have nothing further to say. It is now up to the Police. Please direct your questions to them." As further questions were thrown her way she stood impassively and just stared at them.

Gradually, those at the back began to drift out of the door. Then the rest followed. It took about 5 minutes but then, except for Kyle, the reception area was empty. As the door closed Kyle walked over smiling. "You are a natural. Well done. You also look fabulous. I'm not sure what you have got on your head, but it suits you." He took a closer look. "Is that a hotel napkin?"

"It most certainly is, and I agree – not everyone could carry it off!"

"Come here," he said, laughing. He took her hand and guided her over to the seating area in the corner of reception.

"You do realise that the others are all watching this on the monitor upstairs," she said.

"That's fine. They'll soon get bored." He sat her down in one of the large leather chairs and placed a tablet on the table in front of her. As the receptionist pretended to busy herself behind the desk, he opened it up and switched it on. "Now," he said, waving his hand through the air, "take a good look round the walls and the ceiling and the staircase." Then, he made a few clicks on the keyboard and sat back. "Now, what do you think of this?"

Zoe looked at the screen. In front of her was the reception area. All the features were the same, but the colour scheme had changed. It was light, bright and crisp. The reception desk was now a pale blue with lilac relief on the panelling and the hotel name was picked out in gold. The pale blue brought out the blue in the floor tiles, which were the original ones. The wall behind reception was a darker blue, contrasting with the leaping dolphin surrounded by white and gold crested waves. Kyle rotated the image to show the other three walls. These were in a lighter blue but with the panelled areas in wood, which was now light and probably the original colour. The staircase had a shiny sweeping banister topping gold wavy rods which gave a subtle hint of waves. It all looked so different, but the structure and features were the same. The art deco ceiling lights were now clean and shiny and lit the geometric plaster moulding above. Matching uplighters on the walls lit the wall.

"Kyle, you are incredible."

"Not really. I did some research. That is how it looked when it was first done."

There was a clatter on the stairs, and they looked up. Toby came into view and stopped halfway down. He asked if the two of them were planning on coming upstairs. With Natalie and her father heading south in the morning, they needed to decide what they were all going to do with the rest of the day.

Chapter Twenty-Three

The afternoon passed in a blur. Natalie spent some of it packing but managed to get some alone time with Toby. Wrapped up warm, the two of them went out for a walk. They strolled, arm in arm along the promenade, knowing that they didn't have much time left together as the evening would be spent with her parents, Zoe and Kyle.

Since his outburst on the cave steps, neither had mentioned how they felt about the other. It hung in the air between them. He had said that he loved her, and she hadn't responded. She wanted to, but couldn't bring herself to say out loud, how she felt. As they walked along, hand in hand, he gave hers a double squeeze. She squeezed back and leant in closer. Then he squeezed her hand again. This time he bent his head to her ear and whispered, "I meant it. I do love you, but I am content to wait until a time, if, and when you are ready to say it to me."

She turned and looked up at him, not knowing what to say. He raised a finger to her lips and silenced her. "Shhh. I just wanted to say it again. Just so you know." He removed his finger and kissed her, preventing her from saying anything. His lips were warm and soft. There was a hint of stubble uncomfortably brushing her upper lip, but she didn't mind. Without breaking contact, he steered her into one of the covered seats facing the sea. The wind dropped. They folded themselves into the corner and sat down, arms entwined. He brushed her hair back from her face and looked deep into her eyes and grinned. "I also couldn't let you leave with the lasting memory of me saying 'I love you', as a prelude to finding a corpse."

"Oh, yes," she said laughing, "Wouldn't that be something to tell our children." She gasped, realising what she had said.

"Hah, so, you have been thinking about a future together. It is okay. Don't look so alarmed. I am just kidding. It is early days yet. I know."

Zoe seemed to be newly energised. She showed Kyle round the hotel, introducing him to the staff she knew and introducing herself to those she didn't. Kyle was a little worried that she was 'over-doing' things, but she wouldn't slow down. She seemed to want to see and understand everything that there was to know about the hotel. This was a new Zoe, a Zoe he hadn't seen before. It was both amazing and alarming. He wasn't sure he could keep up.

David and Sharon went for a walk around the town, getting a late lunch down at the harbour. They found an inside table at a small waterfront café and ordered crab. It was the first time that either of them had relaxed since Natalie had phoned them to say Zoe had fallen out of the hotel window. That call now seemed a lifetime ago. Exhausted, they sat in silence, each deep in their own thoughts. When their food arrived, they tucked in. Along with the crab was a small green salad, lemon, and some crusty brown bread. Then the waitress returned with a tray. Carefully she laid out cups and a pot of tea, milk, and sugar. Then she placed a dish of butter on the table and an ornate butter knife. Sharon picked up the knife, slipped it into the butter and scooped out a lump. The butter was firm but not hard. She spread a layer onto her bread and took a bite. Simple but satisfying. She then used her fork to add some crab and finally squeezed some lemon on. Marvellous.

David stuck his spoon into the teapot and gave it a stir and an inspection. Then he poured them both some milk before filling their cups with tea.

"What do you think of Toby and Kyle?" said Sharon.

"Good lads, both of them."

"I can't believe the girls have been so lucky. I hope it lasts."

"What do you think they will do? Do you think Zoe will stay here?" said David.

"I don't like to say this, but I think she will. As for Natalie..."

Chapter Twenty-Four

Natalie and her father set off early. They had a long drive ahead of them. Zoe and Sharon said their goodbyes at the apartment door, Zoe wearing her dressing gown. It was hard and strange, being left. Soon they were on their own with a whole day, and a whole week, ahead of them.

"Right," said Sharon, "What are we going to do?"

"Have a decent breakfast. Let's go down and have a full English, toast, coffee, the works."

"This could turn into a bad habit."

As they walked through reception a couple of people, sitting in the corner, got to their feet and rushed over.

"Miss Spencer," said a short elderly woman with a rosy cheeked complexion and glossy chestnut brown, very straight hair.

Zoe stopped and smiled and looked the woman up and down. There was no notebook, phone, or microphone visible. The man at her side smiled, looking slightly uncomfortable. A little taller than the woman he stooped slightly and blinked persistently.

"Yes," said Zoe. These weren't reporters. If they were, then they were completely different to the others from the previous occasions. Their manner was somewhat deferential; they appeared to be expecting to be 'shown the door' at any minute.

"We wondered," said the woman, "if we could make an appointment to speak to you?"

"What about?"

"Well. Here is my card. Hopefully it will explain." She held out her hand to a jangle of bangles and proffered a small rectangular business card. It said simply 'Belinda Oldham, Medium'. At the bottom were contact details. "We won't take up any more of your time now. I am sure you are busy. My phone number is there if you wish to get in touch. Thank you for your time." With that, the couple headed for the door and left.

"Wow," said Zoe. "That was interesting."

"You aren't thinking of contacting her, are you?" asked Sharon.

"I might. It could be fun. I'd love to hear what she has to say and see if it tallies with what I've experienced. You know – check out if she is a fraud or not."

"Let's just wait and see what the Police have to say. You don't want to go getting mixed up with people like that."

Zoe laughed, "People like *that*!"

"You *know*...!"

"Come on, let's get some breakfast."

After they had eaten Zoe stopped by the reception desk and then the kitchen to ask if everything was okay and if there was anything she needed to be aware of. The staff seemed surprised, but pleased. Initial responses were affirmative, everything was okay. Then, with a little more thought there was the odd, 'Well, actually' and she soon had a list. Top of her thoughts was a daily meeting with Karen and a weekly staff meeting. However, she had an appointment at the hospital in the morning and she also needed to phone the university. She also planned on arranging a meeting with the solicitor and asking the Police for an update.

Kyle joined them late morning. Following Zoe's enthusiastic response to his proposals for the entrance hall he was keen to look at the rest of the hotel's function rooms. Zoe left him in animated conversation with the restaurant manager. The pair were in instant agreement that the art deco features should be retained and updated and were soon suggesting colours which the other received positively. Zoe wandered off wondering if a business 'bromance' was blossoming.

Sharon returned shortly after, having had a walk around the grounds. She had been speaking to the gardener and had hopes that the Dolphin would survive. Talking plants had got the gardener, Ruth, to open up a little more about the family. She hadn't said much but when Sharon had mentioned what Lianne had implied there was an emphatic, "No! Nothing like that." Hopefully she may say more if they talked again.

With Kyle occupied they decided to go for a walk. They phoned reception and asked if there were any reporters outside. There were, and at the garden entrance too. So, they took the lift down to the shore and walked along the beach to the promenade steps. Hopefully, this escape route wouldn't be needed for long. It was good to get out and get a little exercise. The weather was reasonable and, for once, they didn't feel the need to swaddle themselves in scarves, hats, and gloves. After the climb up to the promenade they were both quite warm and Zoe wished she could remove her head dressing and the table napkin holding it in place. It wasn't long before they found a shop selling silk scarves. There was a dizzying choice of colours and patterns, thicknesses, and lengths. It took a while to choose but she managed to find three that she liked. It was going to be a while before her hair grew back, so she may be back for more. Happy with her purchases, and keen to remove the napkin, they found an empty seat shelter and Sharon helped her place one of them on her head.

Despite the cooked breakfast it wasn't long before Zoe was keen to find somewhere for lunch. Together they wandered the narrow streets of the town, checking out all the little alleyways. It was surprising how many small businesses provided food and drink, and they all seemed to have custom, no matter how 'tucked way'. They found a quaint door with a sandwich board outside stating 'Open – fresh crab – sandwiches and wraps, tea and coffee'. It was just a door in a wall. Curious, Zoe pushed it open. Behind it was a dark alley with what looked like a well-lit outdoor space at the end. She looked at Sharon, who shrugged. Together they set off and soon they found themselves in a square courtyard filled with metal tables, and chairs festooned with brightly coloured cushions. The yard was sheltered and sunny and decorated with lavender bushes in big pots. People were seated at the tables. Spotting a free one, they went and sat down. A waitress arrived and deposited a napkin-lined basket of bread on the table along with a jug of water. Zoe guessed that she was the owner. She was probably in her late fifties and her eyes appeared to be everywhere, checking tables and customers' dining progress, ready to offer more drinks and food or the bill, as required. When she returned with their order she cleared her throat, "Er, I hope you don't mind me saying, but aren't you Zoe Spencer, the new owner of The Dolphin Hotel?"

Zoe stared.

"I saw you on the TV last night."

"What? I was on the TV?"

"Yes. Didn't you know?"

"No, I just thought they were newspaper reporters."

"No, the local evening news was there. So, are you down here to escape the paparazzi?"

"Well, we did sneak out the back way, but we are just out getting to know the area."

"Checking out the competition! Just joking, we can't compete with a hotel and lido. Mrs Brammar – your great grandmother, I guess - used to like to come down here. I suppose it was because she rarely ran into any of her hotel guests here. We aren't easy to find. Lovely lady. Shame."

Zoe could barely contain herself. She had so many questions, but, "Shame! What do you mean?"

Eyes ever moving over her customers, the lady excused herself to refill a teapot and bring out a plate of sandwiches from the kitchen. When she returned, she introduced herself. "I am Lindsey White, the owner of the Smugglers' Hideaway. Yes, I knew your great grand parents. I didn't see much of your great grandfather though. He liked to keep himself to himself. Tragic what happened, and now it seems his sister's body has been found. Was it you that found her?

"No, that was my friend Natalie."

"That must have been quite a shock. And you, you've really been in the wars, getting pushed down the stairs like that. Strange woman that Doreen."

"Do you know her?"

"Not really – just what people say – gossip really. Sorry."

"Well, what do people say?"

"It is just gossip. I shouldn't be repeating it. It isn't right."

Zoe said nothing, just waited, encouragingly.

"Well, with Mrs Brammar 'falling' down the stairs, and dying and you being pushed by Doreen, and Doreen being practically the only member of staff who is still here from that time – they are wondering... well... and now another body turns up at the bottom of more stairs."

"Doreen couldn't possibly have been responsible for the body in the cellar, she isn't old enough," said Sharon.

"No, I... realise that, but until it is confirmed that the body is from 1944, people will continue to speculate. It is all over town that Doreen was expecting to inherit The Dolphin. Then, Zoe, you turned up... Then, there were the other deaths, such a lot of tragedy. People still wonder about that."

Back in the apartment they found a phone message saying that Natalie and her dad had made it home. There had been a couple of hold-ups on the M1 but, overall, it hadn't been a bad trip. There was also a message from Kyle saying that he wouldn't be able to take Zoe to the

hospital in the morning, but that Toby would drive
them.

Chapter Twenty-Five

At the hospital Zoe's clips were removed and her head felt a lot better. She no longer had the urge to scratch the area. Once she was able to wash her hair there would be no dried blood to annoy her. When they returned to the hotel Toby drove them straight past. The day's reporters were starting to gather. He dropped them by the back entrance and headed off to work.

Back at the apartment Zoe phoned the university, and the solicitor, and then went down to see Karen. Once again there were reporters milling about, both in reception and on the steps outside. As soon as they saw her, microphones were thrust in her face and questions fired.

"I have nothing further to say. Nothing has changed. Please. This is a hotel, and guests have a right to come and go without having to fight their way through *you* lot. Please leave." No one moved.

Karen beckoned her over and led her into the back office. "We *have* to do something. Guests are complaining and one couple checked out."

"Has there been anything from the Police yet?"

"No."

"How long can it take!?"

"I don't think it will be much longer," said Karen, "but, I expect the reporters won't be satisfied until they have been in the cellar and taken photographs in the cave. They are already creating 'mock-ups'."

"I am not having that lot trooping down there."

"Perhaps *you* could take some photos or ask the Police to release some."

"They won't let me in there."

"I'll phone the station, see if I can get them to make a statement or something."

The next time Zoe went into reception it was clear of reporters. Whatever Karen had said to the Police, it had worked. Over a coffee, Zoe and Karen were able to discuss the hotel. They went over the daily occupancy and maintenance list, staffing, upcoming events, and stock levels. It was dizzying, but something Zoe was going to have to 'get to grips' with. For now, she just listened, content to be led by Karen. Despite it being 'her hotel', she still felt as though she was there on 'work experience'. The deference of the staff still surprised her. No doubt, in time, she would get used to being 'the boss'.

As the week went on, she began to enjoy the meetings and took pleasure in the number of bookings they were taking. Filling the rooms became important to her and news of wedding and other celebration events gave her a little 'buzz'. Seeing her enthusiasm, Karen suggested that she may like to do a little 'serving' at the weekend's wedding. It would be a good way of being involved and a good way to gauge guests' feelings about the event and the hotel. Zoe could walk trays of drinks and canapes through the guests. She loved the idea and soon Karen had her kitted out with the hotel's restaurant uniform, a cream blouse, teal skirt, and matching waistcoat with dolphin logo. She went and found a full-length mirror and did a twirl, thrilled with her appearance. Now, she just needed to find a headscarf to match and some appropriate shoes! After a practice with a tray, it was decided that she would just take out canapes, drinks were too risky with just one hand!

Mrs Walker was pleased with the change she saw. Zoe appeared to be revelling in her new responsibilities. When she found her tripping about the apartment holding aloft a tray of biscuits, weaving through imaginary guests, she laughed out loud. "I don't suppose there is a uniform for me, is there?"

Zoe grinned. Soon the pair of them were holding trays aloft, weaving round the furniture and each other, offering canapes. "Do try a vol au vent, yes, stuffed with dolphin and pimento." "The bruschetta is to die for – topped with dolphin pate and seaweed."

On the Thursday Zoe met with the solicitor and signed the necessary paperwork. Doreen was discussed, but as there was no news as to what was going to happen to her it was impossible to make plans. Zoe was told that her statement would be taken into consideration but as she had been physically injured by Doreen it would be up the Crown Prosecution Service to decide whether to charge her. However, as Doreen's mental state was still uncertain, it would have to wait. Karen had visited her on a number of occasions, but each time Doreen had refused to see her, and the hospital staff would tell her nothing.

Late Friday evening David and Natalie arrived. After brief greetings, they went straight to bed. The 'catch-up' could wait until the morning.

Chapter Twenty-Six

David was up early, woken by Sharon. They had breakfast in the hotel dining room and then headed up to Zoe's apartment. Zoe was pacing up and down. At 10.05 she could wait no longer and knocked on Natalie's door. There was a muffled, "Come in." Zoe burst through the door. Flinging back the curtains, she grabbed Natalie's dressing gown and threw it at her.

"Come on I've got lots to tell you and show you. Get up!"

Natalie, pushed the hair back from her face and grimaced, screwing up her eyes.

"Toby will be here any minute."

That worked. Natalie threw back the covers, grabbed the dressing gown, and headed for the bathroom.

Dressed, Zoe plied her with toast and coffee and Natalie slowly got herself ready for the day, mildly interested in what Zoe was so excited about.

With the arrival of Kyle, who also seemed excited, curiosity got the better of her, "Okay, so tell me."

"We need to show you. Come on."

With Sharon and David in tow, they followed her to the hotel dining room and took a table in the corner, where they had a view of the

267

whole room. "Now take a good look around," said Zoe. Natalie looked. "Now look at this…" Zoe pointed to the tablet Kyle was holding. On the screen was a representation of the dining room but totally transformed. Pale blues, yellows and golds covered the walls and picked out the detailing on the walls, cornices and ceiling. It looked so different, yet it was the same room. Then Zoe produced swatches of material and samples of wallpaper. "What do you think? Kyle did some research and sourced these. It isn't the original design but near as dammit. This is what it looked like when it was first done. Isn't it lush?"

Natalie had to agree. It looked stunning. "Show her the entrance hall and reception area."

Kyle obliged.

"So," said Natalie, "when is this marvellous transformation going to take place?"

"We need to talk to Karen and decide the best time, but I can't wait. He is going to research the bar area next."

A chair was pulled out beside her, and Natalie jumped. Turning she found Toby grinning and settling himself at her side. Their eyes met and she blushed, surprise and delight flushing through her body. "Oh, hi," she said, unable to find a happy medium between acting casual, and flinging her arms around him. Toby smiled and the others laughed out loud.

Zoe got to her feet and hauled Kyle to his. "I suggest we four go out for a walk and leave these two to say hello, alone. I want everyone back in the apartment for 4pm, though. I have a surprise. You're gonna love it."

With the others gone Toby put his arm round her waist and pulled her towards him. "Lovely to have you back. I've missed you." He studied her eyes briefly and then kissed her tenderly, then more fervently. Then, realising that they weren't alone, as the clash of cutlery being laid for lunch filled the room, he pulled back and grinned. "Fancy a drive?"

After a quick word with Karen and a 'No comment' to a stubborn reporter, Zoe, Kyle, David and Sharon left the hotel. David and Sharon headed down towards the harbour, Zoe and Kyle up the street towards the cemetery. Zoe wanted to check out some of the details on the head stones and take photographs of them all. She had no idea how many ancestors were buried there. If fact, she knew very little about her family history; it wasn't something that she had questioned before. When they reached the cemetery gates, they took the longer path to the top of the hill which led round and along the side nearest the sea. Part way up Zoe paused to catch her breath.
"Are you okay?" asked Kyle.
"I'm fine," she said.
He didn't believe her but decided not to 'push it'. He worried about her, but he was

learning that she could be stubborn and challenging her would only make her insist on keeping going. Instead, he turned his attention to their surroundings, to give her the time she needed to recover.

Beside the path was a sizeable monument dedicated to those who had lost their lives at sea. Constructed of weather worn granite it stood defiant; testament to the fortitude of the sailors and fishermen who had lost the battle with the sea: names and ages, dates and dedications fading with the centuries. Alongside it stood a newer monument dedicated to the fallen, who had also lost their lives at sea, but at the hand of man. Zoe wondered if it should have more rightly read 'dedicated to the sunken'. So many names. Nearly all young men. She glanced at Kyle. He wasn't much older than most of those listed. She studied his profile. He was reading names, his face solemn, his shoulders sagging.

"Do you know any of these? Are they relatives?"

He nodded. "These three were my great uncles. These two, twins. We have photos of them in uniform. You know, studio shots before they went to the front. They look so smart, so proud, eager to 'do their bit'."

They walked on a bit. "Then there were those who died at the docks, but they just had family burials, no 'grateful nation' dedication monuments for them. Come on."

David and Sharon strolled down to the harbour, arms linked together. "It is funny," said David, "but it is ages since we were Natalie and Zoe's age, but it seems like only yesterday that we were dating. Do you remember your mother catching us on her sofa and your dad taking me into his shed and having a stern word."

"Uhh, yes. I was mortified."

"About being caught or the 'having a word'?"

"Both, but I couldn't believe my dad could be so old fashioned. I bet he wished he'd had a study for the occasion."

"It didn't stop you seeing me though!"

"No. That was never going to happen."

"Ooh," said Sharon pointing, "look, let's do a boat trip. It takes an hour. Then we'll get a coffee and maybe some lunch."

Toby held open the car door and gave Natalie his hand. She took it and stepped out onto chippings; glad she wasn't wearing heels. They were in a small, secluded car park surrounded by trees. A path led off between the sycamores and blackthorn into denser foliage of hawthorn and hazel. The path was well trodden and easy to follow; it was obviously a popular route. Toby let Natalie take the lead, following the track up and down as it meandered along the hillside. After roughly half a mile the path took a steep downturn and made its way along the side of a valley. Wind whistled in the tops of the trees, getting louder. They rounded a rock outcrop and Natalie stopped and gaped as the view opened out. Ahead was a stone wall with a metal rail on top. The noise she had thought to be wind, now thunderous. Natalie stepped towards the rail and peered over the edge. Spray caught her, but she didn't mind. Water cascaded past her head, crashing into rocks on its way down to a large misty pool about fifty feet below. Above, water poured over and down the rock face, lush vegetation clinging to crevices either side, multicoloured lichen filling in the gaps.

"Keep going," shouted Toby, "there is more."

She turned and saw that the path disappeared into the rock at the side of the waterfall. Intrigued she stepped into the dark entrance, placing her hands on the wet walls. Water ran up her sleeves, cold and nasty, making her yelp. She stopped and shook her arms as Toby laughed. Eyes adjusting, she headed into the dark. Now she could see light ahead.

"Watch where you are putting your feet. It can be wet and slippery".

Another few steps and they were behind the waterfall. She couldn't resist. She held out her hand towards the curtain, and looked at Toby, to confirm that she wasn't about to do something really stupid, but he nodded. She stuck her hand out, finger first, and poked it into the wall of water. Then she put her whole hand in, letting the water batter her palm. Then she pulled it out and shook it at Toby, flicking her fingers and splashing his face.

He stepped back grinning. "You don't want to get into a water fight with me." He cupped his hand and held it out sideways, ready to scoop water her way.

"No, no. I surrender."

"Good. Come here."

Slowly they stepped towards each other. He wrapped his arms around her waist and pulled her close so that her back arched and she found herself looking up at him. As he bent his lips towards hers, she reached up and ran her fingers through the short hairs at the back of his neck. He pulled back briefly, "I really want you to touch me, but that hand is icy cold!"

She tried to apologise but her mouth was soon occupied, and his hands were warm.

At the top of the cemetery the ground levelled out and they walked along until they came to the Brammar graves. Zoe stood back and to one side and, with her phone, took a panorama of them all. Then she went along the row taking close-ups of the individual graves. When she came to Megans's she stopped.

"Do you remember why you attacked the headstone?" asked Kyle.

"Yes, that isn't Megan buried there. That is Edna, and Mary was really upset about it. She needs her own grave, and Megan needs a proper burial."

"I am surprised that the Police haven't dug her up already."

"It has only been a couple of weeks. They probably need permission, or whatever!"

"Yes, they might need your DNA too, to confirm it was Megan in the cave."

"Edna's surname was Green. I wonder if there are any of her relatives in here, or if there are any living relatives."

They wandered up and down the rows of graves for a while scanning the headstones but didn't find any 'Greens'. It was a large cemetery.

"I'll check the Parish Records on-line. That will tell us. This isn't the only cemetery in the area."

"Mary didn't like Edna. She was a nasty vindictive sort, as we've found out. When she wanted something, she didn't take no for an answer. She wanted Jack, even though she was too old for him and Jack, I don't think he cared either way."

"So, with Mary, how aware were you, of her? Was it just like being her. Did you have her knowledge and memories?"

Sitting down on a bench Zoe became quiet and inspected her hands, gathering her thoughts and her words. "No, I was only aware of what was relevant in the moment. I shared her emotions. Whilst I was in the hospital, I shared some of her memories, or rather events, little scenes of her days. Edna came to the hotel asking for Jack. Mary was polite but irritated. She told her where Jack was but soon followed her through the hotel to the dining room. She didn't trust Edna but didn't have a reason to refuse her entry."

"Oh, what was the dining room like? Did it look like my simulation?"

"I've no idea. Mary was focussed on what was happening. The surroundings were of no concern. When Mary reached the dining room, she found Jack on his knees fixing a chair, more intent on that, than Edna, who was trying to give him a scarf. Megan was there and arguing with Edna. She didn't like her either, and Mary was glad at that. She desperately wanted Jack to stick up for himself, but he didn't seem to mind the attention. Mary didn't like the way Edna dressed. She thought her trashy and a slut. Edna and Megan's clothes were virtually the same, but on Edna they seemed different somehow. She was also irritated that Edna managed to draw perfectly straight lines on the back of her legs. You know, pretend stockings." Kyle looked blank. "Silk stockings had a seam up the back. When they couldn't get stockings, women drew a line up the back of their legs. Mary had tried but couldn't manage it. Hers always lacked continuity and were never straight. She was also suspicious of the perfume Edna had, wondering where she got it. Even with her black-market connections Mary couldn't get perfume like that. She wondered what a girl had to do to obtain it."

Toby led Natalie to a spot at the back of the overhang and took out his phone, switched on the torch, and handed it to Natalie. Then he produced three paperclips and crafted a tripod and placed it on a ledge. Natalie was bemused. Then he reached in his pocket and produced a coin sized wooden heart on a chain. He kissed it and held it out for her to do the same. Then he hung it on the tripod. Tiny drips from the limestone ceiling soon wet it. Natalie grinned. "So, do we come back in a thousand years. I've always wanted a heart of stone!"

"Well, that wasn't the gesture I was aiming for. It was meant to denote permanence. I love you, Natalie Walker."

At 3:50pm everyone was back in the apartment, eager for Zoe's surprise. At 4pm the phone rang. A beaming Zoe answered it. "Yes, send her up." Mystified, they all waited as Zoe headed down the hall to meet whoever it was. Kyle shrugged his shoulders; he had no idea what Zoe had planned.

When she returned Sharon let out an exasperated 'humph'! Ignoring her, Zoe announced, "This is Belinda Oldham, she is a Medium."

There was silence.

Tentatively, but a little too brightly, Zoe continued, "She is going to accompany us down into the cellar and tell us what she can find out about what happened down there."

"What?" snapped Natalie. "Are you serious?"

They all gaped at Zoe, who was now almost standing to attention. She clearly was serious.

"I don't believe you Zoe. How could you! Have you any idea how scared and worried I've been the last 3 weeks. At times I have been absolutely terrified. On a number of occasions, I thought you were going to die. I thought I was going to lose you, not to mention the rest of what happened down there. No, no, I'm not doing this."

"It's ... just a bit of fun...," said Zoe.

"No, it really isn't," said Toby putting his arm round Natalie.

Zoe looked at Kyle for support, but he just shook his head and stepped away from her. David and Sharon moved to their daughter's side.

In the silence that followed Belinda Oldham quietly let herself out.

Chapter Twenty-Seven

In the morning the Walkers set off on their long journey south leaving a despondent Zoe on her own in the apartment. They had all dined together the previous evening, but it hadn't been a happy meal. When it became known that none of them were returning the following weekend, and that Toby was going down to see Natalie, Zoe couldn't believe it, blaming the decision on the 'medium' incident. Natalie tried to explain that she had a lot of work to do, and she was exhausted. The travelling was just too much. She would come up the subsequent weekend, probably. Zoe had argued and pleaded, then stubbornly refused to make the journey when Toby had offered to take her down with him.

Just before they left, Sharon handed Zoe a small package. "This isn't the best time to give you this, but you need to see it. The Police delivered it, along with other items from your parents' car, a few weeks after the funeral."

As Zoe took hold of the brown paper packet Sharon said, "It is your grandmother's diary." Zoe immediately opened it. "No love. You get yourself a cup of tea and sit down to read it."

It took her about half an hour to read. She turned immediately to March 16th. There was no entry, but then there wouldn't have been, as there weren't to be any more. Turning back the pages Zoe read backwards, day by day.

15th March – We are going home. We must get her away. We are packed and will leave first thing in the morning. We haven't told her. We don't know how she will react. I have already put our bags in the car boot, the ones she won't miss. Harry has told her we are going to a bird sanctuary down the coast. I hate leaving father so soon after the funeral, but I don't see any other option.

14th March – I can't take much more of this. She is completely unmanageable.

13th March – Harry was battling with her again last night, trying to keep her in their room. Father coping badly. He doesn't need this too.

12th March – The funeral went well. It was a good send off, but Linda became agitated at the grave side, appeared distracted and uninterested in her grandmother's funeral.

11th March – found her in the kitchen again, pulling pans out of THE wall cupboard.

THE wall cupboard. Had her mother been trying to get into the same cupboard that she and Mary had, and her grandmother too? She read on...

Father exasperated with her; saying she is crazy just like I was at her age. He doesn't understand. How could he! He never listened to me.

Finally, she put down the diary. Her cup of tea was cold. Her family had gone. She was on her own, in an empty apartment, in a big hotel. The room seemed very quiet. Then she realised that she had successfully tuned out the sound of the gulls. With that realisation the screeching came crashing back. Irritated, and rebellion rising, she decided to meet with the Medium, anyway. She picked up the phone and dialled.

When she went down for her morning meeting with the duty manager, she passed a couple on the stairs who obviously knew who she was. They seemed excited to see her. She said a polite hello and asked them if they were enjoying their stay. 'Oh, yes, they were. Thank you very much.' She got the impression that they wouldn't have said 'No!', even if they hadn't been enjoying themselves; they were talking to a celebrity. Still, the interaction lifted her mood.

Carl had had a good day off on the Saturday. He and his mates had been kite surfing; the wind and waves had been just right. After a brief explanation she found she really liked the sound of being dragged across the water by a kite and bouncing a kind of surfboard off the waves. Maybe, later in the year, she could give it a try.

The hotel was under control and the kitchen staff had nothing to report so she went for a walk around the grounds. Gravitating towards the Dolphin she was pleased to see that the propped branches remained green. Ruth was in one of the greenhouses filling seed trays. Apart from looking up and nodding slightly there was no other greeting. Zoe dismissed the thought of dismissing the woman and, instead, decided to try her aunt Sharon's tactic of talking plants.

"Morning. What are you planting?"

"Lettuce."

"Oh, we grow our own veg?"

"Yes. The hotel gets through a lot of it, and it is cheaper to grow it."

"What else do we grow?"

"Potatoes, tomatoes, radishes, cucumber, peppers, you name it. Some of it needs to be grown in the greenhouses but a lot of it is outside."

"You must show me sometime. I ought to learn." Sensing scepticism she added, "It wouldn't do me any harm to get my hands dirty."

That created a slight smile, so she plunged in and asked for an update on the Dolphin. Ruth took off her gloves, then placed her hands on her hips. Looking Zoe in the eye she smiled. "Yes, it is going to be okay. It will need support, but I believe that it will look like a dolphin again." Then she looked up to the window from which Zoe had fallen. "What happened? It is very strange that you managed to fall out and land that far away from the building."

"How long have you worked here?" asked Zoe, "Can we have a cuppa and a talk?"

Sitting in Ruth's shed on a packing crate wasn't what Zoe had had in mind, but she'd followed Ruth and stood there whilst Ruth put on the kettle. Hands cradling a cup of coffee she waited until Ruth sat down. Then she began.

"Previously you intimated to Natalie that my great grandfather, Walter, didn't believe my mother, or my grandmother about something, but you didn't say what. I think that whatever it was, it had something to do with what I've been experiencing. You also said all the staff changed after their deaths."

"Yes, apart from Miss Hardcastle."

"So, what didn't he believe?"

Ruth shifted on her packing crate. "I don't know exactly."

Zoe waited.

"It's just gossip."

"Were you working here at the time?"

"Yes."

"Then whatever it is, no matter how ridiculous, just blurt it out."

Ruth opened her mouth, but nothing came out.

Exasperated, Zoe said, "I have experienced being blasted out of that upstairs window, bouncing off that dolphin and landing on the grass, in the middle of the night. I was asleep. I didn't fall. I wasn't pushed. I didn't take a running jump. I experienced what my great great grandmother, Mary, experienced in 1944 when the back of the hotel was blown off by a German bomb. If you can beat that, go ahead." Then she burst into tears. At first Ruth just stared. Then she put down her mug and got to her feet. Gently, she sat down at Zoe's side and put an arm round her shoulder. Then she reached in her pocket and pulled out a surprisingly pristine packet of tissues and handed one to Zoe.

"Another?" and she held out a second tissue, which Zoe took.

"There was something in the cellar. Your mother, Linda, couldn't keep away. Your grandmother, well, it was like she knew why but wouldn't say and your great-grandfather just dismissed it all, as ridiculous: thought they were just being stupid hysterical women. Until the crash, when your mother..." She stopped mid-sentence, unsure whether to proceed, not knowing if Zoe knew.

Zoe looked up and met the other woman's eyes. "Yes, I know my mother caused the crash. What I don't understand is why."

"I'm sorry, love. I can't answer that. The only other person who was here back then is Doreen Hardcastle."

Over lunch Zoe had time to think. It seemed that Doreen was the only person who might be able to shed light on things, but she wasn't allowed to see her, even if she wanted to. Frustration and anger rising she pushed the last of her cheese and ketchup sandwich into her mouth and stomped across the hall to Doreen's apartment. She did a quick re-check of the desk and surrounding shelves but there was nothing that she hadn't seen before. Then she went from room to room. The apartment was smaller than hers with just the one bedroom. Zoe looked around at the décor and scowled. Blue and pink patterned borders ran round each room at ceiling and dado rail heights and matched the frilly swag curtains that blocked a large portion of the view. It was hideous. The whole apartment was stuck in a 1980's time-warp. The bedroom was similar but in green and orange and, to make things worse, there was frilly bedding to match the frilly curtains. It looked like a paint explosion at a jumble sale.

She started with Doreen's dressing table, carefully rummaging through the drawers. She felt uncomfortable going through her things but couldn't stop herself. The lower drawers just contained clothes, but the two smaller upper drawers had a variety of items, hairdryer, unopened packets of tights, clips, receipts, but no other paperwork. The chest of drawers was the same, with a large collection of hand-knitted jumpers. She couldn't imagine Doreen knitting.

In the built-in wardrobe she found a couple of boxes which she pulled down from the top shelf. The first contained a hat: the sort one might wear for a wedding. Zoe couldn't think what Doreen could possibly have worn that to; she wasn't aware that she had any friends, and she didn't think that she had any relatives. 'Wedding! Oh, No!' Zoe remembered that she was supposed to be helping-out at this weekend's wedding. She was meant to be downstairs, learning how to serve drinks. She had completely forgotten. She looked at her watch. By the time she had got herself ready, it wouldn't be worth it. Better that she help-out another time. Besides, she couldn't leave this now. Feeling vaguely guilty then reassuring herself that she was the boss, she could do what she liked, she returned to her search. The second box contained personal paperwork, bills, bank statements etc. Zoe put them back. She checked the lower back of the wardrobe, behind the skirts and dresses, but only found shoes.

Finally, she opened the shallow drawer on Doreen's bedside cabinet. In the back left hand corner was a diary, a familiar looking diary. It was pale blue with gold lettering embossed on the front, just like the other diaries she'd found. The year leapt out at her. It was the year that changed everything; the year she turned 14; the year her parents died; the year that defined her. Then she froze, could this just be one of Doreen's old diaries; after all it was a Dolphin Hotel diary. She rapidly flicked through its pages. Her great grandfather's writing leapt off the pages at her, neat and elegantly scripted. She sank to the floor. Yes, this was the missing diary. Emotions and questions, memories and fears, tumbled together and quickly reached spin cycle. Leaning back against Doreen's bed she shakily turned the pages to 16th March.

16th March – *Christine, Linda and Harry left today. 'Getting her away from here', they said. They didn't tell Linda they were taking her home. Ridiculous.*
Then, in a different pen, as if it had been added at a later date it simply said *CAR CRASH*

Then there was a gap of about a week

23rd March – *Harry's parents making funeral arrangements.*

Flicking back to previous entries she read
...

12th March - *ELIZABETH'S FUNERAL.*
Rest in peace, my love.

10th March – *Staff complaints. Linda wandering the hotel in the night. She is just as bad as her mother. More ridiculous nonsense. Christine says Linda is trying to get into the cellar. Well, the steps aren't there anymore and haven't been since the rebuild.*

So, the cellar steps used to be at the other side of the kitchen. Mary didn't know they had been moved. Why would she! It seemed that her grandmother had also been trying to get into the cupboard.

There were no further entries that were relevant. At the back of the diary was a list on a couple of pieces of folded paper, names and addresses, catering details: it looked like planning for Elizabeth's funeral arrangements.

She needed to see Walter's earlier diaries. Besides the one she was holding, she only had the one year, prior to the deaths, and those afterwards.

When Kyle turned up after finishing an emergency job for a holiday-let client, he found Zoe in the hotel office working her way through all the paperwork she could find, trying to find her great-grandfather's diaries. "He wouldn't have just suddenly started writing ten years ago. There must be others, before that," she told him.

"This is hotel stuff, wouldn't it be amongst Walter's personal paperwork?"

"There isn't anything in the apartment. I've been through every drawer, looked on every shelf, in the boxes under his bed, everywhere. His desk has some of the usual paperwork but no more diaries."

"Doesn't the hotel have any storage rooms it might be in?"

"Yes, but nope. No personal paperwork in there."

"What about Doreen's apartment? I don't know how you'd go on getting permission, but you could use the pretence of needing to look for hotel stuff."

"I've already looked."

"What! You've been through her things! Zoe."

"So! The woman tried to kill me."

"Still... the law may not see it that way."

"Lighten up. Apart from the diaries Karen found, there isn't anything else."

"Well, there must be paperwork somewhere. Everyone has paperwork."

"Right. I'm done," said Zoe. "You're here. This can wait. Let's go upstairs."

In the apartment she led him straight towards the bedroom door. "This, is the first time we have had the place to ourselves," she said with a grin.

Kyle looked a little alarmed, "I really need a shower."

"You smell just fine to me," said Zoe, putting her arms round his neck. "Maybe, we could both shower. I am sure I can find some plastic to wrap up this arm. The shower is quite large. It has a rain forest shower head, safety rail... and jets!"

"Ooh. I've fitted a couple of those and always wanted to try one."

"Well, so long as you get *something* out of the occasion..."

"Oh, I'm sure I shall – jets or not."

Whilst Kyle unlaced his boots and wrestled them off his feet Zoe headed into the bathroom. Soon, splashing water could be heard, and soft, slow, music. By the time he had removed his socks and T-shirt, she was back clutching a roll of cling-wrap.

"Here, help me wrap my arm."

As he did so she used her other hand to unbuckle his belt. Cast wrapped, he threw the roll onto the bed and took her face in his hands, gently kissing her on the lips. Then he ran his hands down her body, his thumbs stroking her nipples on the way past. Stopping at her waist, he undid her jeans then put his hands on her hips, pulling her towards him. She wrapped her arms around him, pressing her fingers into the firm muscles of his back, exploring each ridge and hollow, inhaling his day. His trapezius flexed under her fingers, warm and powerful. She reached down to remove his jeans, but he took her wrists and lifted her hands above her head. Then, he let go, leaving them there, and gently traced the contours of her arms, pausing where they joined her body before continuing down the seams of her cotton top to its hem. Then, slowly, centimetre by centimetre he raised the material up past her navel, over her breasts, her shoulders and her head, placing delicate little kisses on each centimetre of newly revealed flesh. Before freeing her arms, complicated by the plaster cast, he kissed her briefly then said, "Let's get wet..."

They shrugged and kicked and trampled their way out of their jeans and into the shower, a trail of underwear and clingwrap, marking the way.

"Well, I'm starving," said Kyle. "Have you got any food or am I taking you out?"

"How about you take me to The One-Eyed Seagull for a steak and ale pie."

"Then we come back here, yes?"

"Most definitely."

To the sound of Zoe's hairdryer Kyle searched through Walter's wardrobe and found a smart navy-blue shirt. It was a bit tight, and he was very glad that he didn't need to wear a tie with it, but it was better than the paint-splattered T-shirt he had been wearing all day. From his work rucksack he pulled out a spare pair of tan chinos.

The ensemble looked a little strange with his steel toed boots, but he felt cleaner and reasonably presentable. As soon as Zoe was ready, they headed out. In reception, Carl looked them both up and down and then grinned. "Have a good evening."

For a Sunday evening it was quite busy, and they had to weave their way along the pavement occasionally stepping into the road to get round people. "It will get busier as the year goes on," said Kyle, "When the tourist season picks up it can be a real challenge driving down here as there are so many people walking on the road. There has been talk of pedestrianising this stretch. I can't decide if that would be a good thing or not."

Zoe looked around her, up and down the street, and shrugged, "it might work, I could put tables out on the street, but then this side doesn't get any sun for most of the day. Hmm. I don't know."

"Believe me, the hotel does just fine without expanding into the street. Right, what can I get you?" he said, as he pushed open the door of the One-Eyed Seagull.

"A pint of stout to go with my steak and ale pie, I think."

They took a table in the back corner of the pub. From there they had a good view of the place, but by the time their food arrived they could no longer see the door for the number of people at the bar. To the clack of ketchup and brown sauce bottles being plonked on the table they asked what was going on; it had never been this busy when they had been in previously.

"There is a surprise 85th birthday party for one of our regulars," said the waitress. "We are expecting his mates to bring him in at around 7pm."

"Who is that then," said Kyle.

"John Baxter."

"No, he's 85! Really? I thought he must be way older than that." Zoe punched him on the arm, and he explained, "He is one of the men Natalie played dominos with. He knew your great grandfather."

Further comment was stifled as a rising ripple of sound came from the door. Shouts of 'surprise' and 'happy birthday' filled the air, and the great man was shepherded into the middle of the pub. People moved to allow him to sit at a table that had obviously been reserved for the occasion. Pints were passed over heads and to John's apparent disgust someone fired streamers in his direction. "If I'd wanted muck on me shoulders, I wouldn't have used me anti-dandruff shampoo. AND... there had better not be any candles, every breath is precious these days."

"Don't worry, they don't do cakes big enough at the bakery," said Sean.

The lights dimmed and 'Happy Birthday' started, gathering voices as it progressed.

"Oh, bollocks," said John as the crowd parted to allow passage of the pub owner holding a large very dark chocolate cake in the shape of a domino with 8 white dots on one half and 5 white dots on the other.

"Well, that's wrong for a start. You can't have 8 dots on a domino."

"Shut up and start cutting," said the landlord, as he handed John a large cake knife.

Phones clicked madly as John cut, hampered by the odd pat on the back and peck on the cheek.

"You realise this isn't going to do my blood sugar any good."

"By the time its shared round this lot, there won't be much left," said Sean.

"Let me take it, now," said the landlord, "I'll cut it up for you. Don't worry there will definitely be enough for everyone; I have another one out back."

As his cake disappeared John took a sip of his pint and eyed suspiciously the various parcels that were piling up on the table. "I hope there's no 'smellies' amongst this lot. A plain bar of soap is all you need."

"Just open them."

Rustling occurred amongst grumbling and purring, and a pile of coloured paper grew. With the last item revealed, John muttered a "Thanks everyone," and went back to his pint.

From their corner Zoe and Kyle noted that the guests were having more fun than the birthday boy. "Wait here," said Kyle and disappeared to the bar, leaving Zoe playing with a soggy bit of her plaster cast. On his way back he stopped and handed John a packet of Cheese and Onion crisps and wished him a happy birthday. A grateful John grasped Kyle's hand and shook it enthusiastically. Then he pushed back his chair and followed Kyle over to where Zoe was sitting and sat down.

"Best present of the lot that. Thanks. You're Zoe aren't you, friends of that there Natalie. Lovely lass. Is she not here?"

They explained that she had gone back home, and that Zoe was staying to learn how to run the Dolphin. They chatted for a while as John's party continued in the background. When Kyle went to get another round of drinks Zoe broached the subject of her great grandfather and what John might know about the time of her great grandmother's funeral and the car accident which killed her parents and grandmother adding, when she saw his reluctance, that she knew that her mother had tried to get out of the moving car causing the accident.

"This isn't the time or place, lass. Perhaps I could come to the hotel, and we can talk there. I don't have much to say. As I told Natalie, your great grandfather was several years older than me, and we moved in different circles. He was well liked though; I can tell you that. Although, there were folks who thought him harsh, the way he dismissed your grandmother's fears, and those of the other women in the family. Anyway, best get back to looking like I'm enjoying myself."

Chapter Twenty-Eight

Kyle was the first to wake and lay for a while staring at the ceiling. He would have to get up shortly as he needed to go home before going to work. A gentle sigh came from somewhere amongst the covers; Zoe was stirring. An arm appeared and a hand pushed back the flop of blond hair covering her face. There was a brief glimpse of spikey regrowth before she arranged her hair to cover it. When their eyes met, she smiled. "Were you staring at the hole in my head?"

"Actually, I've been staring at the ceiling. Have you been up there?" he said, pointing. Set in an expanse of off-white Artex swirls was a loft hatch. When she shook her head, he leapt out of bed and grabbed a chair. Placing it under the hatch he climbed up and pulled back the securing latch. The hatch dropped onto his waiting hand. In the void above, a loft ladder was visible with cord attached. He stepped down off the chair and moved it to one side. Then he pulled on the cord until he could reach the ladder, unfolded it and let it slide to the floor.

At the door he tried the light switches, finding one that lit up the loft.

"Do you want to go up first?"

"Yes," she said searching the floor and pulling on clothes, wincing as she did so.

"Here, let me help." As he gently fed her plastered wrist into her T-shirt, he laughed. "This is different. I would never have guessed that putting your clothes 'on' could be so, arousing." He pulled her towards him and pressed his lips into hers.

"Shame I've got to go to work."

"Yes, but you'll be back this evening," she said with a grin and began to crab her way, one handed, up the ladder.

"Be careful... Look, wait until this evening."

"I can manage. I'll take it slowly. I don't want to fall!"

"Is it boarded?" he asked as she reached the top of the ladder. She nodded and climbed up out of sight, but she didn't get far. When Kyle climbed up beside her, he exclaimed, "Bloody hell. I'm surprised the ceiling hasn't come down."

As far as the eye could see, which wasn't far as the view was obscured, there were boxes: large boxes, small boxes, tall boxes and thin boxes. Some had labels, others didn't. It was impossible to see the extent of the loft space as the one ceiling light didn't penetrate the depths and there were shadows everywhere from the boxes. Kyle guessed that the space extended at least the length of the room below and probably over the adjoining bedroom and the rest of the apartment. Hopefully, the rest of the space wasn't as full as this. Hopefully, everything had been stacked near the hatch because it was easy to get at.

"Look. I've got to go to work. Let me help you down. I'll pop back at lunchtime if I can. Otherwise, I'll see you this evening," he said as he moved some of the boxes away from the light fitting. "This place is a death trap."

Zoe didn't move.

"I'm serious. You can't stay up here on your own."

"I'll be fine."

"Please," he said more forcefully. "Come down."

Reluctantly she stepped towards the hatch and allowed him to guide her down the ladder. At the bottom he closed the hatch, switched off the light and kissed her again. Then he left, saying that he'd be back at lunchtime if he had time.

She stood for a moment, listening. Then she opened the door, crossed the hall to Doreen's apartment and nudged the mouse on the security camera. She watched as Kyle had a brief word with the receptionist before heading out of the door. Then she headed back to the loft and pulled down the ladder. At the top she stood for a while, slightly over-awed by the task ahead but itching to get going. Taking the lid off the nearest box she found she couldn't see inside very well. Sliding it with her good arm, until it dropped onto the floor, she pushed it under the ceiling light. It was full of bank statements, personal ones. After a brief inspection of the top few, she put them back in the box, which appeared to contain more of the same. She shut the box and pushed it to one side, pulling another box and letting it drop to the floor. This one contained utility bills. The next one was filled with old driving documents, MOT certificates and insurance forms. The next one contained more bank statements. Then she realised that it was one she had already looked in. She needed to label them. She could also do with clothes she didn't mind getting dirty as there was dust everywhere. This was going to be a problem as she had few clothes with her. If only Natalie was coming back up at the weekend.

As she washed her hands and filled the kettle it occurred to her that Toby wouldn't just be going down but coming back up. Maybe she could ask him to bring some of her things. In the meantime, perhaps one of her great-grandfather's shirts would work to cover up her own clothes. Catching her toast as it popped up from the toaster, she took a bite and had more or less finished it by the time she had gathered anything to spread on it. She put another slice in to toast and sat at the table sipping her coffee. There was an unbelievable amount of stuff in the loft. She hoped it wasn't all going to be paperwork. How much could one person collect over the years. Of course, it wasn't necessarily all Walter's, there could be other family items up there. It would be interesting finding out. She crunched on her second slice and wondered what Natalie was up to. Then she thought about her own degree; it would be a shame to let all that work be for nothing.

Stuffing a notepad and pen, felt-tip, and torch into a shoulder bag, she climbed back into the loft. Having re-checked and labelled the first boxes she shone the torch into the bits the ceiling light didn't penetrate. Inching a stack of three boxes to one side, with her feet and hips, she found that there was a narrow passage between the floor to ceiling stacks. Threading her way through she discovered that it turned left and there was a doorway giving access to another roof section. It was only possible to walk upright down the centre of the roof trusses. Shining her torch into different areas she spotted another ceiling light and traced its wire to a switch. Now she could see. There were boxes everywhere but not stacked as deeply or as high. So many boxes, but then a hotel would have a ready supply of deliveries, generally arriving in boxes. Continuing she found that the loft area was u-shaped. Going as far as she could she found another hatch in the floor. This one was bolted from the inside. She knelt down and, hanging onto an attached handle, warily lowered it. She peered down. There was a desk and a computer screen. What she was looking at was Doreen's desk. Shutting and bolting the hatch she went back to inspecting the boxes. She found another light and a light switch and switched that on. Here the boxes contained books: children's books. She crouched on the floor and opened the flyleaf of a book on dinosaurs. Inside was a label, printed in red and gold with black lettering. Beardshaw Primary School, Arithmetic First Prize, presented to Christine Brammar aged 10 years, 12th December 1964. Zoe flicked the pages back and forth. The book had belonged to her grandmother. She sat for a while pulling items from the box. There were other books, some of which were maths textbooks. She hadn't realised that her grandmother had been that clever. There was page after page of marked exercises: 10 out of 10 with the very rare 9 out of 10. In fact, she hadn't ever thought of her grandmother as having gone to school at all. Logically she must have but it hadn't been something that she had thought about. Yet her grandmother must have been a little girl at some point, and that period of her life was all there, in that box. Amazing. Would she find her mother's childhood here too? Unlikely, as her mother hadn't lived at The Dolphin. She'd grown up elsewhere, at her grandparents' house, but what happened to all those things? When her parents and grandmother died, other people had sorted out the family homes; she'd been too young and too distraught. Those days were just a blur now; an enormous dark sinkhole that swallowed and buried her; its sides steep and slippery ready to re-bury her at the slightest attempt to surface. Her family had gone. Her world had gone, taking her childhood with it. Others had made decisions for her and had taken and disposed of what had remained of the family home. Had it all just... gone? She'd been handed some boxes of family photos, and some jewellery, and most of the contents of her bedroom, but she didn't remember anything else. Frantically she started opening boxes at random. What about *her* childhood things, stuff that her mother had kept in a cupboard on the landing, games and old dolls? Random items came to mind; a shoe box with dolls clothes, Woody and her set of Teletubbies, Pokemon cards and her My Little Pony. Nothing. There was nothing here of hers.

Upset and annoyed, she abandoned the loft and went for a shower. Memories of the evening, showering with Kyle, took her thoughts elsewhere and by the time she went down to reception for her morning meeting she felt much happier. A couple of cancellation bookings had been filled by new ones. One of their suppliers had gone bankrupt and the search was on for a suitable replacement. Two of the housekeeping staff had called in sick and it was going to be difficult servicing all the rooms in a suitable time frame. Zoe listened to all this, then realised that there was an expectation to offer solutions, especially to the latter.

"Could I help with the rooms? It is probably good that I learn. I won't be a lot of help with this arm, but I can strip beds one handed."

"Oh, that would be fantastic," said Jackie, the Housekeeping Manager.

"It will help me get to know you all better too," said Zoe. That seemed to go down well, and it was agreed that she would join them later in the morning.

Her signature was needed on a couple of items and a guest had asked to speak to her. This latter was alarming but turned out to be a desire to express gratitude for an enjoyable stay, and maybe a chance to tell others that not only had they stayed in the hotel that had been in the papers and on television, but 'yes', they also 'knew' the hotel owner. She smiled and shook their hands and said she hoped they would come again, and just as she thought that she was getting away they asked if they could take their picture with her. So, she ran her hand through her hair, beamed and posed for a 'selfie' with them. Passing guests saw, and before she could escape she had posed and been posted, hash tagged and shared unknown times.

Kitted out, in a set of The Dolphin's trousers and tunic, Zoe pushed a loaded trolley out of the lift on the 2nd floor and followed Jill, her trainer, to the first of the bedrooms. Jill was a lively bubbly individual who almost bounced when she walked, not pretty, but charismatic, and Zoe instantly took to her. Jill knocked on the door, listened briefly, then opened it. Inside, the room was a scattered mess of bedding and towels.

"Right," said Jill. "If you strip the bed I will start the bathroom. The bedding goes in the laundry bag on the trolley. If you find anything left by the guest, pop it there by the door. We will bag and label it on our way out. If you find anything broken then we need to make a note in this book, for maintenance.

As the morning wore on Zoe honed her bed stripping technique. In the rooms that still had guests staying she learnt how to straighten the beds whilst taking care of guest items on the bedside tables, and how to cope with beds that were covered in the guests' belongings. Rooms differed: some were neat and tidy, others looked like there had been an explosion. Some even had the furniture re-arranged! When restocking the minibars she was amazed at some of the items in them, not supplied by the hotel. One had a pair of trainers in it. Jill wasn't in the least bit surprised.

"I think the worst thing I found was a severed toe," she said.

"What?"

"Yes. Apparently, the guest slipped in the shower with a glass of champagne. His partner had put the toe in the fridge with ice from the champagne ice-bucket but forgot about it when the ambulance arrived. Yes, it was a real fun challenge cleaning up that room; the toe wasn't the only cut."

Zoe enjoyed her morning. It seemed that Jill and the other housekeeping staff competed with each other to see who could do the most rooms and then inspected each other's work, deducting points for anything that had been missed or done badly. She was really impressed and intended to say so at the next meeting. They were a happy bunch and worked well together. She enjoyed working with them and she enjoyed the work, and it surprised her. When lunch time came, she happily joined them in their staff room and felt ridiculously pleased when Jill told the rest of them how well she had done. She planned to do a shift a week and to do the same with the other hotel teams, at least until she was familiar with what they all did.

In the afternoon, Zoe and Jill finished off the rooms and then put the laundry sacks outside, under cover, for collection by the cleaning company. Then they restocked the trolley. By 3pm they were finished for the day and Zoe was exhausted.

Back in the apartment Zoe sat for a while but then went and changed. She couldn't wait to get back into the loft. She felt shattered so decided to limit her visit to labelling boxes whilst looking for diaries. The checking and labelling didn't last long. She opened a box to find an assortment of photo albums and a scattering of loose photographs. Kneeling on the floor she lay an album in front of her and opened it. A photo slid out and she found that others were loose. Tiny corner fixings which once held the pictures in place were now no longer sticking. The album was neatly laid out with descriptions and dates under each photograph but, if she wasn't careful, she wouldn't know what photo was meant to go where. She closed the album carefully and pulled out another. This was newer and the photos were slotted into plastic dockets. She turned the pages, recognising her grandmother, and her mother as a teenager. She recognised the garden they were standing in as that of her grandparents. It was lovely to see it again. Her memories of it were vague and from a different time. She turned the pages, memories flooding back. Tears fell and she had no idea how long she crouched there looking at the photos. When her feet protested she painfully straightened her legs and delicately got to her feet. She put the albums back in the box and pushed it towards the hatch.

When Kyle turned up, she was horrified to realise that she had completely forgotten he'd said he might stop by at lunch time. He had been annoyed when reception had told him she was making beds, but then amused by the thought.

"I forgive you," he said. "So, what was it like being a chambermaid?"

"Housekeeper, if you don't mind."

"Suit yourself but I prefer to visualise you in a blouse, short skirt and tiny pinny. Please ... don't take that away from me and ..., if you have a feather duster..." he said, pulling her towards him.

"I don't, but I can probably find a J-cloth."

"How about a sponge?"

She grinned and took his hand.

When he discovered that she had been back in the loft he was livid, but relieved that she was okay, and soon calmed down. "So, did you find anything interesting up there?" He unfolded his napkin and placed it on his lap, dolphin motif uppermost.

"At the moment just family photographs and some of my grandmother's schoolbooks – textbooks and the like. She was well clever at school. I hadn't realised. She went to Beardshaw Primary School. Do you know it?"

"Yes. I went there, and so did Toby."

They chatted for a while, waiting for their food to arrive. It was both odd and exhilarating dining in her own restaurant. It wasn't the first time she'd done so but this was a meal for two and the staff treated them with both deference and friendly familiarity; trying to impress whilst making them feel 'at home'. The food was excellent, and the staff ensured their wine glasses didn't run dry.

Chapter Twenty-Nine

After her morning meeting she went back up to the loft until her phone told her she had 30 minutes to get ready. At 11.30 the apartment phone rang. Her visitor was in reception.

After initial greetings she offered her guest a seat and a drink, which was declined, and said, "So, what do we do?"

"Well," said Belinda, "I will need to go down to the cellar, but having walked through the hotel I can tell you that I didn't notice anything to be concerned about in the areas I passed through. I would have preferred not to have any prior knowledge. By that I mean what I have read in the papers etc., and to come here with an open mind. I do have to tell you that your grandmother invited me here and spoke to me. The hotel was very different back then. By that I mean, the atmosphere and ... your grandmother ... she was anxious and agitated and, how can I say this..."

"Go on...," said Zoe.

"Not alone. Something had 'latched on' to her. It was weak but desperate and very sad."

"When was this?"

"Probably 1970, 71. She was only a young woman, but old enough to leave home and... I ... advised her to do so."

"And she left?"

"Yes. I think your great grandfather was relieved. He thought she was crazy; had no time for her 'dramatics', as he called them. Your great grandmother was upset, but helped her to leave, not knowing what else to do; her 'dramatics' were upsetting not just the kitchen staff but guests too."

Zoe collected the key and a torch and led Belinda to the kitchen. Ignoring the silent disapproval of the kitchen staff, she unlocked the cellar door and switched on the light. At the bottom of the steps, they stood in silence for a while, Zoe allowing Belinda to take in the scene. Then Belinda walked up and down examining the corners of the space. She turned to Zoe and shrugged. "It is good. Whatever was here, isn't anymore. The space is calm and there is just a lingering... sense of contentment. Where is the cave?"

In the recess she handed Belinda the torch she'd brought for the occasion, whilst she reached into the wall and operated the catch. Then she pushed on the door. It was heavy and scraped on the floor. Why the Police had closed it again, she had no idea. She placed a wedge under its edge to keep it open.

They made their way carefully down the steps: Zoe wishing she had brought two torches. At the bottom she swung the torch in an arc, locating the place she guessed Natalie and Toby had found Megan's body. She had wanted to see this place but been prevented by the Police. Then, when the Police had gone, she hadn't wanted to come down alone and no-one would accompany her, until now. Wishing there was power to the ceiling lights she stepped carefully forward, Belinda close at her side. Without speaking the woman stepped forward and stood looking at the spot where Megan had lain. She seemed to be saying a silent prayer. A solemn Zoe hung her head and felt a cold lonely desolation seep into her soul. How long had Megan been trapped down here before she died?

Belinda finally turned and faced Zoe, a rueful smile on her face. "All is calm here too, now. There is a lingering sadness, but the soul that was here has gone. 'Moved on'. There is no-one to talk to down here. No answers to be gained."

Back in the apartment Zoe related the events and despite her intention of 'giving nothing away' to test Belinda, she told her everything. It was good to have someone to talk to. Over a cup of tea Belinda listened, asked the odd question, and made sympathetic noises in all the right places. When Doreen was mentioned, Belinda shook her head. She didn't have any answers. Edna too, needed to 'move on'.

"Before I go, may I see the room where the bomb hit?"

"Oh, of course, if it is empty. I haven't been in it since that night."

After a trip to reception, key in hand, Zoe led Belinda up to the room at the back of the hotel. She stood in the doorway as Belinda strolled around, stopping in various places. At one point she looked out of the window. Then she moved to the centre of the room and closed her eyes, hands clasped lightly together in front of her. Just when Zoe thought the woman might have fallen asleep, she opened her eyes and looked directly at Zoe, "No, all is good here now. The room is at peace."

As she passed through reception, after showing Belinda out, Karen called her into the office.

"I've just had a call from the hospital. Doreen has asked to see me. I am going to go this afternoon if that is okay. They said 4pm. Would you be able to man the desk until I get back?"

"Of course, yes."

As she headed back upstairs, she wondered what she had agreed to. It might be her hotel, but there was so much she didn't know. The thought of taking charge was quite alarming.

When she presented herself at 3.30 Karen laughed. "You look terrified. Remember, be polite, show interest and if you don't know what to do say you don't know but you'll find out. Then talk to the relevant staff. I probably won't be there long. Have fun!"

No sooner had Karen left than the phone rang. She stared at it in alarm, then answered it, "Dolphin Hotel, Hello."

"Is that reception?"

"Er, yes."

"Could I have some more towels please? A bath and 2 hand towels."

"Certainly." The line went dead, and Zoe put the phone down. Okay, she knew where the towels were kept. She went and quickly got what she needed and headed for the stairs, then stopped. She had no idea what room. She went back to the phone. Was there a last number redial or call log? She pushed some likely buttons but didn't get her answer. Then the phone rang again. "Hello, reception. What can I do for you?"

"Can I have a bathmat as well, please?"

It was the same voice and now she noticed that the room number was flashing up on the display. "Of course. I'll be right up." Breathing a sigh of relief, she collected a bathmat and headed for room 27.

Back at reception a small queue had formed and the person at the head of it was angrily stabbing at the bell on the desk. The doorman, Derek, was standing at his side looking agitated.

"Sorry to keep you waiting, just supplying extra towels. How can I help you?"

"I have a room booked for two nights. The name's Johnson." When she and Natalie had checked in, the receptionist checked the screen, but she'd seen Carl fill in a book on the desk. She opened it now and saw that a Mr and Mrs Johnson were booked into room 19. She handed Mr Johnson the key from the rack behind the counter and gave him directions. Derek disappeared into the lift with the couple's luggage, as they made for the stairs.

The next person at the desk just wanted a local map. That she could deal with. She was even able to point out where the cinema was.

When Derek returned, he waited until the last of the guests had been dealt with and then quietly but politely pointed out that she should just have phoned room service about the towels and that there was a buzzer on the counter to let him know if new guests had arrived. He also acted as porter, as well as doorman. After that he hung around until Karen returned, offering advice as needed. Zoe was very grateful. Karen didn't have much to report from her visit to Doreen, she hadn't stayed long, but would go again. Doreen was doing okay. Zoe was relieved to hand the hotel back to Karen and escape back to the apartment. She had a lot to learn. She sensed that Karen hadn't been that impressed with what she'd done, appearing a little abrasive.

When Kyle arrived, he asked her what was wrong, and pointed out that Karen may be concerned about Doreen getting better, fearing that she may get demoted. Zoe dismissed both the idea and the concern. She had no intention of putting Doreen back in charge of the hotel. She didn't even want her back in the building.

Chapter Thirty

After her unhappy stint on reception, she determined to learn what she needed to know. At 8am she joined Carl, at the front desk, and asked him to teach her. She watched him check-in and check-out guests, answer the phone, deal with queries and complaints, and delegate to other teams, as needed. He took her through the paperwork and showed her how to work the different programmes on the computer. By lunchtime she felt more confident and was greeting guests with a smile and a 'how may I help you?'.

Whilst she was dealing with a guest the phone rang and Carl answered it. She looked up, realising from the conversation, that the call was for her. He handed her the receiver and took over dealing with the guest. The call was from a nurse at the hospital, saying that Doreen wanted to see the hotel owner, if she would be kind enough to visit. Surprised, and curious, Zoe agreed. The visit was again arranged for 4pm.

As the day wore on, she wondered why Doreen wanted to see her. Probably, she was just trying to get Zoe to forgive her for pushing her down the stairs, hoping a word from her would help when she went to court. Zoe couldn't wait to tell her she was wrong. Had she also pushed her great-grandmother down the stairs? Why else would she have Walter's diary which clearly stated that she was the one who had found her at the bottom of the stairs. Had she been questioned at the time? She needed to find the rest of his diaries to see if there had been any other 'incidents' prior to that.

At 4pm she pressed the ward bell and asked for Staff Nurse Collins. There was a click, and the door opened. Staff Nurse Collins led her into the ward, chatting merrily as she went. Apparently, Doreen had brightened and become more communicative following the visit of the other lady from the hotel.

"Karen," Zoe supplied.

"Yes. Karen. She is so much calmer today. She specifically asked for you. Saying you would understand." Zoe raised her eyebrows, but the nurse didn't see. She was led to a side room. The nurse tapped briefly on the door, then pushed it open. The room was painted an off-white with a landscape mural on the wall above the bed. It was bright and overly light but thankfully missed being clinical. As Zoe and Doreen made eye contact the nurse hovered in the doorway. "I can stay if you like. There is a buzzer on the wall if you want me."

Zoe appraised Doreen. She looked her in the eye and knew it was just Doreen in there; Edna, had gone.

"That is okay," she said as Doreen nodded. The nurse left, leaving the door wide open.

Doreen had lost weight. Her hair looked slightly longer, but that was possibly because it was now straight. It was also dull and had a distinct grey demarcation at the roots. She looked older somehow.

"Thank you for coming. How are you?"

Zoe was about to retort with 'How would you be if you'd been pushed down a flight of stairs and needed brain surgery,' but she didn't. Instead, she said, "I'm doing okay thank you. My head doesn't hurt anymore but the scar is still tender. I can't use my wrist, but it is getting better and so long as I don't breathe too deeply my ribs aren't too bad. How are you?"

"It has been a terrible experience. I was horrified by what I did. I never meant to hurt you. It wasn't me. You've got to believe me."

"I do."

"It was like watching a movie..."

"I know."

The conversation was suddenly interrupted by a nurse at the door. "I'm sorry," she said, addressing Zoe, "but I don't think you should be in here. Aren't you the hotel owner?"

"Yes,"

"I don't think that the two of you should be speaking. Please, you need to leave. Now."

In the corridor the nurse said she didn't think, from a legal point of view, that the victim should be talking to her alleged aggressor. Perhaps Zoe should talk to her solicitor. She also didn't think it was helpful for Doreen's condition. Staff Nurse Collins should never have phoned.

Outside, Zoe considered calling George Titherington, but then dismissed the idea. If she and Doreen wanted to see each other then it was nobody else's business.

On her way back to the hotel she stopped at the Police Station and asked for an update. She was lucky, D I Bolton was there and available to talk to her. They were waiting on the results of DNA testing. They had matched Megan's with both Zoe's DNA and Walter's hair sample DNA, obtained from his hairbrush. They were now awaiting permission to exhume 'Edna' and check her DNA with relatives they had traced. He was glad she was there. Would she give permission for a transcript of Megan's diary, from the cave, to be given to the press? Zoe asked for a copy and said she would let him know, after she'd read it.

Clutching an envelope with a copy of the transcript she headed back to the Dolphin. Entering reception Carl asked if he could have a word with her, in the office. When she stepped inside, he closed the door. He opened his mouth and then shut it again, shuffling from foot to foot.

"I don't know how to put this, *but*, there have been complaints."

"What sort of complaints?"

"About Karen."

Surprised, she waited.

"Staff have been complaining that she is snapping at them. One of them has put in a formal complaint of bullying."

Her heart sank. This was something serious and something she couldn't ignore. It didn't sound like Karen at all. She didn't know what she was meant to do about it, and she couldn't ask Karen for advice.

"Do you want to talk to Jez?"

"He is one of the bar staff, isn't he?" She knew full-well who he was. He was the one she had been flirting with on the night she and Natalie arrived in the hotel, and she was fairly certain she had been rude to him.

"Yes. Hear his side of the story before talking to Karen. He isn't on duty at the moment. He'll be back in the morning."

"Right, yes. I'll talk to him then."

Eager to read the transcript she ran up the stairs and was soon back in the apartment. There were 11 typed pages. The first set were photographs of the original sheets laid out on a table. They appeared to have been invoices and crate labels that Megan had written on. She looked at the page with the photographs, but they were difficult to read. So, she turned to the transcript and, taking a deep breath, started reading.

It has been 6 hours, I think. I am hoarse. Edna pushed me down and locked the door. Then the lights went out. I have my torch, but the batteries won't last long. Thankfully there are some candles and matches. It is a real struggle to strike them. My arm looks broken, and I am having to hold down the matchbox with my foot. I am saving my torch to be able to see to relight the candles. My head and my ribs hurt too.

I forgot to wind my watch. Stupid, stupid, stupid. I don't know how long I have been asleep.

I have food and water and candles.

The drink is running out, but I am able to collect water from the walls, in parts.

I think it has been 3 days. Am I to die here. Why has no-one come to let me out.

I am Megan Brammar. I was born 3rd July 1926. My parents are Mary and David Brammar. My father died 5 years ago. I have 2 brothers, Walter who is away fighting the Nazis and my little brother Jack who is a fisherman. I hope he is alright. He was in the cove under the winch,

when the roof collapsed. Mother went up to see and left the cave door open. That is how Edna, Jack's 'beau,' found the entrance. She is too old for him but as there aren't any boys her own age she has set her sights on him. I hate her. I ran past her up the steps and locked her in to stop her telling anyone about the stuff down here. I went to tell ma. Ma said to let her out. Said she would speak to her when she had put out the upstairs light, which was showing as the window had been broken by the bomb and the curtain was flapping. When I opened the cave door, Edna shot out. We fought and she pushed me. I grabbed her gas mask strap, but it broke, and I fell down the steps. The little bitch closed the door and blocked it somehow. I am trapped. I don't know what will happen when the food runs out. Surely someone will come. My head really hurts. Where is mother?

I think I hear the tide when it is in. Two tides equal a day.

All the food has run out, except for the tins but I don't have anything to open them with.

I snapped off a stalacktite and used it and a stone to pierce a tin. I cut my finger but at least I have some food. I have been using cigarettes as lights. They don't last long but they are saving the candles and there are countless boxes of them here.

I don't think anyone is coming. Are they all dead? Have we been invaded? I bang and bang on the cellar door and scream for all I am worth. I have no more tears.

Marking the tides on the wall, to count the days. Think it's been 8 days.

Tides lower now. I don't hear them as readily.

Glad of the cigarettes. As well as the light, smoking them passes the time and I get a little warmth from inhaling them. I am beginning to enjoy the whisky too. Mother wouldn't like me drinking it.

I tried climbing down among the fallen rocks, but I had to come back as I just made more fall. It is too dark to see much and there are too many shadows. I slipped once and nearly fell over an edge. I am thinking about risking it. If I land in the sea at least someone might find my body, and all this will be over.

Couldn't do it. Couldn't risk it. I dropped a rock down, but it sounded to land on more rock. I set fire to some .... and let it fall, but all I could see was a dead end; no evidence of an updraught, or a way out. The sides are too steep and slippery. I couldn't climb back up. My left arm is useless and my head throbs so. Also, I am weak. I have lost so much weight.

So thirsty

I am sorry God. Please forgive me. I shouldn't have locked her in. It was wrong, I know, but I did let her out.

Licking the walls

That was it. There was nothing more. Zoe put the pages down and wiped her eyes. What a horrible way to die. Suddenly she felt the need to get out of the hotel. She needed fresh air. She needed space. '*Licking the walls.*'

Down on the beach she turned into the wind and ran. She ran, forcing her legs to pump, despite the pain in her ribs. She ran, splashing through the surf at the edge of the sea, soaking her shoes and her jeans. She ran, putting gulls to flight. She ran, until she couldn't run any more. Then she stopped, hands pressed against her ribs, willing the stabbing pains to subside, gasping in air. Then, bent double, she sobbed. Then she dropped to her knees and cried out, "Megan. Megan. I am so, so sorry...": her words, lost on the wind, her tears lost in the sea. No-one to hear her cries. No-one to come raise her up. No-one to comfort her.

Kyle couldn't believe the change in her. He noticed as soon as he walked through the door. She was pale and solemn and vaguely dishevelled. He walked slowly towards her, uncertain. She just pointed at the papers on the table. He glanced back at her then picked them up. He read, then reread bits. Then he placed the pages back on the table and took her hand. They sat for a while together until Kyle said, "Come on. Let's get something to eat."

Chapter Thirty-One

At 11am Zoe went down to the bar and found Jez. The bar was empty and so they sat in a table at the window. Feeling slightly uncomfortable she opened by saying that she understood he had made a complaint about Karen, the hotel manager. Would he like to tell her what happened.

He had been clearing glasses when Karen came to speak to Tony, the head barman. He hadn't heard her and turned as she passed. Their elbows clashed and he lost a glass off the tray he was holding. It hit the floor but didn't break. He apologised to her, even though she was equally to blame, but she just turned and said, "What are you, the village idiot!" Then on her way out of the bar she told him to get his hair cut, he looked like a 'Nancy boy'.

"A what?" said Zoe. "I don't even know what that means."

"She meant I look gay."

"So...!"

"She didn't mean it as a compliment."

"I get that. I will have a word with her."

"Is that it? You'll have a word!"

"To begin with. Did anybody else witness the event?"

"Only the elderly man from Room 43, but he just laughed, and he is deaf, so I doubt he heard what she said."

"Okay. Leave it with me." She stood up then said, "I am spending time working with the different teams to get to know them and to learn what they do. When would be a good time to do a shift in here?"

"How about Sunday morning; it usually starts off quiet and then gets busier, ease you in gently."

"Maybe, I am thinking of going back home, I need to collect some things. I will let you know."

On her way back to her apartment she passed a laundry trolley. The room door next to it was open so she stepped inside and said hello to the two ladies who were in there. They chatted briefly, the women seemingly pleased that she had taken the time to talk to them and she was pleased that she had remembered their names.

She put on her great-grandfather's shirt and pulled down the loft ladder. The rest of his diaries must be up there somewhere. She just had to work her way through the boxes methodically. Logically, the diaries were probably put up here anything up to twenty years ago. She went straight to the middle. She checked the contents of a couple of boxes and looked for dates. The first box had stuff from 2011. She moved on. The next box had insurance documents dated 2005, for a boat. He had a boat! She wondered what had happened to that and if it was now hers. Gaining no further clues, she pushed the box to one side. She was in the right area. The last diary she had was dated 2006. She looked at the surrounding boxes. There were five that were the same; probably packed at the same time. She pulled them to her, one at a time, opening them and glancing at the contents. Then she crawled under the eaves and pulled out the last one, hooking it with her foot when it got wedged on a rafter. She opened it. Bingo. Diaries. There was a full set – 1985 to 2005.

With only one fully usable arm she was unable to carry the box down from the loft. Instead, she used the front of Walter's shirt as a sling. Holding its edge in her teeth she took five of the diaries down. Then, bit by bit, she brought the rest.

Over the years the design of the diaries had varied slightly. They were all pale blue with the hotel logo on the front in gold, but the fonts had changed along with the advertising on the backs.

Settling herself down with a coffee she opened the first diary. In 1985 Walter would have been 58 years old and her grandmother, Christine, 32 years old. The medium, Belinda, had told her that Christine left home in 1969 at the age of 16 years. So, there would only have been Walter and Elizabeth living here in 1985. The diary was an interesting social history but didn't contain anything that answered any of the questions Zoe had. She started on 1986. As she read, she began to realise that Walter and Christine had quite a busy social life and it didn't all revolve around the hotel. They often had weekends away, generally to locations in Europe. Paris seemed to be a favourite. She kept reading and became increasingly saddened by the fact that there was very little mention of their daughter Christine and none of their granddaughter Linda. Why was her mother not mentioned? Surely there would have been some interest in their grandchild; Walter was so meticulous about recording other aspects of their life. Then, in the 1992 diary, in the week before Christmas, he wrote,

Friday 18th December – Elizabeth has again invited Christine and family for Christmas dinner. I told her she is wasting her time.

Then:

Monday 21st December – Now Elizabeth is suggesting we all dine out on Christmas Day, saying Christine would come then. I am not paying for us all to have Christmas Dinner elsewhere when we have a perfectly good home, and a hotel to dine in, if we choose.

Friday 25th December – Miserable day with Elizabeth barely speaking to me. We shall be eating turkey until next Christmas. We should have eaten in the hotel dining room, but Elizabeth said the pair of us would look pathetic and just set the staff talking again. I really don't understand why she cares what they think. They aren't paid to think. Gifts exchanged – Sailing book for me, perfume for her.

The phone rang and Zoe answered, expecting it to be reception with an issue to report. It was reception but to say that there was a John Baxter to see her. At first, she had no idea who he was, then she remembered his party in the pub and smiled. "Send him up."

Handing him a mug of tea she sat down opposite and asked him how he was, and how he had managed to get all his presents home.

"I had help. Some of them are still at the pub. I said they could raffle them."

"No! Really?"

"What do I want with shampoo? Anyway, what did you want to know?"

"I guess I want to know why my mother tried to jump out of a moving car and what happened when my great grandmother died. Was that an accident?" There, she'd said it.

"Do I take it there was something suspicious about your great grandmother's death? I don't remember any questions being raised at the time. I didn't go to the funeral, I wasn't that close, but there was the usual talk, 'Isn't it sad', etc. Nothing though, about it being suspicious."

"Okay. Good."

"As for why your mother tried to get out of the car, I don't know. Talk was that she was trying to get back here, some obsession with a cupboard in the kitchen. Walter thought she was crazy. Got right fed up with her. Said she was as bad as her mother. Both talking rubbish. Apparently, your grandmother, Christine, had been a real handful in her teens and Walter was glad when she left, although it broke Elizabeth's heart."

He didn't have any more to add. It all sounded very familiar and was what she had been expecting. She thanked him and promised to join a game of dominoes next time they were both in the One-Eyed Seagull.

Somehow, she managed to miss seeing Karen for the rest of the day. She was relieved as she wasn't looking forward to the encounter. She had no idea how to deal with Jez's accusation. '*Licking the walls*' came unbidden into her head and she felt herself sinking. She took a deep breath to clear her mind. She needed a distraction. Picking up the next diary she started reading, but the phrase wouldn't leave her alone, '*Licking the walls*'. She wished Kyle was there, but he was at work. She wondered what Natalie was doing. It was 3pm; she would probably be in a lecture. University seemed a lifetime away. None of them had called her since they had left. Then she noticed a flashing green light on the phone.

How long had that been there? She pressed play, "Hi love. How are you doing? Give us a call. I'll try again later." It was Aunt Sharon and there were 3 more, similar messages. Zoe picked up the receiver and dialled. It rang and rang, and she thought it would go to answerphone but then a familiar voice said, "Is that you, Zoe?"

It was such a relief to speak to Sharon. When Zoe told her about the transcript from the cave Sharon got angry. "They just gave it you, just like that, with no explanation or warning. You might never have known Megan, but she is still a relative. The stupid man. Are you going to let the Press have a copy?"

"Probably. They aren't camped in the lobby anymore, but they are still about. It might keep them occupied for a bit. Are any of you coming up this weekend? I know you said not."

"Sorry love, no. Toby is coming down. Why don't you come with him?"

"I'll think about it. Would you send some of my clothes back with him; I've only got holiday stuff here."

Chapter Thirty-Two

She awoke to find the light still on and an array of diaries scattered across the bed. She gathered them together and got up. Her reading hadn't gained her any new information, but a picture had emerged of Elizabeth and Walter disagreeing over how to deal with Christine. Zoe needed to find earlier diaries of when Christine was a child and still at home.

The morning meeting went well, with nothing untoward to concern her. Jez seemed a little disgruntled that his complaint hadn't progressed, but she didn't see what she could do about it as it was Karen's day off. She wouldn't be back until the late shift on Sunday. Zoe had a brief conversation with him and apologised on behalf of the hotel. She also told him that she may not join him at the bar on Sunday morning as arranged; she may be going back home.

Reception called her over to the phone on her way past. It was Staff Nurse Collins at the hospital. Doreen was much better and was asking to see her, again. She checked that she would be allowed in, after what the other nurse had said, but was told that the other nurse wouldn't be there. Doreen was adamant that Zoe was the only one she wanted to talk to.

Glancing at the row of family photos as she walked back to her apartment, a picture of

Megan caught her attention. She looked at the young woman. She looked happy, serene, beautiful, posing for the camera. It was a studio shot and she looked like a film-star. Wow! Zoe studied the girl's face, trying to see... what, she didn't know... 'Licking the walls'. No, she couldn't get the phrase out of her head. The thought was horrific; being so desperate. She'd seen the walls down there. She couldn't imagine licking them. She couldn't even imagine drinking water from the walls collected in a clean glass. She shuddered. On impulse she went into her bedroom and changed into her cleaning clothes. Then she went and found Jackie. It wasn't long before she was laughing and joking, her mind focused and back in 'the now'. She helped service three rooms and then it was lunch time. She ate with them, then excused herself: needing to get ready to go to her meeting at the hospital.

She dressed as smartly as she could, though why it mattered she had no idea. It just felt right that she 'make a good impression'.

At the hospital Staff Nurse Collins showed her to Doreen's room and again left them alone, but with the door open.

"I am so glad you came. I wasn't sure you would come back. I... think you know..."

"Know what?"

"I think you know that, well, that it wasn't me, who pushed you down the steps. I would never have done that."

Zoe took a moment. She had assumed that Doreen was aware of Mary and her need to get into the cellar to find Megan. Now she realised that Doreen hadn't had anyone to talk to, who believed her: that it had all been inside her head. Events, as far as Doreen was concerned, had had no confirmation, unless Zoe gave it to her. She tried to remember what she had said at their previous meeting.

Doreen continued, needing to fill the silence, desperate for some acknowledgement that what she thought had happened, really had. "It was her. She was the one who wanted to hurt you, to hurt Mary."

"Who is Mary?"

Doreen blinked, fear flicking behind her eyes. A thick invisible wall shot up between the two of them and Zoe watched Doreen shrink. In front of her eyes, she saw the other woman mentally tumbling backwards, isolation swallowing her. At the previous meeting Zoe had said 'yes', she understood, that she 'knew'. Now, Zoe shrank too. She couldn't do this. She couldn't pretend that she didn't understand, because she did. She completely did, and equally Doreen was the only person who really understood what had happened to her. She didn't know the extent of it, but she would believe and know.

Slowly Zoe reached out. Smiling, she rested her hand on Doreen's knee. Doreen flinched, uncertain, wounded, beaten. Zoe, gently squeezed Doreen's knee, "I am so sorry. Yes, I do know. Doreen, you weren't confused. You weren't delusional. It was all real. It happened." Doreen started to shake, desperate eyes looking deep into Zoe's, seeing and not seeing, what was no longer there. Mary had gone. Zoe took her hands and told her everything that she knew, everything that had happened. Bit by bit Doreen grew back into herself. Her shoulders lifted, her back straightened and she began to relax.

"She has gone," said Zoe, "I can see that – Edna has gone."

"Edna? She was called Edna! Is that who she was?"

"Yes," said Zoe suddenly realising that there was no reason for Doreen to have known Edna's name, despite 'being her'. She hadn't known she was 'Mary' until Kyle had worked it out."

"I don't know what is going to happen to me, but I want you to know that even if I don't go to prison..."

"Oh, it won't come to that," said Zoe without thinking.

"Even if I don't go to prison, I don't want to come back to the hotel. I just don't want to live there anymore. I don't even want to step back in the building. You can put all my things in storage."

Zoe left, mixed emotions vying for attention. Relief and irritation, sorrow and joy. She didn't want Doreen back at the hotel, but she also now felt sorry for her. As Nurse Collins let her out of the ward, she said, "I am glad you came. Your visit will have really helped. She needed to talk to the one person who would truly understand." Then added, as Zoe really looked at her for the first time, "If you ever want to talk, call me. I'll listen."

Zoe left, a new respect for Nurse Collins and a new awareness broadening her beliefs.

Chapter Thirty-Three

At the morning meeting she was relieved to find that Jez wasn't there, as she still hadn't had a word with Karen. Karen had swapped her shift to cover for the night duty manager so wasn't there either and Zoe found that she was leading the meeting. It was a brief meeting as Saturday was their busiest day, when most of the guest changeovers happened. She declined any suggestions to work with other teams in the upcoming week, stating that she might not be there. She needed to speak to Karen before she could decide. Leaving the staff to get on with their day she went back upstairs to a sleepy Kyle and slipped under the covers beside him.

When they finally got up and had satisfied their need for coffee and croissants they ventured back into the loft. It was hot up there, but they determined to get through the boxes. There must be more diaries somewhere. As they worked Kyle grew increasingly concerned about the weight in the boxes, and said so. Zoe, however, wasn't listening, intent on her search. He moved some of the heavier ones towards the hatch and then took them down, stacking them in the corner of the bedroom. They all seemed to be stuffed with documents. He was glad it wasn't up to him to sort through them. There was a squeal from above and he raised his head, listening. There was nothing more, everything seemed to be okay. As he stuck his head through the hatch, she looked up grinning. "I found them. Will you take the box down for me?"

There were 20 diaries. She laid them out in chronological order. They now had a complete set spanning over 60 years. Zoe started flicking through them, starting with the first, when her grandmother was 11 years old. The entries told an interesting story but nothing that answered Zoe's questions. At some point she must read them all, but for now she had other interests. She put it down and picked up the 1969 diary, when Christine would have turned 16. Over a period of three months a picture had emerged. Walter was at first surprised and then increasingly annoyed by Christine's night-time visits to the cellar. Two members of the kitchen staff had resigned, because of her behaviour.

Friday 18th September – Today I fitted a bolt to the outside of Christine's bedroom door.

"What! He locked her in! Can you believe that?"

Kyle just shrugged, "Different times."

Saturday 19th September - None of us got any sleep last night. Constant rattling and crying *coming from her room. Elizabeth not speaking to me.*

A high-pitched siren screeched and wailed. Zoe stared questioningly at Kyle.

"Fire alarm!" he said. "Come on, best get down there."

They joined a trail of guests all heading for the ground floor. At the bottom of the stairs, staff were directing people to assembly points outside, depending on which stairs they had come down.

"Where is your fire panel?" asked Kyle. Then, seeing her blank look, headed for the office behind the reception desk, an alarmed Zoe in tow. The panel was on the wall just inside the office door. A red light was flashing. "Second floor. Looks like one of the back bedrooms. Does this alarm go straight to the fire service, or do we need to call them?"

Zoe didn't know. Kyle stepped out into the reception area to the young woman directing guests, at the bottom of the stairs. Before he could ask her Carl came bouncing down. "False alarm. Room 211."

"Should I get everyone back in?" asked the staff member.

"No, the Fire Brigade should be here any second. We need them to check and give us the all-clear." In the distance a siren could be heard, getting nearer. "Go and do your headcount out front and I'll take over here." On seeing Zoe, he automatically deferred to her, but the look on her face told him that she didn't want that.

"No one has shown me what to do in a fire alarm. I guess I should know but I don't. I just never thought..." she said. "I'll just watch you."

He gave instructions to another member of staff and received a headcount from the assembly point at the rear of the hotel. As he started ticking off rooms the doors opened and in poured the Fire Brigade. The officer marched straight to the fire panel and then set off upstairs with Carl in tow, explaining that he had been unable to find a cause but that it was the alarm in room 211 that had been activated. Zoe wanted to follow but decided to keep out of the way. If it became known that she was the owner, but didn't know what she was doing, it wouldn't be good.

It took a while, but the all-clear was given and the fire panel reset. To Zoe's dismay Carl introduced her to the fire officer, as the new hotel owner. Instead of the reprimand she'd expected, for wasting their time, he praised the staff for a good response. The fire brigade departed, and guests came back inside, some rushing to get on with their day, others grumbling. Kyle excused himself and left for work, leaving Zoe to have a crash course in hotel evacuation.

Whilst Carl explained the fire panel and how it worked and showed her the paperwork involved, she took the opportunity to ask his advice on how to deal with the Karen/Jez incident and wished she hadn't. Another member of staff had made a complaint, being reduced to tears for being late. Apparently, she had needed to take her dog to the vet's and Karen had told her that if she wanted to keep her job she'd have to 'pull her socks up. She was paid to work not do charity work'.

Intent on learning, she stayed on reception. The day wore on and seemed to lurch from one incident to the next. Carl dealt well with most of them but then deferred to her when he didn't know. The trouble was that he knew more than she did, and she began to feel more and more useless. She couldn't wait for Karen to take over but then she would have to confront her about the complaints. When the afternoon duty manager called in sick, Carl agreed to work through until Karen arrived and took over for the night shift. It was incredible how difficult it made things with just one key member of staff being sick. When Zoe realised that neither Jez nor the new complainant were back at work until Monday, she decided to leave talking to Karen until then.

At 6pm Kyle arrived, and Zoe abandoned Carl to manage on his own. Kyle had had a busy day and wasn't in the best of moods. A leak at one of the properties he was restoring had ruined the decorating he had done. It wasn't his fault; he wasn't responsible for the plumbing, but he was the one on site when the owner discovered the ensuing mess. He had been on the receiving end of her anger and dismay. It had also ruined his schedule as the property needed to dry out before he could redecorate. Zoe did what she could to sympathise and soothe, but just gave vent to all the things he had wanted to say in front of the client and couldn't. Feeling irritated she snapped back but then apologised. He apologised too and things settled down, but he was worried how he was going to manage to re-schedule everything. Every hold up had a knock-on effect on his work, and there would be other angry clients.

She took a lasagne out of the oven and added some peas, whilst he poured them each a glass of wine. Then they tucked in.

"So, how did you get on talking to Karen?"

"I haven't yet," she said.

"Why not, you can't just ignore it."

"I'm not. She hasn't been here."

"If you don't deal with it, these things can land you in a world of trouble."

"I will." They ate in silence for a while, cutlery clattering on the crockery. Trying to change the subject to something she thought would please him, she added, "How are you getting on with the design for the bar area? I can't wait to see that."

"Still working on it. I haven't had time."

She tried another tack, "How about we take a drive up the coast tomorrow. You said you would show me..."

"I can't. As I said, I've got to work."

"What! I've been looking forward to that. Can't you do it some other time?"

"No, it needs doing." He emptied his glass. "I'm trying to run a business and build a reputation. I can't just abandon my customers for a trip to an outlet centre...

"I'm sorry, but..."

"You'll soon learn what it is like running a business. Why don't you pass the time getting to grips with the fire regulations and the rest of the Health and Safety stuff you need to know before anything bad happens. Sort out that death trap in the loft before the ceiling comes down."

"I will, I am." *'Licking the walls'.*

"Maybe think about putting something together for the reporters. They are still hanging around out there. Or, let them take some photos in the cellar, then maybe they will stop harassing people."

"Perhaps. Belinda said everything was okay down there now. The hotel was safe."

"Belinda! Belinda; that medium woman! You brought her back here, despite what everyone said. Was it not enough that Natalie had been scared and worried sick about you. That the whole lot of us have been traumatised, beyond anything we could possibly have imagined. We have been terrified and made ill coping with the things that have happened and now, you bring a medium here, when you know how much the rest of us

343

were against it. I just don't believe you." Gathering up their cutlery and stacking their plates he deposited them noisily in the sink.

"Look, Kyle, I'm sorry. You don't need to do that. Leave the washing up, there are more fun things we can do." She slipped her arms round his waist, but he didn't respond. "Kyle, why are we fighting? I didn't mean to annoy or upset you. I can see you've had a hard day. You need to relax and have a bit of fun."

"Life isn't all 'fun', Zoe."

She tried taking his hand to lead him to the bedroom door, but he just flicked hers away.

"No, I'm just... you just don't get it. Look, I'll call you," and he picked up his jacket and let himself out, clicking the door noisily behind him.

Zoe sat, wondering what had just happened. As silence made its presence felt she tried to think back over the conversation, what he'd said, what she'd said. What he'd meant by this and that. Was it over between them? He'd said he would call, but then maybe it was just an escape. She got up and walked about, glancing at the phone. Should she call him? No, he'd be driving. She could leave a message, but what would she say. She picked up one of Walters old diaries but couldn't concentrate and besides, the words were all blurry.

The phone rang and she leapt at it. At first, she didn't recognise the voice. It wasn't Kyle and beyond that her mind refused to engage. Slowly, as the speaker continued, female and familiar, she realised that she was talking to Karen.

"Zoe, would you mind coming down here. Your young man has gone down into the cellar, something about... him... wanting to see for himself..."

"What! Why?"

When she reached reception there was no-one there and the night lights were on. She looked at her watch, surprised at the time. Beyond reception, she could hear the sound of a TV coming from the porters' room, and the intermittent laughter of the duty chef. She guessed the kitchen was empty and her assumption proved correct. The cellar door was ajar, outlined by a weak glow. Puzzled and exasperated she trotted down the steps to where she could see Karen, hovering outside the open cave door, a torch in each hand.

"What is he doing? Did he say why he wanted to go down there, now? Why couldn't' he wait?"

Karen said nothing but just held out a torch. Zoe took it and swept past her, "Kyle, what are you doing? Where are you?" Halfway down the steps she stopped, "Kyle. Kyle." Her voice disappeared into the void. Nothing came back. "Kyle..."

As Karen stopped behind her, Zoe turned and looked up. "Are you sure he is down here?"

She shone her torch into the other woman's face. In the instant before she was propelled violently backwards, their eyes locked. She remembered those eyes.

Chapter Thirty-Four

When he woke, Kyle felt calmer. He was no longer angry, just irritated, mainly with himself. He didn't really know why he had snapped at Zoe. It wasn't her fault that he had had a lousy day. She had only been trying to make him feel better. Feeling lousy, and hating himself for how he'd treated her, he dragged himself out of bed and turned on the shower. The fire alarm, though. She really needed to take running a hotel seriously. He didn't think she had the first idea of the implications of her staff 'messing up'. Then he realised that his irritation was down to him wanting to protect her, but he couldn't do that if she wouldn't take his advice. She'd insisted on going back into the loft, despite what he'd said and despite him getting angry. His muscles ached and he breathed in the Black Pepper and Coriander shower gel, she'd bought him. He started coughing. Then there was the medium. That really irked and his anger fired again.

He arrived at the holiday property in time to strip most of the remaining damage created by the burst pipe, before the DIY shops opened at 10am. Hopefully one of them would have the replacement materials he needed. Some of the tiles had come as a special order from Italy. Mid-morning he tried calling Zoe, but just got her voicemail. Either she was out, working in the hotel and hopefully learning, hopefully having taken on board what he had said or, she was ignoring him. He felt that the latter was the most likely. At 4pm, unable to do any more he packed up for the day and went home. He tried calling her but again the call went to answerphone. "Please call me. I'm sorry I got irritated and walked out. Please call." He showered and dressed, picked up a bunch of flowers from a petrol station, and drove round to The Dolphin Hotel.

Going through reception he nodded at Carl who nodded back, looking vaguely puzzled at the flowers Kyle was carrying. Kyle knocked on the apartment door. There was no answer. After knocking again, he tried the handle. It opened. A quick glance round told him that Zoe wasn't there. He deposited the flowers in the kitchen sink.

Back at reception he approached Carl. "Do you know where Zoe is?"

"No. We've not seen her all day. She's gone home, hasn't she?"

"No. She was here last night."

"Well, at the meeting yesterday morning she didn't agree to join any of the teams, because she was thinking of going home for a while, to get some of her stuff. She just needed to speak to Karen first and Karen was here last night." Seeing Kyle's puzzlement he continued, "I'd have thought she'd have told you though."

Kyle let out a deep sigh, "We had a bit of a falling out. I'll call her on her mobile, when I can get a signal. Let me just go back up and check if her toothbrush is gone."

It was.

Toby was thoroughly fed up. The M1 was nearly static, and the alternatives didn't look any better. Things finally started moving and he wanted to keep going, but his bladder had other ideas, and his wasn't the only one. When he eventually made it to the services at Scotch Corner, he had to wait for a car to leave, before he could park. There was a queue for the loo and a queue for food. The tables were littered and sticky and the noise of fractious kids in the cavernous space stressful. He took his burger out to his car, pushed his seat back, and tucked in. Watching streaks of water trickle down the windscreen he wondered whether he would be back in time to drop off Zoe's clothes. Hopefully he would make it before 9pm.

Kyle phoned Zoe, but she didn't answer. He left a message pleading with her to call him. Then another. Then, "Please, just let me know you are okay. A Smiley will do. Even a 'Frowny'." Damn!

The television did nothing to distract him and when the phone rang, he leapt at it, but it was Toby wanting to know if Zoe was with him, as she wasn't at the hotel.

"No, she's gone home."

"Oh? I've just spoken to Natalie. She didn't say. Maybe she thought I knew."

"It is nearly nine thirty. She should be there by now. Would you ring her again and find out."

Kyle waited. She might be mad at him but surely, if she was going home, she would have got in touch with the Walkers; she'd want picking up from the station. She couldn't 'not get a signal' somewhere en-route. It seemed ages, but wasn't long, before Toby rang back. No, she wasn't there, and they weren't expecting her.

Kyle phoned The Dolphin.

"Dolphin Hotel and Lido, Karen speaking, how may I help you?"

"Karen, it's Kyle, Zoe's friend. Is she there? Carl said she'd gone home but she isn't there."

"Oh, isn't she? We haven't seen her all day."

Fifteen minutes later Kyle and Toby arrived at the hotel. Karen looked up from the phone as they passed, continued speaking but nodded acknowledgement. Taking the steps two at a time Kyle disappeared upstairs, Toby following at a slightly slower pace.

"Her door is unlocked," stated Toby, as Kyle walked straight in.

"She never locks it; no-one comes up here."

Kyle did a recheck of the bathroom. Zoe's toothbrush, make-up, shower gel, shampoo and conditioner, were all gone. Her wardrobe had clothes missing and her suitcase, which normally sat abandoned in the corner of her bedroom, was nowhere to be seen. "Is there a note anywhere? Did she leave a note?"

"No. It looks like she just packed up and went, mate."

"But where to? She should have made it home by now."

"Let's see when she left," said Toby heading for the door. Across the hall, he let himself into Doreen's apartment.

Inside he nudged the mouse on the computer and sat down. The screen came to life. With Kyle looking over his shoulder he ran the recording of the reception desk back to the previous night. "What time did you leave?"

"I don't know, 9.30, something like that. Maybe later, Karen was on the desk. I think she was doing the night shift. So, maybe 10."

Toby scrolled forward, different people came and went, some stopping at the reception desk and talking to Karen, others returning to their rooms. At 10.17 Kyle jogged down the stairs. Karen said something to him, a query of some kind, a look of concern on her face. Kyle didn't stop, just shrugged his shoulders, then flung his hands in the air, with an exasperated, don't talk to me gesture before walking out of the door. Toby looked at him.

"We'd had a row," said Kyle, "I didn't want to talk to Karen about it."

Toby wound forward and then quickly backwards. A blonde head appeared, hair bobbing up and down, and Zoe bounced down the steps. Surprised, Toby wound the recording back. She had run down the stairs, glanced in the back office, listened, and then set off towards the kitchen. He ran it forward, and ran it forward some more. The next person to appear was Karen, who stepped behind the desk and then into the office, out of sight. Then nothing. She came out to the desk a couple of times, but that was it.

"Oh course, she could have returned via the backstairs," said Toby.

"Possibly, but unlikely, it would be a bit of a circuitous route."

Toby ran the recording forward, but Zoe never appeared. If she had come back to her apartment, it wasn't via reception. "Let's go ask Karen if she saw her down there." He stood, and they both turned towards the door, and froze. To the right of the door, unnoticed on their way in, was Zoe's suitcase. Sitting neatly next to it was her bag.

Karen wandered around the kitchen and then returned to reception. Passing the desk she stuck her head into the porters' office. Derek the night porter and Jill the duty chef were happily watching the television, a cup of tea each, steaming on the table between them. She left them be and went back to the office and picked up the novel she was reading. She heard the landing door open and then two sets of feet jog down the stairs. She put her bookmark in place and laid her book on the desk. Then she stood and straightened down the skirt of her suit, ran her fingers through her hair and stepped out behind the reception desk, wearing her best smile. '*Be nonchalant.*' It wasn't needed. The two boys were already part way down the corridor to the kitchen.

The door to the cellar was unlocked, which didn't strike them as odd. Had they had time to think, they may have pondered on the fact. The light was also on. Strange too, but then if Zoe had come this way, she would have put it on, but then surely one of the kitchen staff would have noticed during the intervening 24 hours.

At the bottom of the stairs, they turned towards the alcove, Karen appeared behind with a torch. As the men tried the door, she shone the torch at a large wooden shelf that appeared to have fallen and was lodged at the base of the cave door. Kyle hauled it out of the way and pushed at the enormous shelving unit. As Toby added his weight it groaned and moved backwards, grinding over the rubble on the floor. Karen handed Kyle the torch and he set off down the steps, calling out,

"Zoe, Zoe, are you there? Zoe, where are you? Zoeeee..."

Before following, Toby manoeuvred a wedge in front of the door to keep it open. This would have worked had it been left there. As soon as he was halfway down the steps it was removed. The door swung back into place, filling the gap and leaving Toby stranded in darkness. Instinctively, he turned and stumbled back up the steps shouting to Karen to hold it open, he couldn't see. Then he heard the scraping, and the forcing of the wedge back into the gap. Still not understanding he called out to her, trying to make her understand that the door needed to stay open, but he wasn't talking to Karen. Edna did understand and there was no reply. Realisation dawning, he grabbed part of the door and pulled. Unable to get a decent purchase, it didn't move. Somewhere below him Kyle shouted, "your phone, use your phone." Furious, he ignored the suggestion and pummelled his fists against the wood, but the action failed to hold off the panic that was mounting. There was a clatter on the steps. Light jogged crazily about the walls and Kyle arrived at his side.

"We need to get this open. She's barely conscious. Her lips are cracked and dry and her tongue is, well, it looks ghastly."

Toby, initial anger spent, stepped away from the door. "We need a lever, something to jemmy it with." Following Kyle's example, he took out his phone and switched on its light. A search of the cave revealed very little of use. There were no tools and the piece of wood, that they were able to separate from a crate, snapped. Kyle picked up a rock and hefted it, "If we can't open the door, we'll just have to smash our way through."

Toby found himself a rock and together they began pounding on the door. After half an hour they had made very little impression. The oak had withstood a bomb; it was going to take more than a couple of hand-held rocks to break through it. Kyle looked at his watch. It was 2am. When would anyone start looking for them? There had been no-one in the kitchen. No-one saw them go down there. He lived on his own so he wouldn't be missed until he didn't turn up for work. The lady he was working for would call him, leave voicemails, get exasperated, but would be unlikely to call the Police. Toby's family would notice he was missing, but not until the morning. It would probably be mid morning before they thought to do anything about it. Then they may do nothing knowing that he had had a long drive on the Sunday, unless there was something very urgent at the golf club that needed his attention. Could Zoe last that long?

Making no progress on the door he went back down and crouched at Zoe's side. She was cold, and the jacket he had laid over her was doing little. He lay down beside her and wrapped her in

355

his arms. He spoke softly to her, telling her that it would be okay, that he would get her out of there. She emitted a dry croak, and his heart lurched as he felt a gentle flex of her fingers in the hand he held. It felt so frail. He had no idea if she had any new injuries. The cast on her arm was a soft mess, no longer doing its job properly. She hadn't spoken, and nodded inconsistently to his questions. He didn't know if it was dehydration or confusion. It had only been 24 hours and people could survive for days without water, but the last drink she'd had, had been wine: quite a lot of wine. That wouldn't help.

Between the rhythmic pounding of rock on wood he whispered in her ear, telling her he was sorry they had argued, such a ridiculous thing to do. He loved her.

The pounding stopped and Toby came down to join him, taking off his jacket and placing it over Zoe. "Do you have a signal. I know it is a long shot but... Then you need to turn off your phone, save the battery. I'll switch mine off when I get back up there. I can smash and yell in the dark."

They took it in turns, hour after hour, to pound at the door. Around 5am it seemed that the centre part of the middle panel felt a little softer and tiny splinters came off when picked. Hopefully they were making progress.

As Toby took a breather, at the top of the steps, and silence settled on the oppressive darkness, Kyle heard a drip. He shouted for Toby to stay quiet and listened. Yes, there was dripping. He took out his phone and shone it at the cave wall. A tiny trickle glistened. Desperate, he racked his brain. He needed something to collect it in. It wouldn't be much, but Zoe desperately needed fluid. He'd seen nothing that resembled a vessel when looking for a tool. He checked his pockets, then he checked Zoe's. The only thing she had was a plastic pack of tissues, just a couple. He removed the tissues and carefully propped the plastic packet upright against the wall, using a couple of small stones to keep it in place. Then he left it there, checking every few minutes to see its progress. Before he and Toby swapped places, he was able to give her a couple of sips. He hoped he wasn't poisoning her.

At 6.30, when they thought that the kitchen staff would be turning up, they changed their pounding to three short taps, three heavy taps, three short taps, S.O.S., in the hope that someone would hear and investigate. Every now and then they would shout out, desperation and frustration vying for supremacy.

No-one came.

At 9am Kyle imagined the lady he was doing work for, calling him, demanding to know where he was; she'd been expecting him at 8.30. He couldn't do anything about that. He snuggled up to Zoe, wanting to warm her but not wanting to hurt her. She must have been so scared, down here, all alone. *'Licking the walls'*. The horror of that had got to her. He knew that. Now she had lived the reality. If they died here together, hopefully his presence would give her some comfort.

Toby thought through his day, wondering at what point someone would query his absence with his father and at what point his father would call him. He was usually reliable. His father would think it strange, but how long would it take him to do anything about it. Monday was a busy day, dealing with suppliers. Toby was a grown man. At what point would his father start to question his absence, let alone worry enough to start looking?

Taking over from Kyle he wrapped Zoe in his arms, hoping the heat from his exertions would warm her up as Kyle began his stint pounding on the door. Dot, dot, dot, dash, dash, dash, dot, dot, dot. The sound was jarring and penetrating. When he poured the next dribble of water into Zoe's mouth, he nearly spilt it. Thankfully she was alert enough to swallow and hopefully it would help her. He thought about Natalie. He missed her. What would she do if he died here! How soon would she raise the alarm. She knew that Zoe was missing. Surely, she'd contact his father when she didn't hear from him. She'd think to check the cellar and cave but how long would that take? Would it be in time to save Zoe?

Chapter Thirty-Five

At 8am Karen had handed over to Carl and gone home. Briefly, he'd popped into the kitchen and grabbed himself a mug of coffee. Then he'd set about preparing for the morning staff meeting. Karen had said nothing about the two complaints against her and he hadn't expected her to, but in Zoe's absence was he going to have to deal with them? If so, how? Thankfully, Karen was now off for 2 days.

By 11am the meeting was over, and the staff were getting on with their day. The phone rang. He picked it up. It was Natalie Walker asking if he'd seen Toby. No, he hadn't, and Karen hadn't mentioned seeing him. He hadn't seen Zoe or Kyle either. He agreed to go up and check the apartment.

Twenty minutes later she rang again, "Then please check the cellar and the cave."

"Sorry. The cave! Why would they be in there?"

"I don't know. Just check. Please."

As the phone lay off the hook Natalie waited. What else could she do? Who else could she call. The golf club. She could phone Toby's dad. As she waited, she thought how she could get up there: what trains to get. Why hadn't Toby called, texted, responded to her messages. There had been nothing since he'd called asking about

Zoe. Karen, perhaps if she called Karen. If Carl hadn't found them, she'd ask him for Karen's number. So many thoughts and actions tumbled through her mind. She waited and still she waited, but Carl didn't come back.

When Carl stepped into the kitchen, the staff all looked up. When he marched towards the cellar door, they stared. He tried the door, but it was locked. He was about to go back to the phone and tell Natalie that they couldn't be in the cellar, the door was locked. Feeling slightly foolish he turned to the staff, who were all watching him carefully, and shrugged. They must all be wondering what he was doing. Then the head chef took a couple of steps sideways and reached out. There was a rough scrape, of wood on wood, and a rattle of contents as she pulled open a drawer. She ran her hand rapidly through its contents, then held up a key. A murmur rippled through the staff; a confirmation of their suspicion that she had had it all along. It was the key, THE key, she'd told Zoe she didn't have. With a certain amount of undisguised ceremony, she walked across the kitchen and handed it over to Carl. Then she stepped back and waited. They all waited, and watched.

Inserting the key in the lock, he turned it, then turned the knob and opened the door. The kitchen light illuminated the top few steps but then nothing; beyond was blackness. All eyes on him he stepped inside and located the light switch. He could now see to the bottom of the steps. Part way down he thought he heard something. He stopped and listened. Nothing, he was mistaken. Just his mind playing tricks. He was an adult. He was a grown man. Ridiculous, to be afraid of the dark. He continued down and, finding the second light switch, lit up the cellar. Banging began. Neurons fired and adrenaline surged. Bang, bang, bang, BANG, BANG, BANG, bang, bang, bang. Rooted to the spot he listened, each bang electrifying his nervous system and shooting pain through his paralysed muscles. People. He was looking for people and people made noise. It was coming from the far end of the cellar, the end with the broken bulb; the end where the light didn't penetrate. He needed light. He ran back to the top of the steps.

"Can someone bring a torch. Quickly!"

There was shuffling and a cupboard opening. A torch was produced and thrust into the hand of the youngest and newest member of staff. The lad took it, a mixture of alarm and curiosity spread across his face. Bemused and suspicious of the staff behaviour but eager to see beyond the previously locked door, he followed a retreating Carl into the cellar.

At the bottom of the steps Carl took the torch and shone it into the recess as the young lad stood at his elbow. Bang, bang, bang, BANG, BANG, BANG, bang, bang, bang. The lad leapt and backed away, then quietly retreated to the kitchen. Exasperated, Carl headed for the recess and bashed his fist on the panelling. The banging stopped. He smashed his fist against the wood again and the banging started up once more, rapid and enthusiastic. "Hello, hello, can you hear me," called Carl. "I'll get you out."

There was a yell from the stairs and the clomp of rapidly descending heels. "Nooo," screamed throughout the space. "No, No, No."

"Help," called Carl, "Give me a hand."

The heels ran across the stone floor, "No, oh, no!"

"Karen, help me get this door open."

"Get away. Get out of the way," she screamed, clawing at Carl's shoulder, making him move. He stepped back, clutching his shoulder where her nails had dug in. Annoyed but deferring to his boss he stepped back. He played the torch over the shelves, so she could see. All he could see was a shelving unit. Bottom right was a heavy wooden wedge which, judging by the scuff mark across the flags, had been pushed forcefully into place. If there was a door, that wedge would be stopping it from opening. He lurched to pull it away, but she shoved him back. Had he had time to think he would have been puzzled by her actions. Why was she here? How did she know? She had been working all night, she should be in bed. Now he noticed she was sobbing, and she seemed frantic. Her clothes weren't right. Her blouse wasn't tucked in and not all the buttons were fastened. Her hair wasn't combed. She was normally immaculate.

Bending down she took hold of the wood, but she was moving it the wrong way.

"Let me," said Carl, placing the torch on the floor.

There was a pause, as she thought about this. Then she stepped back to allow him access. She stood behind him as he wrapped his hands round the wedge and tugged. There was a slight movement, but that was all. She picked up the large heavy torch. She shuffled her feet, positioning herself. He tried again and it moved some more. He stood, readying himself for another attempt. With sickening force, the torch struck him on the back of the head. His legs collapsed and he slumped to the floor. As his world swam, shock and disbelief overwhelmed him. He blinked, staring at the dusty floor, trying to orientate himself and process what had just happened. Behind him heels shuffled and he turned and shrank against the concrete. He looked up. Her face was barely visible in the dark, but it terrified him. Rage stalked behind those eyes. Rage inflamed them and plotted. They looked down at him, then through him. Then the torch dropped and bounced, light crazily illuminating random space. Another light, phosphorescent and energetic, grew and filled the cellar. It sought out the corners, probing and testing. It pulsed and popped, imploded and vanished. Silence. The only light that of the torch, mournfully casting shadows.

Karen screamed. She dropped to her knees, horrified and tearful. Frantic!

"Carl, Carl! Are you okay. I am so sorry. Are you hurt? Speak to me."

Carl rubbed the back of his head and got warily to his feet. As he stood, she turned towards the door and tugged at the wedge. He helped and it came free. Karen threw herself at the door and it opened, pulled from the inside.

Toby stepped into the gap, looming monstrously in the torchlight. He flew at Karen flattening her against the wall, sending the torch flying. Shocked, Carl was slow to react, slow to identify Toby. Karen was squealing, struggling to draw in air, winded. Toby had her by the shoulders. He let go pulling back his arm, forming a fist. Released, she dropped to the floor. Toby's fist hit the wall. Carl, leapt at Toby, grabbing his arm. Toby shook himself, trying to break free as Carl clasped him from behind. Karen cowered on the floor, arms raised, gulping in air. It took all Carl's strength, but he managed to pull the bigger man back.

Karen looked up, arms out to defend herself. "She's gone, she's gone. Edna has gone. Toby, she's gone, just now." Tears rolled down her face, "I am so, so, sorry.

Chapter Thirty-Six

Six months later

It had been a short summer and a steep learning curve for Zoe. Running a hotel was a full-time job but she, Karen and Carl had grown into their roles, and Zoe was now confident that Karen and Carl could run the hotel in her absence. Returning to university to finish her degree had been a hard decision, but something she wanted to do. She was packed and ready to leave in the morning.

The newspaper article was the last in the row of frames depicting the Dolphin Hotel and Lido's wartime history. As she placed it on the wall, next to the older cuttings of the bombing, and rebuilding, and those of the lost family members, she reread it.

Bomb victim reburied

The exhumed remains of Edna Green were finally laid to rest in a new grave. Edna's body had spent the last 8 decades in the grave of Megan Brammar. Edna was believed to have drowned at sea on the night a German bomb destroyed the rear of The Dolphin Hotel and Lido. The recent discovery of Megan Brammar's remains in a sealed off section of the hotel's cellar led to a new inquest into the tragic deaths of the two young women.

Zoe couldn't believe how fortunate they had been that the authorities had chosen that Monday to dig up Edna. When later, they had worked out the timeline, it was at the exact moment the grave was opened that Edna left Karen.

Karen had woken, initially agitated, not knowing why. As she got her bearings, she experienced an overwhelming sense of panic and then rage. She'd pulled on the first clothes she could find and had run the three streets to The Dolphin. Reception was empty and all the kitchen staff were staring at the open cellar door. Frantic, she ran down the steps intent on stopping the cave door being opened. It was Megan's fault that she had died in that cellar. She was furious. As she stared down at Carl, about to hit him again, something had changed. She had experienced an overwhelming sense of elation and freedom, of a wrong being righted. Edna had gone. Then she realised what she had done. She lowered her arm, her hand damp around the large rubber torch. They had to be alright. They just had to be.

AND, they were. Zoe was bruised and dehydrated but with no further injuries, just a mild chest infection. She had managed to grab the handrail as she went backwards down the cave steps and this had stopped her going the whole way down. She was exhausted from the fear and terror she had experienced but after a week she was back to herself. The chest infection took a little longer to get over. Carl had quite an 'egg' on the back of his head for a while, but was otherwise fine. He was given a full explanation of events but no-one else was told the truth about Karen's part in their entrapment. As far as everyone else was concerned, Toby and Kyle had got trapped searching for Zoe.

As for Doreen's part in events, they awaited the deliberations of the CPS but were hopeful that her psychiatric report and the fact that she had no intention of returning to the hotel, would help keep her out of prison. Zoe provided a statement, saying she didn't blame Doreen, she hadn't been well. Zoe and Karen both met with her, by mutual consent. When Zoe asked Doreen outright, if Edna had pushed her great-grandmother down the stairs, Doreen replied that she had no idea. When Zoe pointed out that the hotel diary of that time, stated that Elizabeth Brammar had been found at the bottom of the stairs by her, Doreen was puzzled. She then realised that she had only been promoted to hotel manager a couple of months after the funeral, when the previous hotel manager was dismissed. She didn't know why. Maybe Walter's diary would say. It had been in her bedside cabinet. She'd taken it when she'd been organising Walter's funeral; it had all the details from Elizabeth's funeral which were helpful.

With Karen back to her old self she apologised to the staff and smoothed over the complaints without revealing the real reason for her behaviour. She then told Zoe how she should have dealt with them. The staff seemed to accept her apology; her actions had been completely out of character.

Edna Green was laid to rest by family descendants, in a new grave, with a headstone bearing her name. With the families' permission Zoe, Natalie, Kyle and Toby attended; not knowing exactly why, they just felt that they should. Maybe they just wanted to witness the event, ensure that she was laid to rest.

Sometimes a rip appears in the veil separating the living from the dead.
Sometimes the dead can't rest in peace.
Sometimes, the dead won't...

A separate ceremony was arranged for Megan's burial. David and Sharon attended too, along with most of the hotel staff. For Zoe it was a traumatic event. Her emotions were recent and raw. Megan was her daughter and not her daughter and in some way herself. After all, Megan's death was very nearly her own.

Natalie spent the summer at the hotel with Zoe and Kyle, who had moved in. Toby and

Natalie spent a lot of time together, getting to know each other better. As the weather warmed up the two couples enjoyed time in the Lido. Zoe, in particular made a point of trying all the Spa treatments that were on offer, stating that it was important that, as hotel owner, she was familiar with the treatments the hotel was offering. Natalie was very keen to offer a second opinion.

David and Sharon were frequent visitors to the hotel, enjoying both the accommodation and the surrounding seaside resort. They didn't say anything to Natalie and Zoe, but both were looking forward to the time when they could retire and move there.

Over the summer Kyle finalised his plans for the hotel and Zoe was delighted with them, gaining a growing appreciation for art deco. Neither could wait for the new year when the hotel would be at its quietest and the work could be done.

When the university summer break ended, Toby, looking ahead, invited Natalie up to stay with his family for Christmas. When she agreed, he was delighted; he had a big question he wanted her to answer.

Walter's diaries were collected together and given their own bookcase. When Zoe had time to read them all they revealed that, as she'd suspected, the young Christine had met Mary.

As for the iconic topiary dolphin, that had saved Zoe's life, well, it took 5 years, but it finally looked like a dolphin again. AND Ruth, with Zoe's permission, grew herself a steady income selling miniature topiary dolphins to guests.

The End

Thank you for reading my book

If you have enjoyed reading 'When Love and Rage Rip the Veil', do tell your friends, and please leave a review on Amazon. It is lovely to hear what readers think.

Best wishes,

Pauline

If you are looking for something more light-hearted and fun, please take a look at 'Other Books by this Author'.

Acknowledgements

I would like to thank Karol Darnell, of Honesty Press, and author of 'Don't Miss the Last Train Home', 'Going Home' and 'Boxes of Time', for her support in the writing of this book and for her diligent editing.

I would also like to thank Paul Durston, author of 'If I Were Me' and 'If We Were One' for advice on Police matters and for his proof reading and general comments.

Thank you both for your corrections, criticisms and suggestions and the time it took for you to work through my manuscript.

Other Books by This Author

Pauline Potterill is the author of the Romcom/Family Saga Much Meddling series:

Wishing Wells of Much Meddling

Fairy Rings of Much Meddling

Cats' Eyes of Much Meddling

And the compilation of short stories

Twelve Months of much Meddling

All titles available from Honesty Press and Amazon (also ebooks on Amazon).

About the author

Pauline Potterill grew up in the northwest of England, on the edge of the Lake District, but has since lived in many parts of this beautiful country.

"I love local history, tradition and folklore, and believe that everyone should have a sense of their roots and be part of a community. I try to put a feeling of this in my novels, hopefully in an amusing and affectionate way.

I aim to keep readers guessing and like to surprise them.

Ideally, I like to write 'genre-free', because life is."

Printed in Great Britain
by Amazon

49184530R00212